Patsy D

Brother & Sister

Brother
& Sister

JOANNA TROLLOPE

BLOOMSBURY

Published by Bloomsbury, New York and London
Distributed to the trade by Holtzbrinck Publishers

All papers used by Bloomsbury are natural, recyclable
products made from wood grown in well-managed forests.
The manufacturing processes conform to the environmental
regulations of the country of origin

Library of Congress Cataloging-in-Publication Data

Trollope, Joanna.
    Brother and sister / Joanna Trollope.– 1st U.S. ed.
        p. cm.
    ISBN 1-58234-400-0
    1. Brothers and sisters–Fiction. 2. Birthmothers–Fiction.
    3. Adoptees–Fiction. I. Title.

PR6070.R57B76 2004
823′.914–dc22
                                                    2003062649

First U.S. Edition 2004

1 3 5 7 9 10 8 6 4 2

Typeset by Hewer Text Ltd, Edinburgh
Printed in the United States of America by
R. R. Donnelley & Sons, Harrisonburg, Virginia

CHAPTER ONE

From where he sat, Steve could see right down the length of the studio. He could see across the width, too, from one stripped brick wall to the other, and then right up high, right up into the roof space where the seventeenth-century beams—still suggestive, somehow, of the sinuous lines of the branches and trunks they had once been—formed their crooked and purposeful patterns. He'd designed the lighting so that even in the evenings, even on the darkest days, the eye would be drawn upward, as it was in cathedrals and domes. It was comforting to look upwards, comforting and encouraging. He'd spent hours over the last eight years since the studio was finished looking upwards at those wandering beams and thinking about the trees they had once been, about the sky that was still there above them, through the roof. He liked the measurelessness of those thoughts, just as he liked this nameless, neutral time at the end of each working day, when everyone else had gone home leaving him alone to let his mind slip quietly down through all the jarring preoccupations of the previous hours and lie peacefully at the bottom of some still pool of not quite thinking.

It was a running joke in the office that Steve had to be the last to leave. It was the same with the navy-blue name board above the ground-floor window: "Steven Ross and Associates," it read, "Designers."

"And who might those associates be?" Titus said. Titus had worked for Steve for three years. He was twenty-seven, short and square and vigorous, with the elaborate courtesy of manner that sometimes results from an old-fashioned English upbringing. "Because it doesn't *appear* to be me."

"It's a name," Steve said, pretending to read some papers. "It's just a name. To register the company."

"Not *my* name," Justine said. She was straight out of art college and rolled her own cigarettes. She winked at Titus.

"Might be one day," Steve said. "If I think you're worth it."

She liked that. She didn't want straight flirting, but she wanted a challenge from Steve, she wanted him to see that even though she still bit her nails she had drive and focus. When she came for an interview, he'd looked through her portfolio in complete silence and then he'd said, "Good." It was her seventh job interview and nobody had done anything before but sigh and say they hadn't actually got a vacancy after all. She lived for months on that "Good."

Steve stretched himself slowly, luxuriously upright on his stool—Swedish, ergonomically designed—and contemplated his small and satisfying empire. He looked at the original elm floorboards—enormously wide: whatever size could the trees have been?—and the angular outlines of Titus's desk and Justine's desk, and the serene, almost clinical area where Meera did the accounts and administration with heart-lifting orderliness. Steve tried very hard not to indulge himself over order, not to nag about neatness. He endeavored to remember that the precision which seemed to be such a balm to his soul should be properly and appropriately applied to work but should not—emphasize that not—spill over into the rest of life.

It was Nathalie who had alerted him to this. Years ago, before he even found this collapsing urban cottage with all its demanding potential as a workplace, he'd tried to persuade her to move in with him.

She'd looked at him doubtfully.

"Thing is," she'd said, "you're a bit—well, a bit careful."

He'd been wounded.

"You mean fussy," he'd said, "you mean anal."

She sighed. She ran her forefingers under her eyes as if she thought she'd smudged her mascara.

"Well—"

"I don't just take trouble with things," Steve said insistently, "I take trouble with people. I pay attention to *people*."

Nathalie closed her eyes. Steve leaned towards her.

He said unwisely, "Of all the people I've ever met, you need me to do that. You need me to pay attention to you."

Nathalie's eyes snapped open.

"That," she said sharply, "doesn't sound like careful to me. That sounds like *control*."

He'd been chastened. He could remember the feeling still, the hot air of righteous self-justification rushing out of him in a deflating instant. He'd recalled his mother saying, over and over during his childhood and growing up, about some small choice that was absolutely, reasonably, hers to make, "I don't think your dad would like it."

"Sorry," Steve had said to Nathalie. He was full of a thick shame. "Sorry."

There was a photograph of Nathalie in the studio, trapped inside a rectangular Perspex block and fixed to the wall close to Steve's desk. She was wearing a denim shirt and she was holding her long dark hair up with both hands on top of her head in a loose pile, and she was laughing. Beside her was another Perspex block containing a photograph of Polly. Polly was five. She had Steven's soft curly hair and Nathalie's sooty-edged eyes. In the photograph, she was looking straight ahead from under the brim of a flowered sun hat, serious and determined. She had just started school, registered as Polly Ross-Dexter because Nathalie wouldn't give up her surname, and Steve couldn't

3

have the school thinking that he wasn't Polly's father. There'd been a struggle about which name should go first, and Nathalie had only relented in the end on grounds of euphony. This was not a victory, Steve reflected, that had given him any pleasure at all.

He let his gaze travel upwards, from the evidence of Meera's organizational skills to the haphazardness of those of the seventeenth-century roof builders. He'd often tried to work out the stresses among the beams up there, the reasons for their positionings, whether these had been from deliberate calculations or from something altogether more ad hoc, more let's try this, let's try that. It hadn't been a very grand cottage after all, perhaps the house of one of the Huguenot weavers who had fled to England after persecution in France and adapted their competence with silk to an equal competence with the wool that had made Westerham prosperous in the days before the spa waters were discovered and the town became gentrified. When Steve came upon the cottage—he was twenty-seven and humming with notions—it was slumped, decaying, between its more elegant early-nineteenth-century neighbors, and was being used as an indoor reclamation yard, piled with old doors and chimneypieces and floorboards. Its restoration had required a loan from the bank that he was still painfully paying off. When he took it out, he'd wanted to say to Nathalie, "That's hardly being careful, is it?" but he hadn't quite dared to, he hadn't wanted her to have the chance—which she might well have taken—to say, "And exactly who is this great carelessness *for?*"

Of course it was for him. He could bluster about the benefits it would bring for them both, for any children they might have, but he would always have known otherwise, deep in his heart of hearts. He was the one, after all, who lived in the skin of the boy who'd grown up in a back bedroom of the Royal Oak pub out on the Oxford Road, whose father had been so angry at his desire to go to art college that they hadn't spoken for over two years. His mother had crept about between them appeasingly, bringing food parcels to the bedsit the college had helped him find, and always getting back to the pub before opening time.

He'd thought he wanted to be a photographer—that's what he'd set his heart on doing. He'd had fantasies about going back to the Royal Oak and slapping down on the bar, under his father's nose, a national magazine, or a Sunday-newspaper supplement with a double-page spread of beautiful black-and-white shots taken by none other than Steve Ross. But something had interfered with that plan, something had occurred during that first foundation year when everyone else was faffing about making installations out of mirror tiles and painting murals with twig brooms. He'd spent one single morning in the design studio and had known that somehow he'd come home. He'd loved it, completely, immediately; he'd seen the point of the simultaneous precision and creativity, he'd grasped the extraordinary psychological effect of tiny adjustments, in placing or proportion. It was clean, pure, clever, and it was for him. He'd promised himself, cycling to college on the morning of his nineteenth birthday, that he wanted to be—was going to be—a designer with his own studio. He was going to show himself. He was going to show his father.

He got off his stool now, and picked up his waste bin. It was his last task of every day, and yet another source of amusement to Titus and Justine, this rounding up of waste bins in order to tip the contents into the shredder, "Steve's shredder."

"Can't Kim do it?" Titus said, leaning comfortably against Steve's desk.

Kim came in at nine, three evenings a week, to clean.

"No," Steve said.

"Confidentiality?"

"Mmm," Steve said.

"Or," Titus said, folding his arms, "as Kim is probably as interested in the contents of our bins as she would be in a print-out of the Hang Seng index, could it be that she isn't really to be trusted with the *shredder*?"

"Go away," Steve said.

He tipped the contents of his bin into the machine. It would reliably be only paper. So would Meera's. Titus and Justine's bins however hid banana skins and gum wrappers and old Band-Aids. Occasionally, Titus would also leave the tiny packet from a condom, to see if Steve noticed. Titus's sex life seemed, by all accounts, to be a cheerful affair, mostly conducted with girls considerably taller than he was. Sometimes Steve wondered if Justine would have liked to join them.

He put the bin back under his desk and straightened up. The photograph of Polly was directly in front of him, her don't-you-fool-me eyes on an exact level with his own. She seemed quite happy at school, not troubled by anything; in fact, perhaps not troubled enough since her form teacher, Nathalie reported, had gently said that Polly appeared to have some difficulty concentrating and that they should have her hearing checked. Steve touched one ear involuntarily. Nothing wrong with his hearing, never had been.

Downstairs, in the reception area, the street door banged loudly.

"Only me!" Titus shouted.

Steve moved towards the staircase that led down from the studio.

"Forgotten something?"

"I've got someone with me!" Titus called.

Feet crossed the reception area and started up the stairs. A woman's voice said, "This is so *cool*."

"Steve will love that," Titus said. "Won't you, Steve? You'll love it that Sasha thinks this place is cool."

Titus emerged into the studio, pink-cheeked from the cold outside. He wore a vast scarf, muffled up round his neck and ears like a student.

"Sorry to come back," Titus said, grinning. "I know you like us to go when we've gone."

A woman appeared from the staircase behind Titus. She was inevitably much taller than he was, and older, possibly in her mid-thirties, with thick pale hair cropped close to her skull. She held her hand out to Steve.

"I'm Sasha."

"Hello," Steve said.

Titus put his hands in his pockets.

"We're on a bit of a mission," he said. "We had an impulse—"

"I did," Sasha said, smiling at Steve. "It was my impulse."

"Can you spare us five minutes?" Titus said.

Steve said, "I was on my way home, to read to Polly."

"Polly?"

"My daughter," Steve said. He indicated the photograph briefly. "She's five."

Sasha peered.

"Adorable. Five. So it's all Barbie and Angelina Ballerina."

Steve smiled at her.

"Anything pink."

"I love pink," Titus said stoutly. He unwound his scarf and dropped it over the angled edge of Justine's desk. "Explain to him, Sash."

She hesitated.

"It's a bit cheeky—"

"Titus *is* cheeky," Steve said.

"Except that it isn't Titus, it's me."

"Well, then—"

"I'm doing a project," Sasha said. "I'm doing a course, a counseling course, and I'm doing a thesis on identity, personal identity, where we come from, how we define ourselves. That sort of thing."

Steve thought briefly of the Royal Oak. He looked at Sasha's hands. They were long and supple and she had a plain silver band on each thumb.

"The thing is—" Sasha went on and stopped. She looked at Titus.

"Your project," he said airily.

"Titus told me about your wife."

"Partner," Steve said.

Sasha looked briefly at Polly's photograph.

"Sorry—"

"What about Nathalie?"

"That she's adopted," Sasha said.

Steve looked at Titus.

"*Did* I tell you that?"

"Yup."

"I wonder why," Steve said. "I don't usually. I don't think about it."

"Don't you?" Sasha said.

He looked at her. She was very attractive in a bony, bold way, with that pale seal-pelt hair. He smiled kindly.

"No," he said pleasantly, "I don't need to. *She* doesn't need to. It isn't an issue."

"But—"

"Sorry," Steve said, "but Nathalie isn't traumatized. She's always said she's glad she was adopted, that she's had the choice of being who she wanted to be."

"I've never felt like that," Titus said. He put his hands in his pockets. "I know exactly where I come from and almost *none* of it is what I'd have chosen."

Sasha leaned forward.

"I really didn't mean to invade anything—"

"You haven't."

"It's so fascinating, though," Sasha said, "that she doesn't mind."

"She used to tease me," Steve said, "about what she called my battles with my bio-folks. She never had those. Battles, I mean."

Sasha looked at Polly's picture again.

"We shouldn't keep you."

"No."

"But—but do you think she'd talk to me?"

"What?" Steve said. "Nathalie talk to you about adoption?"

Sasha gestured with her big, flexible hands. The rings made her thumbs look oddly truncated.

"It would be so interesting. It would be such a contrast, you see, such a completely other take on the accepted wisdom, such a refreshing *change*—"

"From what?"

"From the acknowledged violence of the primal wound."

"The *what*?"

"Don't get her started," Titus said.

Sasha said clearly, as if quoting, "The abandoned baby lives inside every adoptee all his life."

Steve smiled.

"Not in Nathalie."

"So fascinating," Sasha said again. She thought for a moment and then she said, "Do you think she'd ever talk to me?"

Steve moved away a little to the panel on the wall that controlled the lighting.

"I can ask her."

"*Would* you?"

"Sure," Steve said. "I mean, she may feel it's private, but I know she doesn't feel it's secret. I can only try." He put a hand on the switches and turned to look at Sasha over his shoulder. "Do I describe you as Titus's girlfriend?"

"If you like," Titus said. He picked up his scarf again and looped it round his neck.

Sasha looked down at him.

"If *I* like," she said.

"Down you go," Steve said, "I'm shutting up shop."

Titus went past him and down the staircase with practiced, easy speed. Sasha paused before following him. She was almost as tall as Steve, almost six foot perhaps.

"Thank you," she said.

He pressed the switches and the studio sank silently into darkness.

"Can't promise anything."

"No, but thank you for trying."

He looked at her briefly and indicated that she should precede him down the stairs.

"I'll let Titus know," he said.

Steve cycled home. He'd had bicycles all his life, from what was excruciatingly known as a fairy cycle—given to him by a good-natured customer of his father's—to ride round the backyard of the Royal Oak when he was four, to this twenty-eight-gear mountain bike he'd found behind the cinema with its saddle missing. There was a seat attached to the back of it, for Polly, in which she rode wearing a pale-blue cycling helmet stencilled with cartoon characters from *Winnie-the-Pooh*. They went swimming together by bike, and shopping for all the screws and catches necessary to fix things on the weekends, and to have tea with Polly's grandparents at the Royal Oak. Sometimes Steve wondered if Polly would remember these trips when she was older, the reassuring sight of her father's back, the absurd sight of his safety helmet. Her expression on the back of the bike, Nathalie told him, was both grand and impassive, like a pasha on a palanquin.

The street where they lived was, like the studio, on the edge of one of Westerham's better areas. It was a street of flat-fronted houses built of the pale limestone so familiar locally, with short flights of steps leading directly from door to pavement. Steve and Nathalie had found their flat five months before Polly was born, a long, ground-floor flat with access at the back to a strip of garden with a plum tree and a shed.

"Men like sheds, don't they?" Nathalie said. She had wanted the flat much more than Steve had, because of the garden and being pregnant. "I thought a shed would swing it for you."

Steve had had something else in mind. He'd imagined a first-floor flat, with long windows and molded cornices, something as far away as possible from the dark, crouched rooms of the Royal Oak.

"I could have a washing line," Nathalie said, one hand on her belly and the other on the plum tree. "The baby could sleep out here."

"Yes," Steve said.

"It's got a good kitchen," Nathalie said. "And its own front door."

Steve looked at her. He thought about the studio and his ambitions; he then thought about how both those would seem to him without Nathalie.

"Can we compromise? Can we say five years here and then think again?"

Five years were now up. Polly was five and one month, and her tiny clothes had indeed dried on a line strung between the fence and the plum tree. Nathalie had made the flat very—well, pretty, was the word Steve would choose, charming, comfortable. All those appealing, un-threatening capacities she had displayed at art school—she had specialized, in the end, in textiles—were evident in the home she had made for Steve and Polly. And it was a home, no doubt about it. If you defined a home as the setting of all your domestic life complete with all required emotional and practical attachments, that was what Nathalie had made.

As he cycled up the street, he could see the saffron-colored oblong of his own lit front window, the window of his kitchen–living room where Polly would have eaten her supper off the pine table and possibly drawn him a picture featuring herself, very large, and her parents, some-what smaller, and then, in purple or pink—her favorite colors—the dog she had set her heart on having. She had always liked dogs, even after being knocked over, down some steps, by a bounding Alsatian when she was two.

"So odd," Nathalie said, "I don't like dogs."

He dismounted from his bike and wheeled it into the dank covered area between their house and the next one. He'd had plans for this passage once, visions of pale paint and trellising, and those plans had subsided like so many, subsided into the studio, into family life, into the relentless march of the hours and days and weeks. He sometimes thought about all the *time* he'd had as a child, all those acres of time lying quietly, dully about him, so many of them that sometimes he couldn't think how they were to be filled. Whereas now . . . Well, now time just seemed to bundle him forward, like someone impatiently, ceaselessly dribbling a football.

He let himself into the dark garden. A light fixed to the outside wall shone down on Polly's Barbie bicycle, lying on its side on the paving, and a neat row of flowerpots, under plastic, in which Nathalie was trying to grow auriculas. He put his key in the lock, and let himself into the bedroom, lit only by the light shining down from the passage beyond.

"Home!" he shouted.

There was a thud of feet. Polly came racing down the passage and then stopped, as she always did, several feet away from him.

"I nearly went to sleep," she said.

"You don't sound very sleepy—"

"I was going to turn the light off. I was going to."

He bent to kiss her. She smelled of shampoo and Marmite.

"But you didn't," he said. "And now I'm here."

She turned round and marched back up the passage. Her pajamas were too big for her and gave her the look of a miniature rapper. Nathalie appeared in the doorway of Polly's bedroom.

"He's back," Polly said resignedly.

"Sorry," Steve said, "I got caught up with some scheme of Titus's."

Nathalie liked Titus. He came to supper sometimes and drew dogs for Polly.

"That's OK."

Steve leaned forward and kissed Nathalie's cheek.

"I want Miffy," Polly said.

"Does it *have* to be Miffy?"

"Yes," Polly said.

Nathalie moved past Steve towards the kitchen.

She said as she went, "We saw the ear man."

"What?" Steve said. He looked after her, irritably. She was in the habit of doing that, walking away while saying something he needed to hear.

He followed her.

"What?"

Nathalie didn't turn.

"We saw the ear man. Polly and me. You knew we were going to."

"Did I?"

"Yes," Nathalie said. "You did. We talked about it."

"No, we didn't."

"Actually," Nathalie said, "you're right. No, we didn't. I talked and you didn't listen."

Steve took a breath, glancing to see where Polly was. Then he took another and said in a deliberately friendly voice, "Well, what did he say?"

"There's some malformation. A sort of blockage. Something obstructing the middle ear."

Steve said, more loudly, "There's a malformation in one of Polly's ears?"

"He wanted to look at mine. He wanted to see if there's anything similar in one of mine. He said it was a hereditary kind of thing, a sort of quirk, like a bent finger or the way hair grows."

"And did he find anything?"

13

Nathalie shook her head.

"No."

Polly came into the kitchen, holding her Miffy book.

"Miffy!" she said commandingly to her father.

Steve glanced down.

"Aren't you getting a bit old for Miffy, sweetheart?" He went round to the other side of the table so that he could see Nathalie's face. She was looking down at the table, and her hair had swung forward.

"Nat. Is this serious?"

She said, "He says it's quite a simple operation. It's just the removal of some cartilage really. But lots of aftercare, because ears are so complicated."

"Will it hurt?"

Nathalie nodded. He leaned forward and touched her arm across the table.

He said comfortingly, "They'll deal with that. They won't let it hurt her. They're brilliant at pain control now."

"Miffy!" Polly shouted.

"Two minutes, sweetheart," Steve said. "Nat?"

"It isn't that," Nathalie said. She crossed her arms and held herself, as if she were cold. "It's a simple operation and everything. I know that."

"Well then. Is it her hearing? Is her hearing affected?"

"It is *now*," Nathalie said.

"Yes. Yes, I know. But will the operation improve things? Surely, isn't that the point, isn't the obstruction the thing—"

"I've been feeling sick all afternoon," Nathalie said.

Steve waited. Polly came and stood beside him and held up her book.

"Just a sec, Poll—"

"No secs," Polly said. "*Now*."

Steve bent down and picked her up. She held the book in both hands three inches from his face.

"Miffy."

"Yes. Miffy. I can see."

"I've never felt like this before," Nathalie said. "I've never thought this way. I mean this is a small obstruction in Polly's ear, it isn't even a big, frightening thing that lots of parents have to face, it's just a little thing, a matter of mechanics, really. But—but, well, in his surgery today, I just felt awful, lost. I thought—I thought, what else don't I know?"

Gently Steve pushed the book down with one hand so that he could see across the table.

"Sorry?"

Nathalie raised her head.

"What else don't I know about where Polly's come from?"

Steve looked at Polly. He gave her a wide smile.

"Of course we know where Polly's come from. Don't we, Poll? You've come from Mummy and Daddy."

Polly flapped her book.

She said warningly, "I might get cross."

"It's before that," Nathalie said. "Beyond that. I suddenly felt I was in a space. A void."

Steve adjusted his hold of his daughter.

"You've never talked like this before."

"I've never *felt* like this before."

"You can't mean," Steve said, "that we run up against some small problem in Polly's ear, a problem that it appears can easily be sorted, and you suddenly lose all your confidence?"

Nathalie looked at him.

"Why not?"

"Because—well, because it isn't reasonable."

"This isn't about being reasonable."

She turned aside. She said something in a muffled voice.

"What?"

"I said this isn't about reason. It's about feelings. And feelings—well, feelings have *memories*."

Steve swallowed. He looked at Polly. Her gaze was fixed implacably on his face, indicating that she was simply going to force him to read a book to her that they both knew was intended for three-year-olds. Steve gave Polly a smile. He wondered, even as his mouth stretched, whether it was shamefully appeasing.

"Tell you what," Steve said. He looked at Nathalie. "Polly and I will go and read Miffy, and you ring your mum."

"I thought of that—"

"Well, do it."

"But I think I would rather ring David."

"What is the point," Steve said, his voice betraying the effort of control, "of ringing your brother?"

"Because he'll understand."

"Down," Polly said. "Let me *go*."

Steve lowered her to the floor and stayed crouched beside her, his arms still round her loosely.

"But, Nat, he isn't your real brother, I mean, he hasn't got your ears, or Polly's ears. He's just the brother you grew up with . . ."

Nathalie moved away. Steve turned his face to Polly's. Her eyes were only a foot from his.

"Which ear, Poll?"

She touched one. And then the other, and shrugged.

"Miffy," she said in a baby voice. "Now, now, *now*."

"Yes!"

"Two stories," Polly said, sensing victory.

"OK—"

"Two stories and the train-whistle song."

"OK—"

Steve stood up. Polly grasped his hand firmly. He glanced at Nathalie.

"Are you really going to ring David?"

"Yes."

Steve made a huge effort.

"Give him my best," he said.

CHAPTER TWO

Nathalie had been four when David came to join her. She'd been expecting a baby, not a silent, toddling boy with a big head and big soft hands that he wanted to lay on everything that was hers. There seemed to be, implicit in the way everyone treated David, an extra sympathy and sorrow, so that his speechlessness was allowable, even admirable, and so was the fact that he was ruthlessly determined one second and completely withdrawn the next.

"Don't be cross with him, Nathalie," Lynne and Ralph would say. "He's only little. He can't help it."

Privately, Nathalie thought that *they* could have helped it by not bringing David home in the first place. Life had been fine without David, there had been no need for David. Adding David to the house on Ashmore Road seemed a peculiarly unnecessary, arbitrary thing to do. A baby would have been fine, a baby in a cot or a pram; a baby would not have wanted to challenge or take over the life that Nathalie and Ralph and Lynne had built up together. Nathalie sensed, even at four, that she could have accommodated herself to a baby.

She shut her bedroom door against David. She put her toys in places where David, even though he was learning to climb, couldn't reach. She ate without looking at him and, when he misbehaved at meals, as he often did, hurling his plate to the floor and letting food fall out of his mouth and spill down his front, she fixed her attention on something quite different and stared at it until her eyes watered. When David made Lynne cry with frustration, Nathalie would scream too, to show Lynne that she had good reason for crying. She fought Ralph when he tried to dress her for nursery school and, when he remonstrated, she looked blank and went speechless, like David.

She knew she hated him. She also knew that to say she hated him was not just not allowed, but utterly forbidden. Nobody had ever spelled this out to her, but something in the almost reverential pity that surrounded David made her realize that there were some areas of human conduct that were so fenced about with outrage that penetrating them brought a personal penalty you might have to pay for the rest of your life. She had a sense that if she went down the path of *saying* she hated David, she could never go back. She could say she hated his big head and his dribbling and his dirty nappies and his persistence, but she couldn't say she hated *him*. And it was made worse, much worse, by the fact that he loved her. From the moment he came, he loved her. When he withdrew into himself and sat, bloblike and unresponsive, only Nathalie could make him flicker back to life. It wasn't that she wanted to—she'd have liked him to stay bloblike forever—but that *he* wanted to respond to *her*. When she came near him, his eyes lit up and his hands went out. She hated his hands. They were always sticky.

It took him years to win her over. Lynne told friends that it broke her heart to see David struggling for Nathalie's attention, never mind her approval. Of course you couldn't expect a little girl to appreciate the double deprivation of David's parenting—first the loss through adoption of his birth mother, then the second one of his first adoptive parents in a coach crash on holiday in France—but it was as if Nathalie had hardened her heart to David without even thinking, without even looking at him in the first place.

"And he loves her," Lynne would say, her eyes filling at

the thought of David's infant unrequited emotion. "You can see it in his little face. He *loves* her."

Even then, Nathalie was suspicious of the love word. Lynne used it a lot. Lynne said that she loved Nathalie and so did Ralph, and they loved her especially because they had *chosen* her to be their little girl. If you are chosen, Lynne said, that makes you special. But Nathalie was as suspicious of being special as she was of the love-word. It seemed to her, sitting on Lynne's knee in her pajamas (pale-yellow, printed with rabbits), that when Lynne talked about love and specialness she wanted something back. She wanted Nathalie to gather up all this stuff, and a bit extra, and to give it back to Lynne, like a present, a present which would somehow, obscurely, make Lynne feel better. And Lynne needed to feel better, always. Something in her thin, kind, anxious face made you realize that she carried some sort of ache around, all the time, and she thought that you, in your yellow pajamas, could assuage that ache and comfort her.

But Nathalie couldn't do it. She liked Lynne. She liked Ralph. She liked her life in the house on Ashmore Road and her bedroom, and most of the food that she was offered, and going to school. But she couldn't go further than that. She couldn't fling herself at Ralph and Lynne and want to lose herself in them, partly because she didn't feel the necessary urgency and partly because she couldn't give Lynne what she seemed to want in case Lynne wanted more and more and more until Nathalie was entirely sucked up into her, like carpet fluff going up the vacuum-cleaner tube.

"I always dreamed of a little girl like you," Lynne would say. "And then I got to choose you!"

It was David, in the end, who came to Nathalie's rescue. He began to refuse food unless she fed him, and she refused to feed him if he dribbled. She'd stare at him, a spoonful of mashed carrots poised.

"Don't dribble," she'd say.

He gazed at her, dribbling. She'd put the spoon down. He'd make a huge effort, working his mouth, blotting his chin with his hands. She picked the spoon up again, and inserted it, without comment, into his mouth. It threw Lynne into raptures. The children took no notice of her.

"It's adorable," she'd say to Ralph. "He'll do anything for her."

Except ask, Nathalie thought. When she was six and David was three, it dawned on her in an unspecified way that he never asked for anything. He might demand, incoherently, that she feed him, or insist on sitting next to her, or insert himself in her line of vision, but it was perfectly plain to her that he didn't want anything from her in return, he didn't want anything except to be in her close company for his own satisfaction. And because he didn't talk—couldn't? Lynne worried, or, even more worryingly, wouldn't?—he articulated no need or wish for reciprocity. He just wanted Nathalie there. Like her, he might have been chosen, but he hadn't had any choice himself. Like her, he'd been given something he was expected to be thankful for, he'd been handed a lottery prize at random and told he was very fortunate to have it. But unlike her, he'd decided that in all this avalanche of not choosing he was going to select one thing he liked, one thing that carried no requirement for response or gratitude. And this thing was Nathalie.

And then he grew beautiful. To Lynne's astonished delight, this lumpy, ill-proportioned, almost bald toddler grew into a beautiful little boy, the kind of little boy whose looks somehow penetrated the indifference of even bank clerks and supermarket checkout girls. Taking David about became a matter of intense pride rather than one of defensive apology, a matter almost of competition between Lynne and Ralph. Ralph even took David to his chess club, where he sat on the knee of the club's best player, a senior master who had written an acclaimed book on the strategic challenges of the end-game, and was given a king and a queen to hold. Ralph came home replete with pride. He set David on the floor as if he was a rare piece of statuary.

"He'd charm the glaze off a doughnut," Ralph said.

David's charm lay in his beauty and his passivity. The obtuseness he had seemed to demonstrate as a baby could now be seen, more acceptably, as compliance. He could be left to play for hours with the same two cars on the rug whose stripes made useful roads; he could even be trusted on the rocking horse Ralph made him, rocking and rocking, and rocking, with an absorption Lynne saw as simply being good. It seemed especially good, compared with Nathalie. The older Nathalie grew, the more she seemed to need to do what Lynne's American friend, Sadie, called "acting out". She became provocative and touchy and unpredictable, sometimes clinging, sometimes rejecting Lynne's proffered cuddles. She made intense friendships at school and then gratuitously destroyed them and sobbed wildly over their demise.

"I don't like it," Lynne said. "I don't like the child she's becoming."

Ralph was mending a toy which David had uncharacteristically broken. He didn't look up.

He said slowly, "What you don't like, dear, is that there's a pain you have to live alongside that can't be made better."

Lynne froze. She looked at Ralph's bent head, at his deft hands among the bits of bright plastic. Then she went back into the house and stood by the washing machine, with her fists clenched under her chin, and gave way to a rage that was murderous in its brief intensity. How could he? How *dare* he? How dare he remind her of her abiding disappointment—*hers*—in his lack of potency?

Later that night, she shouted at Nathalie. It was over something entirely trivial, a matter of not brushing teeth or hair, and she horrified herself. She waited, in the midst of her despair, for Nathalie to be horrified too, for tears and trembles and consoling reconciliation. But they didn't come. Instead Nathalie looked at her with an expression that darted between triumph and relief, and then she turned and padded into David's room and climbed into bed with him. Lynne saw David turn to look at her, amazed and pleased, and then she felt she must look no longer, she must leave them there together, saying nothing, side by side.

"At least," she said to Ralph later, exhausted by emotion, by a sense of having let everyone, including herself, down, "at least they have each other."

Lynne still said that. It irritated Nathalie when she said it because it still seemed to Nathalie that Lynne wanted to be reassured about it, even thanked, and even though Nathalie loved Lynne, even though she acknowledged what a support Lynne had always been to her, how Lynne had ever been on her side, she still could not get her mind comfortably around the idea that Lynne felt she owed her something.

This problem over Polly's ear was exactly a case in point. Polly was Lynne's granddaughter and Lynne would want, would expect, to be included in any anxiety surrounding her, large or small. It would be a mark of the closeness between Nathalie and Lynne—a mark of the *no difference* there was between their relationship and that of a natural mother and daughter—that Nathalie should confide to Lynne all maternal preoccupations, everything that had to do with this bond that Nathalie had now achieved so properly, so primitively, with Polly.

But David had silently taught Nathalie otherwise. Watching him as he grew from a child to a boy to an adolescent, she had seen that he quietly went round things; he didn't charge through the middle, breaking the china. He made it plain that if Nathalie needed to break the china he was prepared both to share the blame and help clear it up, but that she didn't have to do things that way to get what she wanted. Over time, cushioned by his undemanding constancy, she began to relinquish some of the assertiveness of her power over him, to begin, even, to seek him out to give her the unarticulated satisfaction of his presence as hers had always seemed to give him. Leaning against the kitchen wall now, about to dial David's number, she suddenly had a memory of herself, crouched on the landing floor outside the locked bathroom door in Ashmore Road. David was inside, singing. He was about fifteen and he was obsessed with being a blues singer. He talked about bayous and catfish and getting no satisfaction and he was saving up for a slide guitar. Crouched on the gray marl carpet, Nathalie could hear him singing "This Train" and she knew he'd be lying in the bath, with everything but his nose and mouth submerged in the water, fixin' to die.

It made her smile, remembering that, remembering him writing songs with titles like "Ain't No Way Out", remembering him before he met Marnie and became a businessman, and a father of three. She was still smiling when she picked up the receiver and dialed his number.

"You sound happy," Marnie said.

"Oh," Nathalie said, "I was just grinning about something when I picked up the phone—"

"Polly?" Marnie said. In Marnie's steady, practical, comfortable life, most sources of pleasure and humor lay with children.

"No," Nathalie said. She began to twist her hair up behind her head as she always did when unrelaxed. "No, not actually. It was about Dave, remembering something about Dave when we were kids. Is he there?"

"Well, no," Marnie said.

"Shall I guess?"

"Wednesday night, Nat—"

"Chess club. Of course. I should've known. What *is* it with men and chess?"

"Only some men—"

"My father," Nathalie said, "Dave—"

"He wants Daniel to play," Marnie said. "But he won't."

"Why?"

"He says he's not interested."

"Perhaps he isn't—"

"Exactly what I say. At ten, he knows what interests him. Of course, his refusal makes Ellen want to play and David's taught her but you can see his heart isn't in it. She's not a boy."

Nathalie pictured Marnie standing in her hallway, looking at herself in the mirror that hung by the telephone. She'd be looking at herself, with the kind of easy acceptance with which she looked at most things, touching her thick, majestic fair plait which she wore pulled over one solid shoulder. Sometimes Nathalie imagined how the plait would look when Marnie was older, wound into a dense carved bun like an illustration from *Heidi*. When David had first met Marnie—capably running a small private nursery school—she'd sometimes worn her hair loose, a heavy corn-colored curtain, crinkled from so much plaiting.

"Anything I can help with?" Marnie said.

"Um," Nathalie said. She paused and then she said untruthfully, "It's a Mum thing."

Marnie said nothing. In her view, David and Nathalie were lucky to have Lynne, lucky to have a mother who lived close enough, and was enthusiastic enough, to be an excellent grandmother. Marnie's own mother lived in Winnipeg, where Marnie had grown up, and lectured on company law at the university. Every summer—with or without David—Marnie put her three children on a plane and took them to Winnipeg for a month. Every summer the children came back saying loudly that they would far, *far* rather live in Canada. Their grandmother took them on camping trips to her cottage on a nearby lake and every meal was a cookout.

"Anybody can do that for a month," Marnie would say to Lynne. "It's the Monday to Friday stuff that counts. It's the Monday to Friday that *I* value."

"We all want each other's mothers," Nathalie said.

"Oh, I want mine all right," Marnie said. "It's just that I don't want her all the way off in Winnipeg."

Nathalie let her hair fall. She liked Marnie, loved her even for giving David such a rooted, equable life, but every so often she ran up against something that was unavoidably like complacency, something that slid quietly from the accepting to the smug and seemed, in so doing, to imply judgment.

"It wasn't anything much," Nathalie said. "I just needed to have a little whine."

"Why don't you whine to me? I have the time. I'm giving the kids supper late tonight. Ellen's got a rehearsal."

"Because," Nathalie said, abruptly irritated by the vision of comparative domestic busyness and order conjured up by Marnie's last speech, "you make me feel bad about whingeing about her at all."

"She's a good woman," Marnie said. "A good mother."

"There you are!" Nathalie cried. "Listen to yourself! Anybody normal would have said, 'No, I don't, do I? God, how awful, I really didn't mean to, d'you want to know what drives me mad about *my* mother?' "

Marnie said calmly, "I don't think that way."

"No. Nor you do."

"I'll tell David you called. Do you want him to call you back tonight?"

"No," Nathalie said miserably. "The moment has passed. The fire has gone out."

"I'm glad I could help—"

"It was a *real* fire, Marnie. It *meant* something."

"I'm sure David will call you from work tomorrow."

Nathalie shut her eyes.

"Give my love to the kids."

"You bet," Marnie said, comfortable, collected and Canadian.

"Bye."

Nathalie put the receiver back in its cradle on the wall. She leaned against the wall beside it. From Polly's bedroom, she could hear Steve's voice reading the elegant humorous cadences of Beatrix Potter. He had plainly triumphed in the matter of Miffy, but then, once she had re-established her dominion over him, Polly would have allowed him to triumph. She also openly preferred Beatrix Potter, loving the way the animals took their clothes off when they reverted to behaving like animals, loving the language. She was reading along now with Steve, her voice slightly strident to prevent his skipping so much as a syllable.

" 'I am *affronted*,' " Polly shouted. " 'I am *affronted*, said Mrs. Tabitha Twitchett.' "

Nathalie peeled her shoulders away from the wall and slid into the nearest kitchen chair. Across the table's dully gleaming surface she could see a scattering of crumbs and a smear or two of milk or yogurt left over from Polly's supper. She reached out and pressed her forefinger down on some of the crumbs.

"That's real," she thought, "*real*. That's *here*. So's Polly. So's Steve. They're real like they were yesterday, like they'll be tomorrow. Nothing has changed. Nothing is going to."

The telephone rang. Swivelling in her chair, Nathalie reached behind her to unhook the receiver from the wall.

"Am I interrupting your supper?" Lynne said.

She always said something like that: "I'll only be a moment," or, "Is this a good time?"

"I haven't started it," Nathalie said. "In fact, I haven't even thought about it."

Lynne laughed. She admired that in Nathalie, that modern female nonchalance which felt no compunction about not setting regular meals before men. Ralph was undemanding, heaven knows, but Lynne still felt an obligation, a need, to lay tables at seven in the morning and seven at night and place upon them these—well, they were kinds of offerings really, offerings of affection and dutifulness. And mollification. Try as she might, Lynne could never quite leave conciliation out of any relationship.

"I rang to see about Polly," Lynne said. "I was thinking about you. All afternoon."

Nathalie looked at the clock. The appointment with the ENT consultant had been at three-fifteen. It was now ten minutes to eight. She leaned her head against the wall.

"He was a really nice man—"

"Was he?"

"He's got children of his own. It makes a difference, don't you think?"

"Oh *yes*," Lynne said, with fervor.

Nathalie knew she was waiting for more.

She said, "He was very kind to Polly. Very thorough."

She stopped. Lynne waited.

Nathalie said, "He examined her for ages. Both ears. He told her to put her hand up if he hurt her and she said, 'Can't I scream?' "

"Bless her," Lynne said.

"He said, 'No, because you'll wobble my instrument.' She thought that was terribly funny. She loves words like wobble."

"Nathalie," Lynne said carefully. "What did he say about the problem?"

"What problem?"

Lynne sucked in her breath, a tiny almost inaudible gasp. She had always done that when her patience was tested, drawing in a quick little breath as if this was a necessary physical check on a rising temper. Nathalie had played on it as a teenager, idly provoking and provoking until Lynne conceded a victory of nerve and took her betraying breath.

"The problem with Polly's hearing, dear. The reason why she is having difficulty at school—"

27

"She isn't having *difficulty* . . ."

"The reason, then, for her not seeming to be able to concentrate very well."

Nathalie said easily, "It's a tiny thing."

"*Is* it?" Lynne's voice rose in relief.

"Oh yes. A tiny thing."

"What kind of tiny thing?"

"A little extra piece of cartilage blocking her ear. Like a little spur."

"Can—can he take it out?"

"Oh yes," Nathalie said, almost carelessly.

"But that's wonderful. What a relief. Did he say why she might have it?"

"Have what?"

"This little extra piece of cartilage. I mean, could it be hereditary? Did he examine you?"

Nathalie looked at the ceiling.

"No. Why should he?"

Lynne said tiredly, "Never mind."

"Mum, he examined Polly and found she has a minute malformation, which he will correct."

"Yes."

"No big deal."

"No. Will he do it soon?"

"In the next three months."

"I'm so glad, dear. Really I am—"

"Me too."

"I was worried," Lynne said. "I was thinking about you." She let another small silence fall and then she said, "Would you like me to babysit this weekend?"

From her bedroom, Polly was shouting " '—which much disturbed the dignity and repose of the TEA PARTY!' "

"I don't know what we're doing yet," Nathalie said. "But thank you. I'll let you know."

"Give Polly a kiss from me . . ."

"I will. Mum, thanks for ringing."

"I'm glad all's well—"

"Yes."

"Night night, dear," Lynne said.

Nathalie slammed the receiver back in its cradle. Then she went over to the fridge and took out a plastic box of fresh pasta and half an onion on a plate and some minced beef sealed in thick white plastic and threw them on the table. Then she went back across the kitchen and found her bag and rummaged in it for her mobile phone.

"Mummy will come," Steve said from the passage, "but *not* if you get out of bed."

Polly wailed something.

"You've *got* a drink of water. *And* blue rabbit. And Barbie has both her shoes on, they are *not* lost."

Nathalie pressed the buttons to send a text message. "Ring me," she wrote, "soonest." David's number came up on the tiny screen. Steve appeared in the doorway.

"Will you say goodnight to her?"

"Of course—"

"The phone rang—"

"It was Mum. Wanting to know about this afternoon."

"And?"

"I told her it was a tiny thing and a tiny operation."

Steve looked at the phone in her hand.

"True or false?"

"Literally, true."

"Mummy, come *here*—"

"Nat, I thought you said—"

"At *once!*" Polly shouted.

Nathalie slipped past Steve into the passage. It was dark, as was Polly's room except for a nightlight shaped like a small glowing teddy bear plugged into the electric point by her bed.

"Daddy only read a tiny story—"

"No, he didn't. I heard him. He read you all of Tom Kitten."

"I really wanted Mrs. Tiggywinkle," Polly said. "I wanted that *so much*."

"Tomorrow," Nathalie said. She leaned down over Polly and breathed her in.

"Will I have a bandage?" Polly said.

"When?"

"When the wobble man does my ear. Will I have a bandage? Will it go all around so I have to suck through a straw?"

"No, darling. It will be a tiny cut right inside. You won't even be able to see it."

"I *want* to see it."

"Polly," Nathalie said, "it is sleep time now. You can talk your head off in the morning but not now."

"Blah blah blah," Polly said, turning on her side away from Nathalie. "Blah blah *blah*."

"Same to you," Nathalie said. She kissed Polly's cheek, "Sleep tight."

"Only," Polly said, her eyes shut, "if I don't *wobble*."

In the kitchen, Steve was slicing the onion. He sliced like a chef, using a big knife and rapid, precise practiced movements. There was a glass of wine beside him, and another glass on the table, which had been cleared of crumbs.

"Titus has a new girlfriend," Steve said.

"Oh?"

"Rather gorgeous, in a weird way. Sort of Jamie Lee Curtis type. About a foot taller than he is, as usual."

"It would be hard to be a foot *shorter*."

"He has no trouble pulling them, does he?"

Nathalie opened a cupboard by Steve's knee and took out a skillet.

"He's very attractive. As a person, I mean. Funny and sympathetic."

"You," Steve said, taking the skillet from her, "like anyone who's nice to Polly."

"Of course. And if they're nice to me too, I adore them."

"Like me."

Steve poured olive oil into the skillet and set it on a cooker ring.

"Titus wanted me to ask you something. Or at least he wanted something on Sasha's behalf."

"Sasha being the new girlfriend?"

"Yes."

Nathalie picked up the bag of mince and tore it open.

"She's doing some kind of counseling course. She's got a project on identity, how we identify ourselves, whether or not we need to know where we've come from." He lifted the board on which he had chopped the onion and tipped it into the skillet. "She—well, she wondered if she could possibly talk to you."

Nathalie carried the split bag of mince over to the cooker.

"Why?"

"Because Titus told her you were adopted and I said it had never troubled you."

Nathalie let the mince fall into the onion.

"How does Titus know I'm adopted?"

"I must have told him—"

"How many *other* people have you told?"

"Nobody. No one. I can't actually remember telling Titus, but he said I did—"

"Does it *matter*," Nathalie said, "my being adopted? Does it make any *difference*?"

Steve began to break the mince up with a wooden spatula.

"Not to me, Nat. And I thought not to you."

She said emphatically, "Certainly not to me."

"Then that's what *does* make you different. Apparently. Not feeling set apart. That's why Sasha would like to talk to you."

Nathalie turned back to the table and picked up her glass of wine.

31

"Well, she can."

Steve turned round.

"She can?"

"Yes. Why not?"

"I thought—well, I thought after what you said just now about feeling lost, about being so thrown in case you don't know everything Polly might have inherited, that—well, that you wouldn't want to talk to anyone. I felt I had to ask because I told Titus I would but I didn't think you'd say yes."

Nathalie said quietly, "Well, I have."

"Did you talk to Dave?"

"No. It was a chess night. I forgot."

"But—"

"It doesn't matter now," Nathalie said. "Sorry about earlier. Anything to do with Polly—"

"*Tell* me about it."

"I know. I'm sorry."

"So I can tell Titus that this Sasha woman could at least ring you?"

"Of course," Nathalie said.

She picked her hair up and began to twist it behind her head.

"I don't mind telling her how I feel."

Steve watched her, spatula in hand. Behind him, the onions and meat spat and sizzled.

"Which—is?"

"That being adopted," Nathalie said, "allows you to choose to be the person *you* want to be. I can shuffle the cards of my past at will." She smiled at him. "You can't do that. Nor can she."

CHAPTER THREE

When David Dexter was eighteen, he told his parents, Lynne and Ralph, that he wasn't going to take up the university place he had won to read business studies. He was going instead, he said, in the flat voice he had learned to use if telling them something that might cause a stronger reaction than was comfortable for him to deal with, to agricultural college in the West Midlands to study horticulture. He intended, probably, to be a landscape gardener or something of the sort. He wasn't sure. He just knew he didn't want to go to Leicester, and study business.

Ralph thought of all those weekends spent cajoling David to help him in the garden.

"But you don't even *like* gardens, David."

"Perhaps," Lynne said quickly, anxious as ever that none of the children's apparent enthusiasms, however hard to understand, should go without encouragement, "he just doesn't like *this* garden."

David said, "I just want to learn about something living. That's all."

Ralph, who had run his own small engineering company until it was bought up by a rival, rattled the change in his trouser pockets.

"I think you'll find there's something pretty *living* about the business world—"

"*Directly* living," David said. "Cyclical. Organic. Something I can *touch*."

They let him go. They had to, just as, Ralph had pointed out, his own father—whom he had detested—had had to recognize that Ralph was not going to follow him into accountancy. Ralph's father had expressed his resentment by leaving the bulk of his meager estate to Ralph's sister, which decision, Ralph suspected, had no doubt given him considerable vengeful satisfaction. So David went off to horticultural college with everyone's hearty outward blessing, and gained an adequate degree and then proceeded to set up a small lawn-mowing and hedge-trimming business which had now blossomed into a busy garden-maintenance company with three vehicles bearing his name on the cab doors, and a staff of ten.

It was, in his very early days, cutting the long, sour privet hedges in front of a row of substantial Victorian detached houses, one of which had a nursery school in its basement, that he had met Marnie. He'd heard her voice—American, he thought—organizing her little chattering charges in a way he found immediately attractive. She'd sounded friendly and interested and affectionate, but also as if she knew what those children should be doing, and she also knew that very soon they would all be doing it, without argument. David had played a kind of game with himself, wielding his electric hedge-cutter out of sight of the owner of that appealing voice, imagining what she would look like. She was possibly in her mid or late twenties: she was quite tall, and slight, with perhaps Nathalie's coloring, pale skin and darkish hair and those clear, strongly colored eyes which give their owners such a particular intensity of gaze.

When he finally trimmed his noisy way round the hedge and into view of the back windows of the nursery school, he found, to his intrigued excitement, that he had only been right about one thing. Marnie was tall, almost as tall as he

34

was, taller if she wore anything other than the peculiar blue canvas sandals she was wearing then. But she was young, not more than twenty-two or -three, and solid with the big supple grace of a girl brought up on sport. And she was fair, very fair, Scandinavian fair, with her hair pulled smoothly back from her face and hanging right down her back in a thick, even pigtail. There was no ribbon on the end of the pigtail, only a plain rubber band of the serviceable kind used to bundle up mail.

Three days later, having covertly watched her as she came and went from the school—on foot, carrying a backpack rather than a handbag—David lay in wait for her. He was in his work clothes, his hands and forearms smeared with green from the hedges, having not given any thought as to the impression he might make on account of being so wholly taken up in his mind by the impression that Marnie had made on him.

"I looked up," Marnie said later to Nathalie, "and there was this *fabulous* man."

He asked her if she would have a drink with him. He told her that it was her voice that had caught his attention, and her manner with the children. He said he'd never asked an American out before.

"Canadian," Marnie said. "Winnipeg. Listen to my r's."

They drank cider on a peeling bench outside a pub on the edge of the canal. Marnie said she had done preschool teacher training in Canada and had come to England because she needed to get out of Winnipeg and had felt that Toronto wasn't far enough. She had almost immediately landed a nursery-teaching job in West London, where she had so impressed one of the mothers there—"She's been so good to me, but really, she wants to run my life for me, and live it too"—that she had been helped, within two years, to set up her own school in her benefactor's home town. She was twenty-four.

"Me too," David said. "Do you play tennis?"

"Sure," she said.

She played golf as well, and swam and skied, and was taking climbing lessons on the purpose-built wall at the local sports center. She appeared to possess none of the mysterious complexities and maneuverings of the girls David had been involved with before; he didn't feel, as he so often had, that he abruptly had to leave the straight-forward highway and plunge off into the shadowy labyrinths either side, in pursuit of a girl who'd suddenly gone elusive and baffling on him. Yet even he was baffled now. Here he was, irresistibly drawn towards this uncommon girl, almost exotic in her seemingly serene otherness to all the English girls he'd known—and she wasn't remotely like Nathalie. David had always supposed, hoped even, that when he found the girl he would like to share his life with she would be so like Nathalie that he would feel no sense of added loss. It was, after all, the loss he had always dreaded, the loss he had wrestled with painfully when Nathalie met Steve Ross at art school and began to turn away from David, in the ineluctable way of a sunflower turning its face towards the sun. He'd always imagined, after that, that his consolation would come in the form of finding a girl just like Nathalie. But Marnie wasn't like any woman David had ever met, even up to the point of, within eight months of meeting, directing her warm brown gaze straight at him and suggesting that they get married.

He was astonished, astonished and relieved.

He leaned across the Cheddar ploughman's lunch they were sharing in a pub outside Westerham and said firmly, "Of course."

Marnie smiled.

"When it's right, go for it."

It was all so easy. He could hardly believe it. Lynne and Ralph were delighted, and Nathalie was too taken aback by Marnie's complete absence of challenge to her on any grounds to do anything other than echo them. Marnie took him to Winnipeg and introduced him to her kind, straightforward academic parents and a handful of approachable, easygoing brothers, and David had an eerie sensation that all this had somehow been guided by an unseen hand, and that the path that had been so treacherous and stony in his early life was now being superbly smoothed for him as a kind of almost unearthly compensation. He looked round his new Canadian family and considered his English one and it suddenly seemed to him that all kinds of disturbing inner battles had not so much been won as simply melted away without a blow being struck. He told Marnie he loved her in a voice that even she, almost dazed by him as she then was, could hear was heavy with gratitude. It was deeply, wonderfully thrilling.

They were married in England (Marnie's decision), honeymooned by hiking (Marnie's decision) through the Pyrenees from France to Spain, and returned to set up house in a cramped flat ten minutes' walk from Marnie's nursery school. Ellen was born—and named for her Canadian grandmother—eighteen months after they were married, and Daniel two years after that. The gardening business expanded, as did the nursery school to new premises with enough space for fifty children, and they moved to a detached house with a long garden—long enough to hit a cricket or tennis ball—running down to the edge of Westerham golf course. On weekends, Daniel collected lost golf balls from the bushes along the fairways and behind the greens, and sold them back to the members for five or ten pence depending upon what he thought he could get away with. From the lawn of the long garden, Ellen watched this minute commercial enterprise with scorn: her own aim was to be famous, but whether as an actress or as a tennis player she had not yet decided.

After nearly fourteen years of marriage, Marnie became pregnant once again. The result—Petey—turned her instincts all homeward, and she gave up the nursery school to gratifying laments from all the parents, in order to devote herself to motherhood and domestic life. After all, she said to David, she'd never had the full-time chance for either, and she was going to take it now, while Petey was still small.

"Of course," David said. He had said, "Of course," a great deal in the fifteen years they had been together and most of the time he had meant it. But this change in Marnie's life was weirdly disconcerting and his "Of course" didn't have quite its usual ring of conviction.

He wondered, staring at the input invoices for Value Added Tax on his computer—he still preferred to do these quarterly returns himself—what it was that alarmed him about the prospect of Marnie's not working. It wasn't really the money, because in the first place he was doing well enough to keep them all comfortably if not luxuriously, and in the second, the nursery school had never been run for a profit. It was more, he thought, scrolling pointlessly up and down, how their life would be when all Marnie's quiet, formidable energies were focused in just one area instead of two.

You couldn't, exactly, call Marnie bossy. She didn't domineer or nag or insist for no good reason. But she had a very clear, certain view of how human beings should conduct themselves, both as individuals and even more importantly in relation to one another. Marnie saw people in terms of community; she talked in terms of groups and teams and families. This had worked wonderfully at the nursery school where such principles were both practical and healthy. But when it came to family life, it didn't seem to work out so naturally. Marnie made it very plain to David, as the children came along, that he was no longer a priority to himself, nor even to her, but rather a leading team member in this new group, and the new group took precedence over everything. *Everything.* Family, it became clear, was Marnie's religion.

Part of David loved this, adored it, believed that it was helping to restore, deep down, the great torn gashes left by having his own blood family ripped away. He would look at his children asleep and feel an intensity of possession that was to do with something far more visceral than even paternal love. But for all this savage sense of physical belonging, part of him still strayed away by itself, part of him that was still engaged upon the lifelong struggle—he supposed every human to be similarly engaged—of discovering exactly who he was and how to live with that person. This struggle, which seemed to preoccupy the less conscious parts of his mind for most of the time, was in no way eased by his unquestioned love for either Marnie or his children. Only two things eased it, two things that he knew Marnie felt were, if not actually disloyal to the family, at least not contributory to its welfare. She would never prevent him from doing either, but she silently conveyed to him the fact that she considered the time and energy he devoted to these other pursuits was time and energy the family both deserved and could well have profited from. These two pursuits were playing chess, and seeing his sister Nathalie.

Ralph had taught David to play chess when he was seven, and even at seven, David had sensed a kind of rivalry at stake which excited him. Ralph was a good, steady player, a member of a local club, and he had said to Lynne that he wanted to teach David various skills and games that they might share, perhaps, when talking was simply too difficult. Lynne thought it was a wonderful idea. Her eyes shone. They shone with a gratitude to Ralph, which she was always thankful to feel, because it diminished her abiding sense of being let down by Ralph in the matter of babies.

Ralph had a soapstone chessboard that Lynne had given him, and a set of heavily carved wooden pieces which had belonged to his grandfather. He set David down one side of the board on a stool.

"Now," he said. "Before I tell you what's what I want to tell you two things. One is that, because all the moves in chess are up to you, you soon find out your own limitations. The second thing is—you could beat me."

David's head came up. His eyes were bright.

"*Beat* you?"

"The only aim in chess is to checkmate the king. You could capture all the other pieces on the board and still lose. But if you checkmate the king, you win. So a boy can win over a man."

It was evident quite quickly that David was going to be good, very good even, better than Ralph had bargained for. By the time he was twelve, Ralph, saying bravado things like, "Well, I always said the game was greater than the players," ceased to play with him. David noticed this, but took no account of it, so obsessed was he by then with this mesmerizing activity, where thought seemed to replace action, where he could move without really exposing himself, where he felt both his emotional and intellectual defenses were safe.

"Why do you play?" Nathalie said, declining to let him teach her. "Why do you keep on and *on* playing?"

He was tearing an envelope into smaller and smaller squares.

"Because I can control it."

"No, you can't. You don't always win. When you lose, you've lost control."

"But I can play again," David said. "There's always another game. Every time I lose, I look forward to winning the next one. It keeps me hoping." He balled his fist up round the envelope pieces. "And I can't get lost."

"*What?*"

"There's always an end game. There's always a resolution. If you play chess, you can't get lost."

"Yes," Nathalie said.

"See?"

"Yes," Nathalie said again.

"I don't have to surrender—"

"OK, OK," Nathalie said, "I get it. I've *got* it. But I still don't want to play."

David started a chess club at school and another at horticultural college. When he met Marnie he suggested that he teach her, but she was sure enough of him then not to need to learn. In any case, chess seemed irrelevant to her; it was deliciously foreign, a game emerging from the labyrinthine coils of Byzantium, from all the ancient, sophisticated, decayed civilzations of the past. For David to play it appeared to her eccentric but also cultivated, and somehow gentlemanly. It was only as time went on, and she saw that he was drawn back to it all the time, as if to an opium pipe, that she began to sense uneasily that this game represented something more than just a game to David, and that some atavistic workings-out lay beneath the deceptively civilized black-and-white surface. But then, she told herself, is it completely crazy to be suspicious— jealous even—of a *game*? Suppose he played golf all weekend, or spent all their money on boats or vintage cars or flying round the world in support of a football team? Chess, she told herself, was no enemy; couldn't be. Chess was like doing the crossword, a challenging intel- lectual exercise of great beauty and history. Chess was not arbitrary or demanding or emotional or vulnerable. Chess was not like Nathalie.

Marnie liked Nathalie. She was sure she did. From their first meeting, Nathalie had shown Marnie only affection and acceptance, and, even if this affection and acceptance denoted a supreme confidence on Nathalie's part about her own significance in David's life, it was, Marnie was sure, genuine in itself. Wasn't it? After all, there was everything in David and Nathalie's past to excuse and explain the bond between them—pure chance, Nathalie had said to her, because they might just as easily have loathed each other from the start—but the fact that they were *not* blood relations was something you could not, if as intimately involved with them as Marnie was, entirely overlook.

Marnie was one for friends, not particularly girlfriends. She attempted, in her customary, modestly confident way, to make a friend out of Nathalie, to establish a relationship quite separate from the one either had with David. But Nathalie eluded her. She was a pleasant sister-in-law, an excellent aunt, she wasn't greedy about time or attention, but she could still stir something in David, whatever his mood, that transported him, very slightly, out of Marnie's reach. And when he was out of her reach, she felt herself to be inaudible and invisible in a way that nobody else in her life had ever made her feel. And at those moments too she felt herself to be living far away from Canada.

Standing now beside the telephone in the hall, with Petey asleep in his cot upstairs—it was really time, she knew, to move him to a bed—and the prepared vegetables just waiting to be cooked for supper in the kitchen, Marnie thought hard about Nathalie. Nathalie had not rung to complain to David about Lynne. That was perfectly plain. Nathalie had rung about something quite different, some-thing she was not prepared to tell Marnie about, something which related to that place where she and David had first clung together after the shipwreck of their early lives. Marnie looked at herself, at the regularity of her features and teeth, at the way her striped cotton shirt had been competently ironed. A small but unmistakable anger rose up inside her, hot and red. You'd think, she said to herself, that I'd done enough, wouldn't you? You'd think that to give a man the first three blood relations of his life was the most any woman *could* do?

Nathalie drove out of Westerham in the rain. There was something oily and sticky on the windscreen and an exasperating long smear formed and re-formed with every sweep of the wiper blades. She sat leaning forward in her seat, craning this way and that to see round the smear and devoting far too much energy to the decision as to whether to stop and get out into the rain and clean the glass with a sheet of last week's local paper which was lying in the floor-well by the passenger seat, or whether to stay dry and dangerously maddened. She chose the latter, and drove on, muttering.

David had rung and asked her to meet him at a site he was working on seven miles from Westerham. It was the substantial garden of an impressive mock-medieval house whose new owners had asked David to design the basic lay-out of the garden as well as get it into shape. David was pleased about this. It was the best creative commission he had yet had and he was enjoying it. He wanted Nathalie to see it in its worst state, at the very raw beginning, before he started to impose pattern and order on it; he could show it to her while she said to him whatever it was that she wanted to say.

In the drive of the house stood a little Mercedes town car, a big four-wheel drive and two dark-green pickup trucks with "David Dexter—Gardens" painted on the doors in cream. Nathalie pulled up beside one of them, reached into the back seat to retrieve the Minnie Mouse umbrella, complete with big black ears, which Lynne had given Polly, and got out into the rain. It had slowed to a drizzle. Nathalie squinted up at the sky and put up the umbrella. Then she made her way around the house to the gardens beyond, where David had said she would find him.

The whole area seemed to be nothing but a sea of mud with islands of heaped building materials here and there. A small digger was chugging purposefully up and down and in one corner, huddled together as if for mutual comfort, stood a sad collection of spindly trees, their roots bundled up in sacking. In the middle of this discouraging scene, David was standing, holding a plan sheathed in plastic. Nathalie called out to him.

"Dave!"

He turned and waved. Then he shouted something to the boy on the digger, and came stamping through the mud towards her.

"Very sorry," Nathalie said, gesturing at the muddy desolation, "but I cannot begin to see what will emerge from this—"

David bent to kiss her cheek. Then he straightened and waved his right arm.

"Long terrace there, raised grass terrace all down that side, curved stone steps, lawn, grove, space for swimming pool, formal garden, brick paths."

"If you say so," Nathalie said.

David glanced at her umbrella.

"Like the ears—"

"It's Polly's," Nathalie said unnecessarily.

"There's a sort of pavilion over there," David said. "A summerhouse thing. We could go there for five minutes. Are you OK?"

He put a hand under Nathalie's bent elbow.

She said, "I don't usually ring you if I'm OK, do I?"

He put his garden plan in his pocket and began to guide her round the edge of the mud.

"I like to think I have a *sense* if you're not OK—"

Nathalie thought briefly how oppressive she would have found such a remark if Steve had made it.

She said, "Well, you did. You wouldn't have rung back if you hadn't. You'd have texted me, saying, 'What's up?' "

"Yes," he said. "What *is* up?"

Nathalie said nothing. She concentrated on putting her feet down carefully to divert herself from thinking of how she was going to say what she was going to say. She let

David lead her up a short flight of crumbling stone steps to a little grass platform on which sat a greenish wooden building shaped like a pagoda. She looked at it.

"Is this staying?"

"Certainly not. Fake, pretentious and out of keeping."

"But dry—"

"Certainly dry," David agreed, pushing open a half-glazed door.

She stepped inside. The interior was raw and untreated, and contained nothing but a broken plastic chair and a drift of dead leaves.

"Charming—"

"I'm replacing it with stone. Circular, like a little dove-cote."

"Dave," Nathalie said abruptly, "you know how we've always been—"

"How?"

"Not looking back, not saying 'if only . . . ,' not wishing we had what we haven't got—"

He closed the door behind them and stood looking out into the faint rain.

"Yes?"

Nathalie glanced at his back.

"Well, something's happened."

There was a pause, and then he said, "Tell me."

She looked at his back again. He was wearing a waxed jacket over overalls, and the wax had worn thin here and there and she could see dark patches where the damp had seeped through to the underlying cotton.

"I want you to help me do something," Nathalie said.

He turned round.

He said, smiling, "Nat, you only have to ask—"

"But you won't like this."

"Won't I?"

"No. Because I've sort of broken the rules."

"What rules?"

"The pact we have. About making something of being adopted, about making it a plus not a minus?"

"Yes—"

"Well, I'm going back on that."

He waited. Nathalie realized that she was still holding the Minnie Mouse umbrella over her head even though she was inside. She lowered it carefully to the floor, crumpling the ears.

"Dave—"

"Yes."

"I want to find my mother."

David gave a small, sharp intake of breath. He put his hands out towards her and then pulled them back abruptly and jammed them into his jacket pockets.

"You—you *can't.*"

"Why not?"

"You'll upset everything. Everyone. Mum, Steve, Polly, yourself. Me. There's no point."

"I need to," Nathalie said.

He looked at her. His face was full of misery.

"But why? You never—"

She put a hand up to stop him.

"No, I never did before. I never wanted to before. Or at least, I never let myself want to. I told myself that I wasn't going to be that kind of adopted person, lugging a grievance around and wanting people to make allowances for me. But suddenly—" She leaned forward and looked earnestly up into his face. "*Suddenly* I do need to. I need to for Polly, but I need to for me. I need to stop being this person of my own creation and find out what really happened. I need to stop feeling so separate."

He said hopelessly, "You've got me—"

"You're separate too."

"*Please*, Nathalie—"

She shook her head.

"Sorry, I can't not. It started with Polly's ear thing, and

then I had this session with Titus's girlfriend and I could hear myself coming out with all this stuff about being a lottery determined by no one but me except I have more numbers than most, and I suddenly thought I can't stand this crap anymore, I can't stand hearing myself lying about liking my life story beginning with me, I can't stand pretending any more, I can't stand not admitting that I have to confront whatever it is, whatever *she* is—and make good somehow."

He said, almost in a whisper, "But it's *been* good. It *is* good."

She moved to grasp the damp folds of his jacket.

"But not anymore, Dave. Something has changed or got unblocked or got released. I used to want to give back to the adoptive process, d'you remember? When we were having such trouble making Polly, d'you remember me talking about adopting myself because I'd been so lucky? Well, I don't believe that now. I wonder if I deep down believed it then. I want to be like people who know where they've come from. I want Polly to know. I want to look the truth in the face even if I don't like it." She shook his jacket. "I want to find my *mother*."

"You've got a mother—"

"Shut up."

"You'll break her heart."

"Possibly. And Dad's. And maybe my own. I won't start without telling her."

David shivered.

"I suppose you want me to help you tell her?"

"Yes."

He closed his eyes.

"Let me adjust a bit. Let me think—"

"There's something else."

He opened his eyes again. She was still holding his jacket and her face was very close.

"Go on."

"I want you to do it too."

He stared.

"Me—"

"I want you to look for your mother, too. I want us to do this together."

He stepped back sharply, yanking his jacket out of her hands.

"No," he said. "Sorry."

"Dave, please, don't you see—"

He put his own hands up to his ears.

"No, Nathalie. Not that. I don't want to, I don't need to, I can't even *think* about it."

She stood in silence, watching him. He took his hands away from his ears.

He said, "Sorry, Nat. No. Now and forever, *no*."

"Dave—"

His face was suddenly completely desolate, as if he'd heard that one of his children was hurt.

"She gave me away!" he shouted. "She bloody *gave me away*!"

Nathalie moved closer and slid a hand up against his cheek. He put his own hand up to cover it. He was shaking.

"Don't ask me."

"No. Sorry."

"I'll help you," David said, "if that's what you want, if that's what you really want, but don't ask me to join in."

Nathalie said softly, "You aren't really controlling things by just being passive—"

"We're not talking about control."

"Aren't we? Aren't I trying to take it?"

"Don't go on, Nat, don't go on at me—"

"Sorry—"

He took his hand away from covering hers and put his arms round her.

"I'll have to tell Marnie."

"Of course. Don't you tell her most things?"

48

"Most." He took his arms away. He said in a different voice, looking away from her, "I've never told her about the cutting."

"That was years ago. You were fifteen, sixteen—"

"Nobody but you knows about the cutting. She thinks the scars were some skin allergy."

Nathalie looked up at him. She remembered standing guard outside the bathroom door while David's meticulously organized sessions with razor blade, tissues, disinfecting cream, plasters were silently, appallingly performed, and how he'd look afterwards, relieved as if he'd had a holiday from himself.

She said comfortingly, "It's over, the cutting. I'll never tell anyone about it."

"No—"

"Why—why did you mention it?"

"Because when you told me what you wanted to do, I suddenly felt like I did when I needed to cut, I suddenly felt that everything was spiraling out of control, that I couldn't keep hold of things, that I couldn't keep hold of you—"

"You'll always have hold of me," Nathalie said.

He gave her a shaky smile.

"Just don't ask me to do more than I can—manage."

"Forget it."

"I'll help you—"

"Dave," Nathalie said, "please don't worry. I shouldn't have asked you. I'm a selfish cow."

He gave her another doubtful smile, then he stepped back and opened the door of the summerhouse and took a gulp of damp air.

"No. You're brave."

She put a hand out and touched his sleeve.

"Can't I be brave for both of us?"

He didn't look at her. Instead, he took his plastic-covered plan out of his pocket and stepped out into the rain.

"No," he said, over his shoulder. "*No.*"

CHAPTER FOUR

The coffee shop was furnished with chic metal tables and chairs imported from the Continent with, at the back by a window looking into a small paved garden somebody had devised for the use of summer customers in optimistic defiance of the climate, two black-leather sofas. On one of these Sasha was sitting, leaning back with one arm along the back of the sofa and her long legs crossed. She wore black trousers and a little cream-colored cropped jacket and the kind of heavy black laced-up boots that Steve associated with long-ago Mods and Rockers. He also noticed—he hadn't seen this on their first meeting—that she had a tiny jeweled stud in her nose, which flashed when she turned her head, a glint of blue-green, like a kingfisher.

He sat opposite her on the second sofa, leaning forward, his elbow on his knees. He had bought them both lattes—hers with an extra shot of espresso—and these were on the low table between them in heavy white mugs. When Sasha had rung to thank him warmly for passing on her request to Nathalie, his first impulse had been to say, "No problem, glad it worked out," and put the phone down. But something else had intervened, an uncomfortable something about the way Nathalie was behaving at the moment, about the atmosphere of distinct but undefinable edginess there was in the flat which was making—no getting round it—both Polly and Steve behave edgily too.

So instead of putting the phone down on Sasha, he'd found himself asking her to meet him for coffee, and then was disconcertingly pleased when she didn't sound even much surprised, and said she'd love to.

"A sort of debrief," she said.

He'd given an anxious little laugh.

"All above board—"

"Oh yes," Sasha said. She managed to sound both reassuring and at the same time shocked that disloyalty to Nathalie was even a possibility. And now here she was, almost sprawled on the black sofa, telling him with perfect ease all the things he realized he'd needed to know, to be comforted about.

"She was wonderfully straightforward with me," Sasha said. "I mean she said, 'Look, absolutely no therapy-toting, understood?' "

"She hates that—"

"Of course. It can be such an intrusive approach. Anyway, I was there to ask, not tell, thanks to you."

Steve's eyes fell from her face to her boots. They had scarlet-edged eyelets and scarlet laces. They were brazenly unwomanly and therefore—Steve swallowed.

He said, "Nothing to it. She wouldn't have agreed if she hadn't wanted to see you."

"She told me her father's theory. So interesting. He used to tell her and her brother that adoptive parents don't feel as guilty about their children's personalities as birth parents do, so that frees them from the responsibilities that encourage resentment. And I don't know about you, Steve, but my family *heaves* with resentments, and we're all *far* too involved with each other. Nathalie said she's always had space, that her parents have always given her space."

Steve thought of Lynne, of those persistent unspoken needs and wishes, of the anxious, silent pleadings for recovered hope. He picked up his coffee mug.

"Of course we talked about it when we first met. We

talked about it a lot then. But she really wasn't bothered and if she wasn't, I wasn't going to push her."

"You wouldn't need to," Sasha said, "she was perfectly clear. She said she was thankful to be free of all that genetic claustrophobia. She said she knew all she needed to know about herself from her birth papers but that she'd far rather have had the freedom to make herself and her own way than have the path mapped out for her, which is what would have happened if she'd known any more. She said she never doubted she'd been loved."

Steve took a mouthful of his coffee. Then he smiled, almost privately.

"Oh no."

"I can think," Sasha said, "of so many of my friends who can't say that of their *natural* parents."

Steve thought about his father. Then he considered mentioning him and decided, reluctantly, against it.

He said instead, "I wonder why people still feel so uneasy about adoption?"

"Oh, that's just numbers," Sasha said. "It's just less common. IVF, legal abortion, less stigma about illegitimacy. One study I read said there are only about a quarter of the adoptions now than there were thirty years ago." She uncrossed her legs and leaned forward to pick up her coffee. "Social attitudes are so different. I mean, in Nathalie's day there were two social improprieties to wrestle with—her natural mother being not married and too fertile and her adoptive mother being married and *in*fertile. All that's gone, thank heavens."

"Has it?"

"Oh yes," Sasha said confidently. She smiled at Steve over the rim of her mug and her nose stud blazed with a sudden tiny turquoise fire. "As a society, we talk about *everything* now, don't we? I mean, can you imagine Nathalie's mother and mine having the kind of conversation Nathalie and I had?"

"No—"

"She's a stunning woman," Sasha said. "Lucky you. A stunning woman with no hang-ups."

Steve said awkwardly, "I just had a feeling that maybe I wasn't doing enough, being sympathetic enough. That maybe this whole adoption thing *was* some kind of problem for her and I wasn't helping, I was just making assumptions—" He stopped and then he said awkwardly, "I'm grateful."

Sasha's eyes widened.

"Who to?"

"Well, you. You've—you've set my mind at rest."

"Good," Sasha said. She smiled again. "Just think of the selection procedures Nathalie's parents went through to get her. Pretty rigorous. They must have wanted her very badly."

Steve looked into his coffee again. He nodded.

Sasha said, "Can you imagine wanting anything that badly?"

He shrugged.

"Career things, maybe. I certainly wanted my daughter, but far more when she was actually here than before she was born."

"Of course," Sasha said. She leaned back into the sofa again and draped her arms out sideways. "It's often so difficult to *visualize* what we want, isn't it?"

Steve grinned at her.

"Did you visualize Titus?"

Sasha laughed. She threw back her head so that Steve had an uninterrupted view of her neck rising smoothly out of the collar of her jacket.

Then she said, "You couldn't *visualize* Titus, could you? I mean, you couldn't exactly *invent* him."

"He's a clever boy."

"Oh yes," she said, "and huge fun. We met doing yoga."

"Titus does *yoga?*"

53

"Of course not. He'd come with a friend, with the sole purpose of making fun of us all."

"Tantric Titus—"

"He only came to one class. Hopeless, of course, but so funny."

"I'll remember that," Steve said. "It'll come in very useful." He put his hands on his knees. "I'm really sorry, but I ought to get back to the office."

She smiled at him, without moving.

"Of course—"

He stood up.

"Thanks so much for seeing me. And—and what you said—"

She was still smiling.

"My pleasure, Steve. Any time. Thanks for the coffee. I'm going to stay here and finish mine."

He moved away, his hand raised in a half-wave.

"Bye, Sasha."

She waited until he was half a dozen steps away and then she called after him, "See you soon, Steve," and laughed when he went on walking.

Back in the office, Meera was typing from Steve's dictation tapes with her headphones on, Justine was on the telephone and Titus was pinging pellets of waste paper into his bin with a rubber band.

Steve said, passing him, "I don't pay you to do that."

"I'm thinking," Titus said. "I can't think unless I'm doing something else." He slid off his stool and followed Steve across the ancient, polished floorboards. "Have a good time?"

Steve stopped and turned to stare at him.

"What's up with you?"

Titus grinned.

"She tells me everything."

"Very unwise."

"Actually, thanks for asking Nathalie—for setting up this thing. It meant a lot to Sasha."

"Well, good," Steve said. He hitched himself half on to his stool and leaned forward to move the mouse for his computer. He said, not looking at Titus, "Nice girl."

"Yes," Titus said. He put his hands in his pockets and yawned. "I could kick myself, though."

"Why? Is she pregnant?"

"No," Titus said morosely. "It's just that I really like her."

"So?"

"Well, I don't *do* that," Titus said. "It's the *girls* who really like *me*, usually. Remember Vannie?"

"Oh yes," Steve said.

Vannie had had the kind of body and sheer physical presence that was impossible to overlook, but all the same when Titus dumped her without ceremony she had sat for days in the downstairs reception area, huddled and sniffing and—dreadful to witness—pleading with him to take her back. Steve glanced sideways at Titus.

"Why should you worry? I'm sure she likes you too."

"But *does* she?"

"Titus," Steve said, "I have a meeting to plan for and you have the Gower logo to finish."

"I nearly have."

"Go away," Steve said. "Tell Justine about your feelings."

"She's not interested," Titus said. "She thinks I'm an upper-class twerp with an emotional age of seven."

Steve didn't look at him.

"Well?"

"I may be a twerp," Titus said, "but I think being in love is *shit*. Aren't you supposed to feel on top of the world?"

Steve said resignedly, "I left her finishing half a pint of latte in Caffe Roma. Go and find her."

"Blessings," Titus said.

"And then stay until that logo is finished."

"It's a deal."

55

"I don't actually think you're a twerp," Steve said, "but you *are* bloody annoying."

"I know," Titus said happily. He blew Steve a kiss.

Steve watched him briefly as he slip-skidded across the floor and vanished through the door to the staircase. Justine put the phone down and looked across at Steve.

"Love," Steve said with ironic emphasis.

Justine made a face. He glanced up at the wall beside him, at Nathalie laughing, in her blue shirt, at Polly just *regarding*, from under her hat. He thought of Sasha, lounging on the café sofa, telling him all the things he needed to know, all the things he knew he was daft to worry about but needed reassurance over all the same. He smiled at the photographs and felt, simultaneously, a mildly superior pity for Titus's anxiety. He would cycle home, he told himself, past the Union Street flower stall, and buy Nathalie a love token. Iris, if they had any.

"There was no need," Marnie said quietly, "to speak to him like that."

She was standing behind David in the little room he used as an office, off the hallway. Since she had been at home, the office had been considerably more orderly, with the introduction—unquestionably an improvement but also mildly admonishing—of box files and a year planner which now hung on the wall above his desk.

David continued to look at the computer screen.

"I've told him about golf balls over and over. I've told him he can putt to his heart's content but he can't practice drives in the *garden*."

"It wasn't what you said," Marnie said in the same even, reasonable voice, "it was the *way* you said it."

"Marnie," David said, "could you possibly concentrate on bringing up just the children, and refrain from including me?"

There was silence. In it, behind his back, David could sense Marnie wrestling with this remark. When they were first together, she would merely have laughed, or thrown something—very accurately—at him. But over the years, she had become rather less equable about anything that amounted to criticism, anything that implied that there might be faults or flaws in the blatantly, palpably fair-minded way she was trying to deal with family life, with David. Sometimes David summoned up an image in his mind of that athletically built girl in her blue canvas sandals swinging into the nursery school with all the calm assurance of someone who understands the kind of life they have, and knows how to handle it. That image, if he was feeling tired or low for any reason, could sometimes make him feel sharply nostalgic.

He took a breath now and said, still looking at the screen, "Sorry."

"That's OK," Marnie said. Then she said, in a softer tone, "What's up?"

He shrugged.

"Oh, work—"

"But it's going well—"

"Yes."

Marnie moved from behind him to beside him. She put a hand out towards his computer mouse, almost as if she'd had a thought of turning the machine off, and pulled it back again.

"Want to talk?"

David sighed.

"Come into the kitchen," Marnie said. "I'll make some coffee."

Marnie always made coffee. In her grandmother's kitchen—her Scandinavian grandmother, who had bequeathed Marnie her smooth, fair coloring—the coffee pot had been the great domestic totem, sitting all day on the back of the stove, strong and bitter and familiar.

"I don't really want coffee—"

"But you want to talk."

"Not want—"

"David," Marnie said, "when do we ever want to do the things that need to be done?"

He got slowly to his feet.

"I'm going to have coffee," Marnie said. "It's not important whether you have any or not. It's only important that you talk."

She went out of the office and down the hall to the kitchen. David looked out of the office window, at the hornbeam hedge he had planted and which was not thriving, closed his eyes, counted to ten, opened them again and followed her.

She was standing in the kitchen measuring coffee into a red enamel jug. David stood in the doorway and regarded her. She was wearing clean jeans and a navy-blue polo-necked sweater, and her pigtail was pulled over one shoulder and fastened at the end with a clip decorated with a row of ladybirds. Ellen had given her mother that clip. Ellen knew it was hopeless to give her mother anything remotely funky: ladybirds, however, were acceptably orderly and unostentatious.

"I'm sorry," David said.

Marnie looked up. She smiled.

"I don't mean to patronize you—"

He came further into the room and pulled a chair out from the table. He watched Marnie pour boiling water into her enamel jug.

"And I don't mean to yell at Daniel."

"Don't you think," Marnie said in her nursery-school voice, dipping a long spoon into the coffee and stirring, "that we do these things we don't mean to do because of something else? Like we're scared or upset?"

"Well, of course," David said irritably. "When was that ever new?"

"Doesn't have to be new to be true. Sure you don't want coffee?"

He leaned back in his chair and sighed.

"Oh, OK. I'll have some."

Marnie unhooked two mugs from a row above the counter.

"I'm going to help you," she said. "I'm going to tell you that my instinct about how you're feeling right now has to do with Nathalie."

David grunted. Marnie put a strainer over one of the mugs and began to pour.

"She called here the other night. She wanted to talk to you, she said. She wanted to discuss something to do with your mother. But I kind of felt that wasn't really why she'd called. Fair enough not to want to tell me the real reason, but you can bet your mother wasn't it."

"No," David said.

Marnie turned and put the coffee mugs on the table. Then she sat down opposite David and pushed a mug towards him.

"So my guess is, she's called you and she's told you whatever it is and it's bugging you."

David said, staring past Marnie and out through the window behind her where he could see Daniel practicing erratic, impatient swings with a golf club, "I told her I'd tell you—"

"Sure," Marnie said.

"It's not a secret, it's not even particularly private, at least, it won't be for long, it can't be—" He stopped.

Marnie waited. She put her hands around her coffee mug, and waited, her eyes on the tabletop.

"She wants to find her mother."

Marnie's head jerked up.

"Holy *smoke*."

David said again, dully this time as if resigning himself, "She wants to look for her mother."

Marnie let go of her mug and put her hands down flat on the table.

"What brought this on?"

"I don't know exactly. She gave me some reasons but they sounded pretty flimsy to me. I—I wonder if this has been brewing a long time, I wonder—" He broke off and shifted his gaze from the window to Marnie. "It makes me wonder a lot of things."

Marnie shook her head.

"She always seemed so sure she didn't need to—"

"I know."

"Maybe," Marnie said, "what she said and what she thought were two different things."

David gave a little shiver.

"Don't," he said quietly.

Marnie leaned forward.

"Does she mean to involve you?"

He nodded.

"How?"

"She wants me to help her tell Mum."

Marnie said, "It will half kill your mother."

"She knows that."

"She *knows* that?"

"She just needs to do this thing very badly. Desperately, even. I pointed out all the people she'll hurt and she said she knew all that and maybe she was a selfish cow but she couldn't go on pretending any more."

"Pretending?"

"Pretending she didn't mind not being like people who know who their parents are."

Marnie leaned over the tabletop and scratched at something on the surface with a fingernail.

She said, almost impersonally, "It's called rubber-banding."

David looked at her.

"What is?"

"What Nathalie's doing. What's happened to Nathalie." Marnie raised her head. She said with precision, "The return of unresolved griefs from childhood in adult life is called rubber-banding."

"How on earth do you know?"

"I looked it up."

"Looked it up?"

"On the Internet," Marnie said. "There's a lot about adoption on the Internet."

David said angrily, "What were you doing on the Internet?"

"Just looking—"

"You mean sneaking—"

"I don't sneak," Marnie said. "I'd have talked about it as much as you wanted. *If* you'd ever wanted to talk."

David pushed his chair back.

"Talking doesn't solve everything."

"No. But maybe it *explains* some."

"Like what?"

"Like why Nathalie's decision has thrown you so."

"It's Mum," David said. "And Dad. And Steve and Polly—"

"And yourself?"

He stood up. He nodded.

"David," Marnie said, "could you just look at the positive? Could you just consider your upbringing and your present life and family situation? Could you just reflect on the fact that whatever the circumstances and tragedies of your early life I chose to stay in England and marry you and have your children? I *chose* that."

He looked down at her. There was a pause and then he bent towards her and said fiercely, "I was only chosen by you after I was rejected by *her*."

Marnie looked back.

"Her?"

"Yes," David said. "*Her*."

"Not—not Nathalie?"

61

"No."

Marnie swallowed. "You mean your birth mother."

"Yes," David said with emphasis.

Marnie turned her face away. She put up one hand and held the end of her plait.

"We seem—to be in real deep here—"

David said nothing.

Marnie said, "Nathalie's—kind of ripped the wounds open, hasn't she, even if she didn't mean to—"

"She asked me to go with her."

"Go where?"

"On this journey. To find—to find our mothers."

Marnie let her plait go and sat bolt upright.

"She asked you to find your mother too?"

"Yes."

"Anything else I should know?"

"No!" David shouted. He closed his eyes and turned his face to the ceiling.

"And will you?"

"No!" David shouted again.

Marnie waited a moment and then she said, "Why not?"

"Because I don't *want* to! I don't need to! I don't want to have anything to do with her, *ever*."

"Look at me," Marnie said.

Slowly David bent his head forward until his gaze rested on Marnie. She was sitting straight-backed with her hands flat on the table. Her hands were ringless. She had never worn rings, not even a wedding ring. "Why?" she'd said. "Why does a ring make us any more married?"

"What," he said now.

"Listen—"

"Look," he said, interrupting, "I don't want any half-baked claptrap off the Internet—"

She ignored him.

"Nathalie decides, for reasons we don't know, or maybe understand, that she wants to find her mother. She tells you. She has never given you any reason previously for wishing to do this, so it's a shock for you. But it's more than that. It's unhinging something in you, it's digging up something from the past you thought you'd buried, maybe even buried with Nathalie's help. It seems to me there's only one solution." She stopped and brought her hands together, as if to prevent them from gesturing and thus making the whole situation more emotional than it already was.

Then she said, "You have to agree."

"I *have* agreed," David said. "I've told her I'll help with Mum."

"No."

She looked steadily at him, and he had a clutch of recollection, a memory of those children in the nursery school who were going to do what Marnie told them to do because, in the end, she knew what was best for them.

"No," he said again. His voice sounded far away and thin.

"Nathalie's right," Marnie said. "If she's going to look for her mother, you have to look for yours, too—"

"Marnie—"

"You do," she said. "Or you'll never be at peace again. Not now."

CHAPTER FIVE

The upstairs sitting room of the Royal Oak had been decorated by Evelyn Ross to provide a distinct contrast to the public rooms below. The Royal Oak—apart from the improbably green tree on its signboard—had apparently always been painted black and dark red, with gold lettering, and nothing would shift Ray Ross from the conviction that this was somehow a historic tradition that it was his duty to uphold. When he had first become the licensee, all those years ago, Evelyn had begged for at least cream instead of black, or even, inside, some color for the window frames and doors less profoundly redolent of beer than the chipped tan they had always been, and had been met with complete resistance. The pub would be repainted every ten years, Ray said, in the livery it had always worn, and if she wanted to display her artistic flair she could do it in the areas well away from the dignity of his business.

"This isn't a bloody café," he'd said. "You can do all your nonsense upstairs, Evie. Do it where the customers can't see."

So she had painted her sitting room lilac with white woodwork and furnished it with a sofa upholstered in cream leather which had been in a clearance sale at a furnishing store. The store had also provided the nest of brass-legged occasional tables and the imitation onyx lamps with pleated shades. Ray never sat on the sofa: he said it was impossible to stay on. Instead he used an easy chair inherited from Evie's father, which she kept covered with a piece of tapestry-woven fabric because all Ray's clothes smelled of beer and frying.

"You be thankful," he said every so often, "that I'm not a bloody fishmonger."

The sitting room was a small haven for Evie. On the rare occasions when she wasn't required in the kitchen or behind the bar, she would settle—with difficulty—onto her leather sofa and watch old movies on the television, luxuriously conscious of not being part of the noise and activity and smells of the pub below. Sometimes, during longueurs in the movies, she thought about how life would be in two years' time, when Ray retired, and they bought the bungalow in Ferndown they'd always talked about, and Ray had no official occupation. Quite where she could go then to escape the heavy, demanding seductiveness of his presence, she couldn't think. Her daughter, Verena, Steve's older sister, who lived on the Isle of Man and only came down to Westerham once a year, said that she should get a job herself when Ray retired.

"Just a little job, Mum. Just something to get you out a bit. Dad'll drive you crazy, otherwise."

Evie didn't think Ray would like her to have a job, even a little one. He would be affronted by it, insulted. Working for him in the Royal Oak was one thing—for Ray, after all, a publican like his father, the Royal Oak was almost a vocation—but slipping out to earn money from another source was quite another. It would be seen as a disloyalty. She could possibly do some voluntary work in a local hospital, or a library, or an old people's home, but she didn't think a paid job would be possible. It was all very well for Verena, married to a man of a completely different generation from Ray's, a man who almost *expected* his wife to have a life of her own, just as it was all very well for Evie's daughter-in-law, Nathalie. Steve had always been so good to Nathalie. Steve saw Nathalie as a person in her own right in a way Evie knew Ray could never do, a way which he would regard as unmanly. Evie had never said to Steve—or, indeed, to a living soul—"I wish your dad was more like you," but sometimes, sitting on her leather sofa with her feet up on its matching ottoman, she wanted it so badly she almost cried.

She loved it when Steve brought Polly round. Polly was a source of delight and fascination to both her grandparents at the Royal Oak—she was the one person in the world Ray Ross would stop whatever he was doing for—and the recipient of endless presents. Evie knew Steve didn't like the kind of things she bought Polly, but Polly loved them. Polly and her grandmother shared an excited appetite for the excessively feminine, for glitter and flowers and Hello Kitty handbags. Evie kept the things she bought for Polly in a velvet-padded chest—it was really a dressing-table stool—behind the cream sofa. Polly called it her treasure box. She also understood that most of the items in the treasure box belonged at the Royal Oak in a way that could not be translated to Steve and Nathalie's flat, thus constituting a small conspiracy with her grandmother that Evie relished. Only over a few items, such as the Barbie bicycle that had been her fourth birthday present, did she fight so remorselessly to be allowed to take them home that Steve felt it would have been both unkind and excessively priggish not to let her. Some afternoons, before evening opening time, Evie opened the treasure box and gloated over its tinselly contents, imagining Polly's face—often profoundly serious when truly affected—when she saw the new additions, the sparkling toenail polish, the stick-on butterfly tattoos, the jeweled bow hairslides. Although she always loved seeing Steve, it was an acute disappointment to Evie if he came to the Royal Oak alone. The sight of his bike, chained outside with Polly's little seat on the back, gave Evie the same fluttering rush of feeling that the sight of Ray

Ross's motorbike had once given her, more than forty-five years before.

Polly's been, she'd tell Verena, on the line to the Isle of Man, and Verena would sigh. Verena had two boys for whom their grandparents at the Royal Oak constituted no more than a peculiar annual week's holiday, punctuated by plates of chips and flavored uncomfortably by their mother's tension. "She's a wonderful child," Evie would tell Verena, "wonderful. She has such an imagination," little suspecting that in the Isle of Man, Verena was rehearsing the phone call to her brother that she'd make the moment Evie put the receiver down.

"Thanks a million," Verena planned to say to Steve. "Thanks a million for thrusting Polly down Mum's throat, thanks a million for making sure she never gives Jake and Stuart a thought, thanks for being the perfect son, dancing bloody attendance, showing me up, cutting me out."

She never actually made the calls. She never rang Steve at all, except at Christmas, and if he thought of her in return, he gave little sign of it. He told Nathalie that that was how his family were, how they'd always been, that they didn't make a big deal of one another, didn't need each other really. Nathalie always smiled when he said that, as if she knew, as if he was demonstrating yet again that natural families couldn't, in the end, hold a candle to chosen families, that real family life was a matter of free will and love, not of blood. And so it was a surprise to Steve to find himself climbing the back stairs of the Royal Oak towards his mother's sitting room, impelled by an unease he could neither quite define, nor tolerate alone.

Evie was on her sofa, her knees covered by a blanket she had crocheted herself out of squares of mauve and purple wool. She gave a little start when Steve came in, pointing the remote control of the television at him involuntarily, as if it were some kind of defensive weapon.

"Ooh, I thought it was your father—"

"He's downstairs," Steve said.

Evie struggled to get up from under her blanket.

"No Polly? Where's Polly?"

Steve bent to kiss his mother's cheek. Nathalie had taught him to do that. Before Nathalie, it had never crossed his mind.

"She's at school, Mum. Nathalie's picking her up."

Evie pushed the blanket onto the floor.

"Why didn't you wait till you could bring her? I've got something for her."

Steve paused, and then he said awkwardly, "Today's a bit different, Mum."

Evie looked up sharply. She stopped trying to get up and stayed where she was, on the edge of the sofa.

"What's happened?"

"Nobody's hurt, Mum. Everyone's safe."

"What's happened?"

Steve lowered himself into the easy chair his father used. He sat leaning forward in it, staring at the carpet.

"It's nothing bad, Mum—"

"Then why are you here?" Evie said. "Why are you here without Polly?"

"I wanted to ask you something."

An expression of instant wariness crossed Evie's face. It was an expression very familiar to Steve, an expression he'd known all down the years when Evie was steeling herself to decide to do something for her children in defiance of her husband.

"Don't worry, Mum," Steve said. "No action. Only an opinion."

"I've never been afraid to act, have I?" Evie said, her voice rising on a tiny note of resentment.

"No. You never have."

"And I wouldn't be now. Especially if it was for Polly."

"This isn't about Polly," Steve said, "it's about Nathalie. About Nathalie and me—"

Evie looked hard at him.

"You never—"

"No," Steve said. He made a wide gesture with both hands, as if utterly dismissing the notion that there could ever be anything wrong between Nathalie and himself.

"I always said you should get married," Evie said. "It isn't fair on Polly. I've always thought that."

"I know," Steve said. He shut his eyes for a moment. He had no energy for embarking, yet again, on his defense of Nathalie's strongly expressed desire to live with him, but not to be married to him.

He said firmly, "It's not about that."

Evie bent sideways to pick up the blanket and began to fold it.

"What then?"

Steve said carefully, "You know how Nat's always been about adoption and stuff, you know how she's always said she wasn't bothered by not knowing her real mother, by not having a natural family?"

Evie patted the folded blanket on her knee, as if it were a cat.

She said placidly, "She's always been good that way."

Steve looked across at her.

"Well, it's all changed."

Evie stopped patting.

"What has?"

"Everything. How she feels, what she wants. Everything. Almost overnight she's gone from saying she's fine about it to saying she isn't fine at all and she wants to find her mother. Her—natural mother."

Evie shook her head.

"What's brought this on?" She looked across at Steve. "What've you done?"

He shrugged. He felt the anger he'd always felt when his mother used that tone to him, when she'd cornered him by the door to the cellar, or coming out of the bathroom, or in

69

his bedroom, and said, "What've you done to upset your father?"

He muttered now, as he always used to, "Nothing."

"Well, if it's nothing," Evie said, "what've you got to be upset about?"

"I'm not upset—"

"Then why are you here? Why haven't you brought Polly?"

Steve looked down again at the carpet between his feet. It was beige, trellised in darker beige with a bunch of stylized pinkish flowers in every diamond shape. He tried to re-member what Nathalie had said, how Nathalie had ex-plained to him that his mother only used that sharp tone to him because she daren't ever use such a tone to his father.

He said as patiently as he could, his gaze still on the carpet, "Mum, I don't know where I stand."

"Well, you would," Evie said, "if you were her husband."

Steve's head jerked up.

He almost shouted, "I am her husband! In everything that matters!"

Evie gave a little jump. She set the folded blanket beside her and got up from the sofa. Then she pulled the ottoman across the carpet until it was close to Steve's chair and sat down on it.

"Sorry, dear."

"This isn't about doing the respectable thing," Steve said. "This isn't about what the neighbors think."

"No, dear."

Steve looked miserably at his mother.

"It's been a shock, Mum."

Evie put out both hands and took Steve's nearest one between them. Her hands felt familiar, broad and warm and surprisingly soft after all those years of kitchen work.

He said, "She even told—someone we know—how fine she was about being adopted only ten days ago. When Polly had her ear seen she said it shook her a bit but only for a moment. She talked to Dave and I thought that'd sorted it. But it hasn't. It's done the opposite. She's now absolutely set on finding her mother. She just came out with it. Out of the blue. I'd put Polly to bed, we'd had something to eat, we were just sitting there talking about nothing much and wham, bam, she says it. Tells me she's made up her mind, says it's the thing that's been missing all along, that nothing I can say will stop her so I might as well help all I can." He glanced at Evie. "She's getting the details of a search service."

Evie squeezed Steve's hands. He could feel her rings, gold bands set with diamond chips, now worn to mere slivers, pressing into his own fingers.

She said, "What's upset you then? What's upset you about this?"

He looked down again.

He said gruffly, "That she just tells me. Doesn't ask me, doesn't—consult." He paused, and then he said, "And—and it makes me feel I'm not enough. Not enough for her."

"Well, dear," Evie said. "You'll never be her mother."

"She's got a mother."

Evie considered. There'd never been any difficulty, as far as she was concerned, in dealing with Lynne. They got on fine, the two grandmothers, Lynne's superiority in being the first grandmother because of being Nathalie's mother nicely balanced by Evie's quietly complacent knowledge that she was the grandmother with the blood connection to Polly. This superiority was not something, she discovered, she cared to have challenged. She took her hands gently away from Steve's and folded them in her lap. The sudden image of a new competing grandmother, a grandmother with *all* the cards, was both disconcerting and unpleasant.

She looked down at her hands and adjusted her rings. "Does Lynne know?"

"Not yet."

"It won't be easy. Not for her."

"No, I know. I've told her that."

"And David?"

"She's making him do it too."

Evie stared at Steve.

"*Making* him?"

"He doesn't want to. But they've persuaded him between them, Nathalie and Marnie."

Evie looked across the room at the framed color photograph of Lake Ullswater at sunset which Ray had given her several Christmases before.

"Suppose her mother doesn't want to be found—"

"Why wouldn't she?"

"Oh," Evie said with emphasis. "*Plenty* of reasons."

"Well, I think Nathalie'll risk that."

"She's risking a lot, isn't she?"

Steve sighed.

"She says she's risking more if she doesn't look." He put his elbows on his knees and laced his fingers together. "She says she's never felt so strongly about anything, except having Polly."

Evie said slowly, "Well, you'll have to let her, dear."

"It isn't a question of let."

"Then you'll have to help her."

"I know. I said so, didn't I?"

"I didn't like my dad," Evie said suddenly. "Sometimes I hated him. He was a real pig to my mother. Probably that's why I—" She stopped and took a little breath. Then she said, "But at least I know who it was I didn't like."

"Same as Dad and me," Steve said.

"Don't say that—"

"It's true." He glanced at her again. "Will you tell Dad about all this?"

"He won't like it," Evie said. "He doesn't like apple carts being upset."

"Me neither."

Evie patted his hand.

"Maybe it'll settle things—"

"They weren't unsettled, Mum!"

Evie straightened her back. She looked across the room again at Lake Ullswater, and then she said, "Then why is she doing it?"

Titus was waiting by the railings that ran round two sides of St. Margaret's Church. Sasha had said she would meet him there at six-thirty, so he had arrived twelve minutes after six-thirty with studied carelessness and found that she was even later. It was, in fact, now ten to seven. Titus had read the painted board announcing the name of the Vicar and the times of services and the proud boast that this was the finest Arts and Crafts Movement church in the area several times. He had also examined the façade (not his chosen architectural period), counted the railings (over-engineered and certainly nineteenth century) and vowed to wait only two more minutes before pushing off, only to break each vow a second later. Girls, Titus told himself, did punctuality in the same way that they minded about clean cups and glasses and knew where the car keys were. Girls liked plans and arrangements: they were the ones who wanted to know what time and where so that they could decide what to wear and whether to put any makeup on. It was girls, Titus reminded himself, while silently promising he would not look up at the clock on the church tower again, who were the halves of relationships that got anxious about the impression they made, who seldom had the upper hand, who felt this pleasing need to be accommodating and understanding. At least—Titus irritably kicked the stone curb into which the railings were set— that is how they had always been—seemed—for him. He knew he was a short-arse. He'd realized, at about fifteen, that he was going to be his mother's height and not his father's, and he'd made his plans accordingly. At least he was broad, even if he was short, and there was nothing the

73

matter with his face or his tongue or his hair or the quickness of his wits. It was soon plain that there was nothing the matter with his ability with girls, either. He'd gone through so many girls by the time he was twenty that his brothers were forced to cover their envy with sad attempts at mockery and derision. Titus affected to ignore them. Instead of rising to the baits, he merely nicked their girlfriends from under their noses, and carried on. And on, and on, until he met Sasha.

He unwound his muffler and laced it fiercely in and out of several railing spikes. Sasha. What was it about Sasha? Sure, she was gorgeous, but she was idiotically tall, which made him look a prat, and she could be appallingly earnest and New Agey and she dressed in a kind of fake butch way he couldn't stand. He hated her boots, hated them with a passion, and she wore them all the time. When she wasn't wearing them, when they were lying around next to his on the sitting-room or bedroom floor, he'd say, "*Look* at those! They look as if they belonged to some bloody *navvy*," and she'd smile and say idly, "Upset you, do they?" and he'd have to show her that he was man enough to disregard all the boots in the world. He'd once tried to buy her sexy boots, boots with spike heels and tight ankles, and she'd laughed at him. She'd just laughed. And then she'd turned and walked away, taking huge strides in her bloody navvy boots. Titus gave his muffler such a vicious tug that the wool creaked under the strain. Above, the church clock struck seven.

"Wow, you're punctual," Sasha said.

She was standing behind him, in the long naval overcoat she'd found in a forces' surplus store. He began to unwind the muffler.

He said, deliberately not turning round, "You are half an hour late."

"I'm dead on time."

"You said six-thirty."

"I said seven."

"Balls," Titus said. "Bollocks."

"You use such weird language," Sasha said. "Wherever were you educated?"

"You know perfectly well."

"If you're going to sulk," Sasha said, "I shall find someone else to play with."

Titus whipped round.

"I'm not sulking."

Sasha bent a little and kissed him on the mouth. He felt the brief sliding wetness of her tongue. He snapped the muffler off the railings and round her neck in a single deft movement.

"Gotcha."

Sasha waited a moment and then ducked her head free.

Titus said, "I've been here for half an *hour*."

Sasha sighed.

"We've had that conversation."

"We didn't finish it."

"I did," Sasha said. "Are you going to shut up about it or am I walking away?"

Titus hesitated a moment, then he pulled his shoulders back, slung his scarf over one shoulder and took Sasha's hand in a purposeful manner.

"Sorry," he said. He grinned up at her. "I've had a pretty crap day."

"Ah," Sasha said. She began to walk pulling him with her.

"What's 'ah'?"

"It's 'I've had a crap day so I'm going to give someone else a crap evening,' is it?"

"No," Titus said, "I'm not."

"What kind of crap?"

"Steve—"

"Ah—" Sasha said again. She swung Titus's hand a little. "I like Steve."

Titus made a huge effort not to say, "He's married," and

said, instead, in a goody-goody voice he would never have dreamed of using in front of his brothers, "I like him too."

"So?"

"He was in a mood. A big *mood*."

"We all get moods."

"But this was a touchy-feely mood. Steve doesn't have those. Steve goes mental if you leave a pen on your desk out of alignment, but he doesn't do emotional. So it means he doesn't get any practice and therefore when *he* is upset, he's upset like someone being thrown into a pool for the first time and told to swim. All thrashing and splashing. And *obsessed* with the alignment of pens."

Two teenage boys on skateboards went screeching past, sniggering at the discrepancy between Sasha and Titus's heights.

Sasha looked after them briefly, and then she said casually, "What was he upset about?"

They paused to cross the street.

"I dunno—"

"You must do," Sasha said. "You can't share a space that size all day and not have some kind of clue."

Titus glanced at her sharply.

"Why do you care? Why are you so interested?"

Sasha set off across the street, towing Titus behind her.

"Why do you think? Because of Nathalie, of course. Because of what I saw of Nathalie."

"Well," Titus said crossly, "you saw all wrong, didn't you?"

Sasha stopped walking. She stood stock still on the pavement and took her hand away.

"No, Titus," she said, in the voice she used for explaining psychological theory to him, "no, I did not read Nathalie wrong."

He smiled.

He said with a little air of triumph, "Then why is she trying to find a search service to look for her natural mother?"

Sasha said nothing. She moved away from Titus to stand in the lit square that fell from a newsagent's window. Titus followed her. He put a hand on her sleeve and stroked it.

"Sorry."

Sasha paused a moment and then she said, "What happened?"

"He just came out with it," Titus said. "When the girls went out at lunchtime, I said what was he being such a pain about, and it all came out."

"Exactly what did he say?"

Titus looked up. Sasha's features were thrown into deep relief by the harsh shadows cast out of the shop window and she looked like some wonderfully dangerous Valkyrie. He swallowed.

He said, "Well, it looks like she didn't tell you the truth or something. She's decided she wants to find her natural mother and she's making her brother look for his mother too."

"Her brother?"

"Her adopted brother. Dave the digger. He does gardens." He peered at Sasha. "Aren't you upset?"

She smiled down at him.

"No," she said. "Why should I be?"

"Well," Titus said, shifting a little, "you got it wrong. She fooled you."

"Or herself," Sasha said. "That's what's so interesting."

"*Interesting?*"

"It proves the theory," Sasha said, "the theory that *all* adoptees are interested in where they come from. At bottom, they are. Lack of interest is merely a defense."

"But you believed her!"

"I wonder," Sasha said. "I *wonder* if I did?"

"Come *on*—"

"I asked her about work," Sasha said. "I asked her what she did, with all her artistic talents, and she was very evasive. I couldn't get a sense she did anything much, just bits and pieces for friends, odd things, little jobs. And of course, that's classic."

"Classic?"

"The rejection adoptees suffer doesn't just affect their relationships. It spills over into work. They become paralyzed by the fear of being turned down so they won't even try. It looks like laziness, but it isn't. They often want to be better than the best, but they can't make themselves."

Titus took her hand again.

"Bor*ing*," he said, smiling.

"Not boring for Nathalie—"

"Very boring for me—"

"Not," Sasha said, smiling back, "boring for Steve."

"I want a drink," Titus said loudly.

"Do you?"

"I want a drink, with you, and then another, and then possibly another and then a Thai green curry and then—"

Sasha bent and kissed him again. Her tongue lingered a little this time and Titus was appalled to hear himself give a little gasp. Sasha took her mouth away.

"We'll see," she said. "We'll do the drink anyway."

CHAPTER SIX

Daniel lay on his bed. Or rather, he lay across it with his head balanced on one edge and his feet propped up against the wall at the opposite side. The wall had posters on it, exclusively of sportsmen, and Daniel had arranged his trainered feet around them in order not to obscure one of Ian Thorpe's ears or Andrew Flintoff's nose. Daniel wasn't much of a swimmer, but he was passionate about cricket, could recite accurately—if there'd been anyone around who gave a toss about such things—all the names of the major county and world cricket teams, including Bangladesh and Sri Lanka.

He moved his feet a little, tapping Thorpe's chin.

"Attapattu," he chanted silently. "Sangakkara. Jayawardene—"

He lifted his feet off the wall and brought his knees down onto his chest, pressing hard, pulling his thighs down with his hands so as to blot out all consciousness of the interminableness of this afternoon, the endlessness of these unwanted holiday days in which his mother urged him to devise his own amusements. She was very keen on that, very keen on Daniel and Ellen learning to be proactive, rather than merely reactive, in their leisure time. She explained, in her reasonable way and in order to forestall a torrent of complaint about unfairness, that this requirement did not apply to Petey who was both too young to understand the value of constructive self-diversion and also too young—lucky Petey, as usual—to know what it was to be bored. When Petey was older, Daniel's mother said, he too would need to learn how to interest himself, just as Daniel and Ellen must learn now.

Daniel pulled his knees down even further and parted them so that they could slide past his face and rest beside his ears. It was his mother's theories in this department which meant that he was the only boy he knew—and possibly the only boy in the known universe—who did not have a personal computer in his bedroom. The only computer, apart from his father's business one, was an old family one which lived downstairs in the same room as the only television and suffered from the same rigorous rationing of use. Daniel raised his knees and attempted to fit them into his eye sockets. It seemed to him sometimes that his parents must both have had some kind of amnesia, the kind that prevents you from ever remembering what it was like to be anything other than old and boring.

Of course, his mother had had *her* childhood in Canada. That, Daniel considered, gave her a monstrously unfair advantage and in consequence no excuse whatever for inflicting such unbelievable quantities of boredom on her own children. His mother had spent absolutely all her childhood time, obviously, as Daniel spent those precious summer weeks in Canada, fishing on the lake and making fires and building cabins and playing tennis with her brothers, those godlike uncles who represented to Daniel all the glories of accomplished male prowess otherwise reserved for England's World Cup cricket squad. Daniel's Canadian uncles could do anything they pleased with a rod or a bat or a gun or a pickup truck and, to be fair, his mother wasn't far behind them. It was just when you took her out of Canada again, and put her back in Westerham, that she seemed to remember all her restrictions again, seemed to lose all the sense of proportion that properly recognized extra cricket coaching to be infinitely more worthwhile to Daniel's development than reading a book or making a model or, heaven help us, *cooking*. Cooking was beyond Daniel's comprehension, not because it was girly but because it was so entirely pointless to spend hours chopping and mixing and stirring when more satisfying tastes could be instantly conjured out of ready-made packets and plastic pots and foil dishes. When asked once what he would like to eat most in the world he said a cheeseburger and chips in a really good seat at Lord's during a Test Match, and then he paused and added that the burger and chips didn't, actually, matter very much.

He put his feet flat on the wall below the edges of the posters, and pushed until his shoulders were off the bed and he could reach behind him and put his hands on the floor. Ellen could do handsprings. She could also walk some way on her hands and was exceptionally good, for someone of twelve, at tennis. At this moment Ellen was at the Westerham Tennis Club's junior afternoon practicing her service with a bucket of balls at her feet. She had cycled there, and when it was over, she would cycle back again and come into the kitchen wearing an expression of expectation of approval that would make Daniel want to hit her. Ever since he could remember, Ellen had possessed the capacity to make him feel that being a mere raw boy was most truly a misfortune.

He considered doing a back roll off the bed and decided against it, instead slithering down gracelessly and banging his tailbone on the floor. Then he got to his feet and wandered over to the window. A golfing four was just leaving the green that lay nearest to the bottom of the garden, pulling their trolleys behind them, a sharp spring wind filling out their anoraks in comical little balloons here and there. Daniel had been forbidden to scavenge for lost golf balls and sell them back to the players but he had not, in his heart of hearts, accepted the ban as final. He had chosen, rather, to hear it as something his parents would prefer not to know about rather than something he would be punished for persisting in.

He crossed the room and opened the door extremely quietly. His mother, he knew, had taken Petey to a toddlers' swim group and his father was having an afternoon of catching up with paperwork which meant that, although he was technically babysitting Daniel, he was not actually alert to Daniel's presence, let alone his needs. Daniel tiptoed across the narrow landing and looked down into the hall. The door to his father's office was ajar and Daniel could see his sweatered back and the bright glow of the computer screen beyond. The thing to do, Daniel decided, was to slide seamlessly down the stairs, along the hallway, calling, "Just going into the garden, Dad," in an offhand voice and then escape outside, thereby hardly causing a flicker in David's concentration about anything other than his figures.

Daniel reached the bottom of the stairs with slightly more speed, and therefore noise, than he had intended.

"That you?" David said. He didn't turn.

"Uh-huh," Daniel said.

"What've you been doing?"

Daniel sighed.

"Nothing."

"Like what?"

Daniel sighed again. He edged reluctantly across the hall until he could see into his father's office. The computer screen did not have figures on it: it had a chess game. Daniel could see the black pieces grouped together in the top-left corner and the white pieces scattered over the rest of the board. He edged nearer.

"What are you doing?"

"Playing chess," David said. He moved something. "Very badly. Look. The queen's rook is still where it started. It never pays to play wait-and-see in the middle of the game."

Daniel shifted a little on his feet. Chess made him uncomfortable. His father had wanted to teach him chess for three years now, ever since he was seven, and he didn't want to learn. He wasn't indifferent to learning, he was adamant that he didn't want to, and his father was hurt. Daniel could see that, could see the bruised look of hurt in David's eyes. He didn't want to cause hurt like that, but he couldn't see what else he could do. Something in him simply shrank from chess, shrank from whatever absorption it was that so held his father in thrall, held him, Daniel considered, apart from his family; the regularity of those chess nights, the arrangements with chess friends, the—well, the *absence*, in Daniel's view, of exactly that team spirit that seemed to him so wonderful. It did not occur to him, standing there uneasily behind his father and staring at the neat little pieces on the screen, to ask why his father was playing chess instead of doing his business paperwork, but it did occur to him to wonder why his father was playing chess at all. He shuffled his feet.

"Why are you?"

"Why am I what?"

"Why are you playing chess?"

There was a pause, then David moved the mouse and the screen abruptly went blank.

He said, still staring at the blank screen, "Because it comforts me."

The next question, Daniel knew, should have been "What's the matter?" but it was a difficult question. Sometimes you wanted it asked very badly and sometimes you hated having it asked, and if you had to do the asking there might be all kinds of stuff that followed that made you feel like you did when you tried to pull just one towel down out of the airing cupboard and the whole lot fell out instead and came out of its folds and turned having a simple shower into an episode. Daniel shuffled again.

He muttered, almost automatically, "Sorry."

David gave an abrupt little laugh. He turned round and looked at Daniel.

"What have you got to be sorry for?"

Daniel shrugged.

"Nothing."

There was a short pause and then David said, "Would you like me to come and bowl for you?"

Daniel nodded vigorously. His father's office seemed to go suddenly from being monotone to being highly colored. David stood up and stretched.

"Might as well—"

Daniel drooped a little.

"Do you mind?"

"No," David said. "No, I don't mind. It'll do me good. It'll stop me thinking."

It had taken Nathalie over a week to gain enough courage to telephone the adoption search service. It was called FamilyFind, and the telephone number had been grudgingly given to her by the woman in social services who had wanted Nathalie to use an official agency, something government-run or at least with national standing. She had looked at Nathalie with something close to dislike, Nathalie thought, as if she, Nathalie, was behaving in an ungrateful and unappreciative manner when she ought to have known better. She reminded Nathalie of her first primary-school teacher who had been quite unable to disguise her distaste when Nathalie threw a tantrum about not being chosen as Mary in the Christmas Nativity play, and Lynne was so sweet and consoling to her and, in response to all this sweet consolation, Nathalie had bitten her hard, on the hand, hard enough to draw blood. The implication then had been that Nathalie was biting the hand that fed her, and it was no different now. She looked at the woman from social services and said that she was a special case and needed special treatment.

"In what way?"

"There are two of us," Nathalie said.

84

"*Two* of you?"

"My brother and myself."

"With the *same* mother?"

"Oh no."

"Well, then—"

"It's a double journey," Nathalie said. "We need particular treatment in case we don't feel the same."

"You certainly won't," the woman said. She pulled open a drawer and took out a sheaf of long blue leaflets held together by a rubber band. She said, almost disagreeably, "You could try these people."

Nathalie looked at the blue leaflet. It had a drawing on the front of it, a little silhouetted row of figures, two men and two children and in the middle a woman looking as if she didn't know which way to turn. Above the drawing it said, "FamilyFind" and underneath it said, "We offer a complete search service for anyone adopted and their natural relations." She turned the leaflet over. There was an e-mail address on the back and a London telephone number.

She said hesitantly, "Do I just ring?"

"Of course," the woman said. "*If* you want to."

Nathalie put the leaflet away in a kitchen drawer when she got home, not hiding it exactly but placing it nonchalantly among the paper napkins and cardboard plates left over from Polly's last birthday party. She read it, very quickly, before she put it away and discovered that its presence was more complicated than she had thought, more compelling, as if it held the key to all kinds of possibilities which were far from being certainly benign. And it wasn't as if she could give a very coherent reason for this volte-face, this sudden desire to do the very thing she had always resolutely said she wasn't interested in. She'd told Steve and Lynne that it had been started by Polly's ear trouble, but even she knew that that had been only the tiniest, flimsiest of beginnings. After all, it didn't look as if Polly's ear was anything other than a small natural aberration; it was nothing hereditary and nothing really frightening like damaged eardrums and the consequent need for cochlea implants. She'd even gone to meet Titus's girlfriend feeling quite blithe, feeling that she could airily brush aside all the familiar questions, all the wearily patronizing assumptions that people who weren't adopted made so readily—eagerly almost, Nathalie thought—about those who were. But it was when she was coming away from that meeting that something had hit her, not an anger exactly, nor even the feeling of lostness she had tried to describe to Steve, but more a sensation of shame. She stood on the pavement twenty yards from the coffee place where she and Sasha had met, and felt a great wave of shame surge over her, the kind of burning shame associated with a public humiliation that is unquestionably deserved. How could she have done it, she asked herself, how could she have passed herself off— eloquently, frequently, confidently—as being one kind of person all these years when she was in fact quite another? How could she pretend—well, lie was the word she *ought* to be using here, wasn't it?—to all these people like Lynne and Ralph and Steve, who loved her and who had believed her? How could she have insisted that not only did she not mind being adopted but that she actually *preferred* it, when all along she knew that she was treading a separate, fragile, unhappy path which Polly's longed-for arrival had only somehow served to accentuate?

Or was that really how it had been? Had she in fact earnestly believed one thing and did she now, equally earnestly, believe another? Were her feelings all part of her inability to be able to stick at things, to make a career instead of just fiddling about with a string of little jobs that drove Steve mad because he said they were such a waste of her talents? And how, Nathalie thought, staring at the innocent pine front of the drawer that concealed the blue leaflet, was this journey to find her mother supposed to help with any of that? What if her mother was *dead*?

But—and this is what all her hot, circling thoughts always came back to—she had to do it. She knew she wouldn't settle until she'd done it, she knew she'd be like someone who can't concentrate because they are always waiting for the crucial phone call, the deciding knock at the door. She'd tried to explain this to Lynne, tried to make Lynne see that it wasn't any inadequacy on Lynne's part, as a mother, that was making her want to find the woman who had actually given birth to her. Lynne had stood there, in her garden, where she had taken Nathalie to look at the spring bulbs, and she'd said, over and over, "But I thought you'd got everything you wanted!"

"So did I," Nathalie said.

Lynne bent down to set a leaning narcissus upright.

"You always said—"

"I know, Mum. I always did."

"It's hard not to take it personally," Lynne said, propping the bent flower against a straighter one.

"Mum—"

"I always had this feeling," Lynne said, kneeling now, on the damp grass, "that I'd somehow rescued you and David. Even when I was battling with my own disappointments, I used to tell myself that I'd done some good in the world at least, that I'd helped two children to have a chance they mightn't otherwise have had. I know you shouldn't think like that, but it's hard not to when people keep telling you that you've done a good thing."

"You *did* do a good thing," Nathalie said.

"I used to say to myself, 'I want a baby, I want a baby.' Dad said I shouldn't say that. Dad said I should say instead that I wanted to bring up a child." Lynne looked up at Nathalie. "If you find your mother, can't you see what that makes me?"

Nathalie shook her head.

Lynne said miserably, "I go from being the rescuer to the woman who took another woman's child."

Nathalie crouched down beside her.

"You won't change, Mum."

"No, I won't change. Not as a person. But what I'm seen as will change. What about Polly? What kind of granny do I become when Polly has this new granny?"

"It mightn't happen—"

"What mightn't?"

"I mightn't find her. I mightn't like her."

"Then why are you taking such a chance?"

"Oh, Mum," Nathalie said, leaning forward and holding Lynne's arms hard. "Because I have to *know*. Even if I don't like it, I have to know. *You* know, don't you? You know who your mother was?"

Lynne pulled herself free and stood up.

"At least David—" She stopped.

"At least David what?"

"Doesn't want to join in all this."

Nathalie stood too.

"Mum, he does."

"No, he doesn't want to. You are forcing him."

"I couldn't *force* him, Mum. I couldn't if I tried. He's scared, like me, but he's going to."

Lynne took a step away and began to fiddle with a flowering currant bush.

"Daniel was here yesterday. He helped Dad in the workshop. He's good with his hands."

"Mum," Nathalie said, "*nothing* is going to change between you and your children or you and your grandchildren."

"You don't know that," Lynne said.

Nathalie put her hands over her face.

"Please trust me!"

Lynne said nothing.

Nathalie took her hands away and said furiously, "Look, I didn't *have* to tell you or Steve or anyone. I could have just telephoned this search-service person in secret and gone to meet my mother—if indeed she's still alive—and none of you would have been any the wiser. But I didn't. I *didn't*, did I? I've told you all everything, right from the beginning, and if that doesn't show love and trust and all the things you imply I'm failing in, I don't know what does!"

Lynne put a hand out and adjusted a spray of leaves on a philadelphus. The moment she took her hand away, the philadelphus adjusted itself back to its original position.

"I don't want to go back to the past," Lynne said.

Nathalie said nothing. Lynne laid hold of the philadelphus again.

"It's not that I don't understand what you want to do. I'd never try and stop you. You know I wouldn't. But it's just such a risk, it just opens up so much that I thought was healed over, all those things I thought I'd come to terms with."

Nathalie closed her eyes. She and Lynne had had a long and anguishing conversation about infertility when she had discovered that she was, at last, pregnant with Polly, and she had, at this moment, less than no desire to have it again.

She opened her eyes and said, in as neutral a voice as possible, "Will you tell Dad?"

Lynne let the philadelphus spring back.

"Oh no."

"What do you mean—that you won't or that he shouldn't be told?"

"Of course he should be told," Lynne said. "You should tell him yourself."

"I thought you'd like to—"

Lynne spun round. She was someone who could be relied upon never to lose her temper, but she had lost it now. Her face was quite diminished by the concentration of her fury.

"Nathalie," she said, "Nathalie. I don't like *any* of this."

Titus, Steve noticed, had left his computer on. His screensaver, which no doubt he had designed himself, was a series of serenely flying pigs, some of them wearing spectacles. Steve stood and watched their stately floating progress across the screen for some minutes and then he leaned forward and turned the computer off. On the desk around the keyboard lay a nonchalant scattering of little objects— paper clips, rubber bands, a dice, a crumpled bus ticket, a liquorice toffee in a black-and-white-striped wrapper—that caused Steve simultaneous irritation at its presence and envy that its presence was of neither annoyance nor significance to Titus. He bent over the desk and scooped all the mess to the edge with the side of his hand. Titus's bin, he noticed, was almost full and apparently with items of rubbish that had absolutely nothing to do with work. Steve took a breath. There was a fine line between being punctilious and being paranoid, and peering analytically at the contents of someone else's waste bin was definitely a symptom of the latter.

"Fussing," Nathalie used to say to him, "isn't sexy." She'd said it affectionately, laughing, in the days when she could get away with saying anything. That wouldn't happen now, no good pretending otherwise. In the first place, she wouldn't be laughing and in the second she wouldn't get away with it. Steve gave Titus's waste bin an inaccurate, childish kick and went across the studio to his own desk.

"I just hope," he said aloud and angrily to Nathalie's smiling face on the wall, "that you know what you're doing."

"Steve," someone said.

He spun round. Sasha was standing holding the door that led to the staircase. She was half hidden by it, like some cool modern version of a fan dancer, so that he could see only one eye and one ear and a long slice of dark clothing.

"What are you doing here?"

"I was looking for Titus—"

"How did you get in?"

Sasha emerged from behind the door. She was wearing a

kind of naval overcoat, strongly made with emphatic shoulders and buttons.

"The door wasn't locked, only latched. The street door."

"That was Titus," Steve said. He looked at her. She had her red-laced boots on again. He said, "I've no idea where he is."

"It doesn't matter."

Steve said nothing.

"I'm glad to see, you," Sasha said. "Actually."

Steve shrugged.

He said, almost nastily, "I wonder why."

Sasha moved towards his desk, unbuttoning her coat. "Sorry?"

"Well," Steve said, "having made such a superb diagnosis of Nathalie's state of mind, I imagine you've come to justify yourself."

"Oh no," Sasha said easily.

"So you feel not one twinge of conscience in being one hundred percent wide of the mark and persuading me to think likewise?"

"Of course not," Sasha said. "I'm not a bloody *doctor*."

Steve grunted.

"I just find it all riveting," Sasha said.

"What, getting things wrong?"

Sasha leaned against the side of Steve's desk. Underneath the coat she was wearing a tight red T-shirt and black trousers tucked into her red-laced boots.

"The thing is," Sasha said, "that now she's come clean Nathalie falls completely into the pattern. The almost universal pattern. And all those years of denial, as if she knew, all along, what she really felt and couldn't face it."

Steve moved a little until he was quite close to her, close enough to see her eyelashes and the tiny sharp angles of her nose stud.

He said, "Am I going to have to spell it out?"

"What?"

"That I am angry with you. That I am really *very* angry indeed."

She smiled at him.

"No, you're not."

"Excuse me—"

"Steve," Sasha said, "you're angry, for sure. You're angry and frightened and puzzled. Who wouldn't be, in your situation? But you aren't angry with *me*."

"Don't you be so sure."

She smiled again.

"Well," she said, "I don't accept it. I don't accept your anger. You'll have to find somewhere else to dump it."

"But you made me *believe*—"

"I didn't do anything," Sasha said. "I merely told you what Nathalie told me. Which was, as it's turned out, what she wanted to believe and you wanted to hear. In fact, you should be thanking me."

"How—"

"You should be thanking me," Sasha said, "for being the catalyst, for being the force for change, for truth, at last."

Steve turned away and put his hands in his pockets.

He said, staring off down the studio, "This is all a bit much for me."

Sasha said nothing. She hitched herself onto the edge of Steve's desk and swung her foot.

Then she said, in quite a different voice, "I know."

Steve blinked. He could feel, to his distress, that tears were bunching up in the back of his throat.

He said unsteadily, "It's—" and then he stopped.

Sasha watched him, swinging her foot.

"It isn't," she said, in the same soft tone, "as if she'd found another man."

"It's worse."

"Worse?"

"It's another territory," Steve said. "Feelings that were there long before I knew her. Feelings I've no part in—"

"But not a *threat*."

Steve sighed.

"There's David."

"David?"

"It's all tied up with David, too. It's all part of this fucking club we can't join."

"But they have different mothers—"

"And the same situation."

"Steve," Sasha said, "I've never met him, but are you jealous of David?"

Steve gave a little bark of near laughter.

"Oh yes."

"Why?"

"He knows things I'll never know. He shares things I can't share."

Sasha said curiously, "What's he like?"

Steve gave another little bark.

"Big, blond and beautiful."

"Well," Sasha said, "you are big and beautiful."

"I'm losing my hair."

"All the better."

Steve turned round.

"What are you after?"

She looked at him calmly. She had a red bead on a leather bootlace sitting precisely in the hollow of her throat above the neckline of her T-shirt.

"Making you feel better."

"Why bother?"

"Because this is an unusual and very emotional situation and you are a nice guy."

Steve said awkwardly, "I thought you were looking for Titus."

"I was."

"Well, then—"

"He isn't here. He said he'd be here until six and it's long after."

"He likes you," Steve said.

"And I like him."

"No, I mean more than that. I mean that he's really keen."

"I'm just a challenge," Sasha said. She glanced sideways at him. "We all like challenges."

"I don't much like mine—"

"You could learn to."

He said nothing.

"I could teach you," Sasha said in a cool voice.

"Do you seriously expect me to have any faith in your powers of discernment?"

She regarded him. The light from one of the ceiling spotlights fell directly on the smooth pelt of her hair and made it shine like something unearthly, like a nimbus.

"Yes," she said.

Steve snorted.

Sasha said, bending a little towards him, "You're angry because you were wrong. We hate having our safe patterns disturbed, we hate disillusion."

"And who," Steve said with heavy sarcasm, "are you quoting now?"

"Steinbeck."

"*Steinbeck?*"

"Yes."

Steve moved away from his desk and began to pace. Sasha stayed where she was, and watched him. She watched him until he had circled Justine's desk and come slowly back to her.

He said, "D'you know something?"

"Tell me," Sasha said.

"She always said being adopted was no big deal, but now I come to think of it, she was always coming back to it. Always."

"Yes."

"When I think about it, I don't think a week went by—"

"No."

"I'm so *obtuse*—"

"No."

He glanced at her.

"No?"

"You're not in thrall."

"To what?"

"To what is known as early attachment figures. Like a rejecting parent."

"I think," Steve said, "that I've had enough of this kind of talk—"

"Pity," Sasha said. "I like it."

"Can you do any other kind?"

"Try me."

He smiled. He straightened his shoulders and put his hand out for his jacket, hanging on a steel peg in the wall.

"Over a drink," Steve said.

CHAPTER SEVEN

Marnie was running Petey's bath with the kind of attention to ritual that is comforting when other areas of life seem to be slipping out of control. His towel—a square towel, hooded at one corner, left over from his babyhood—lay ready on the bathroom chair and his pajamas were hanging on the heated towel rail. Petey himself was not in the bathroom however, but was instead in his bedroom where he was lying on the floor having one of the intense and almost soundless rages that had overtaken him since just before his second birthday.

In theory, Marnie, of course, knew about these rages. She had written sheaves of notes, during her years of conscientious nursery-teacher training, about the small child's need to have some powers transferred to himself from his omnipotent parents, and how this need often manifested itself in tantrums. But somehow, the reality of Petey's rages was something she couldn't seem to handle with anything like the calm assurance she had felt and displayed when Ellen and Daniel were at the same stage. She remembered, clearly, both the energy and the consistency she had been able to bring to discipline and to distraction then, the confidence she had felt in shepherding these two little creatures from babyhood into the first stages of independence. Both children had shown, she knew, a highly developed sense of recognition and responsibility for other people by Petey's age. She remembered Daniel's acute concern when a carelessly flung toy had caught her a sharp blow not far from her eye. The resulting bruise had distressed him for days. But Petey was not like Daniel. He had been an obliging and easy baby but it was as if, as his second birthday approached, he had decided that he had been altogether too amenable for too long and must make up for lost time. That evening, for example, having been whining round her while she painstakingly made his supper, he had seized his plastic dish when she set it before him, plunged both hands into the contents and then spattered them far and wide, gazing at her blankly and fixedly while he did so. Then, when reprimanded, he had fallen instantly into one of his near silent, heaving, paroxysms of rage. Forty minutes later, he was still in it, jerking on his back on the rug by his cot, his silky pale hair fanning out like the tentacles of a sea anenome, his face in a rictus of utter temper.

Marnie knelt by the bath and swished her hand in the water. She thought that, if Petey hadn't stopped in five minutes' time, she would call Ellen to come and help her. Ellen was good with Petey's rages because they in no way alarmed her. She made it very plain to Petey that his tantrums bored her, that mostly she couldn't even see that he was having one because they were indeed so very, very boring. She would go into Petey's room, looking as if she were thinking of something else, and step over him as if he were no more than part of the carpet, and begin to play, very casually, with something he prized, or, even better, something he was only permitted to play with very occasionally. It was often only a matter of seconds before Petey had shed his rage as if it were no more encumbering than a cloak and would be clamoring to do whatever Ellen appeared to be so engrossed in. She could, Marnie knew, have summoned Ellen as soon as Petey's baked potato and peas and grated cheese began to be hurled around the kitchen, but she hadn't. And she hadn't—she shut her eyes and swished her hand harder in the water—because she didn't want Ellen taking charge, she didn't, at the moment, want any more evidence, however small, that the domestic control and competence and satisfaction that had always, up to now, been so—so *sweetly* hers was in any way diminished. What with David's new preoccupations—however much she had urged them, however much she had known she was doing the right, loving, wifely thing in urging them—and his consequent increased withdrawal from the family, from her, Marnie didn't think that she could, just now, stand any more relegation, not just from the center of things, but from the supreme maternal role she had chosen—yes, *chosen*—when Petey was born.

Ellen appeared in the doorway. She was wearing the pink shorts in which she had played tennis earlier that day, and an uneasy little top which outlined the diffident small buds of her breasts and exposed her pale young midriff.

"Petey's having a thing."

"I know."

"D'you want me to sort him?"

Marnie put her hands on the side of the bath and pushed herself to her feet.

"I think we'll just leave him."

"Why?"

"He threw his supper all over the place."

"Maybe he's hungry."

"Then he can stay hungry."

"And screaming?"

"Ellen," Marnie said. "This is the third child I've raised." Ellen tweaked her top.

"You can't be right about everything, always. Nobody is."

"Some things I do know about."

"What I hate about this family," Ellen said, "is that everyone thinks they know everything about something. Dad knows all about chess. Daniel knows all about cricket.

98

You know all about children. When I have children I'm going to make sure I know a little about a lot of things—I'm not going to be Mrs. Supreme Opinion about *any*thing. No wonder Petey has his things."

Marnie bent and refolded Petey's towel.

"You'll find experience dictates your knowledge. And validates it."

"Then I'll have to have a lot of experience, won't I?"

"Ellen," Marnie said, "I don't have enough energy for this kind of conversation right now."

"Well, why won't you let me see to Petey?"

Marnie turned away. She bent to re-smooth Petey's pajamas and her plait swung forward, the heavy, solid, flaxen plait that had been swinging over her shoulder for more than twenty years. Twenty years—she caught her breath suddenly, seized by the image of herself twenty years ago, before coming to England, before the nursery school, before David, before two-year-old Petey, lying on his bedroom floor in a fury that was quite beyond either his or her control. She straightened up slowly.

"Go get him," she said tiredly to Ellen.

She heard Ellen's feet pounding along the landing and then her voice, light, indifferent, in the doorway to Petey's room.

"Hello," Ellen said, "you tedious child."

Marnie looked at herself in the bathroom mirror. White T-shirt, dark cotton overshirt, clean skin, good teeth. Perhaps it was time to cut her hair. Perhaps it was time to jettison the T-shirt and the overshirt and let Ellen take her shopping. Perhaps it was time, in the midst of all these dark passageways opening up around her, to reassess how she felt in all these wonderings about identity, how it was for her, a girl from Winnipeg, who had hitched her hopeful wagon to a foreign star and found that—please, God, not forever—it had lost its pulling power.

She went out of the bathroom and down the landing. She

stopped outside Petey's bedroom and looked in. In the middle of the room, and regarding herself as best she could in Petey's baby looking glass, ringed with blue rabbits, Ellen was dancing a fair imitation of Kylie Minogue. And from the floor by his cot, upright on his bottom with his thumb in his mouth and his legs neatly crossed at the ankle, Petey was peacefully watching her.

Justine almost never stayed in the office for lunch. It wasn't only that she needed to get out and walk but also that she needed to show Steve that she could assert her independence and go out, and also be reliably depended upon to come back in an hour, give or take five minutes or so. Going out also saved her from having to acknowledge that Meera never left her desk at lunchtime, but sat there eating, very unobtrusively, a neat packed lunch from a pristine plastic box. This was, Justine thought, what Steve would have liked them all to do, as long as, like Meera, they left no detritus, no crumbs or smears or smells. Justine imagined sometimes the kind of lunch Titus might bring—hideous leftovers full of garlic and chili, lumps of overpowering cheese, mangoes, oranges—and thought of how Steve would react, the distaste, the disapproval of the distaste, the struggle between the two, and Titus oblivious in the midst of it all, licking his fingers and hurling fruit peels towards his bin.

Justine had slightly hoped that, seeing as they were under pressure to finish work for the Greig Gallery that week, and she had volunteered to forgo her lunch hour, Titus might offer to forgo his too. She had a brief fantasy about him asking her what kind of sandwich she would like, and then him going off to get it and coming back with something quite different, and very messy, like prawns in Marie Rose sauce filling, and them having to eat the sandwiches together in a kind of giggling, furtive conspiracy. Being clever and state-educated, and only the second person in her family to go on to further education, Justine naturally despised someone like Titus. His confidence, his thick dark hair, his voice, his apparent supreme indifference to the defects of his class and height were all in their way powerful reasons for finding him anathema, and no more than yet another example of the stupid upper-class has-beens who her father said had made such a laughing-stock of the Conservative Party. Justine had been brought up with a very clear idea of which social groups were beneath contempt, and Titus fell fair and square into the middle of most of them. When she talked to her sister about work, she referred to Titus as "Sloane Brain," and her sister, who was currently going out with a professional activist—Justine was not quite sure for which cause—said she didn't know how Justine could stand working with a tosser like that.

Sometimes—often, even—Justine didn't know how, either. It was indisputable that Titus was good at what he did, especially at layout where he excelled, and that when he wasn't in the office an indefinable electric charge went out of the atmosphere, like a spotlight being extinguished. But setting all that aside, so much about Titus was unbearable, especially his indifference to other people's opinions. No, Justine thought, it's his indifference to other *people*, the way he breezes round the office not noticing if anyone needs anything or wants anything. Or has a new haircut.

Justine wasn't sure about her haircut. She'd had her hair long all her life, well past her shoulders, sometimes carelessly skewering it up on top of her head with a pencil. And then she'd cut it. She'd cut it all off, really short, and was unable to decide whether it was radically becoming or unbecoming because whichever it was it was certainly radical. She'd waited for everyone to notice and at last Meera had said, "Very pretty" (her own hair was black with a blue gloss and hung to her waist), and Steve had said, "Brave!" and Titus had said nothing. And you could be forgiven, couldn't you, for thinking Titus liked short hair if his current girlfriend was anything to go by, you could at least expect a wink and a thumbs-up, couldn't you?

Justine finished her solitary sandwich—cheese and cole-slaw, not a wise choice—and looked again at her lettering for the Greig Gallery. A modern take on rococo was what they'd asked for. Whatever that meant. Behind her, Meera snapped shut the lid of her plastic lunch box and went briskly past on her way to the lavatory downstairs from which she would emerge smelling of toothpaste and Issey perfume. Justine sighed. Perhaps it was time to look for another job, to look for a place where you didn't have to work with people from the unacceptable Land of Posh. The street door slammed. Titus's voice could be heard down-stairs performing a parody of an operatic tenor singing the theme from *Titanic*. Justine bent intently towards her computer screen and fingered the wisps of hair in the nape of her neck.

"It isn't necessary to meet," the woman from FamilyFind had said. "We can do it all over the telephone if you'd rather. It's entirely up to you."

Nathalie had been sitting on the floor, squashed into a corner the far side of the bed, like a child in trouble, with the telephone pressed to her ear.

"I don't know—"

The woman had waited. She was called Elaine, she said, Elaine Price. She had sounded patient and practical, in the way you hope hospital nurses will be.

"I'm sorry," Nathalie said, "I don't seem able to decide very well, I don't seem able to think—"

"Could you," Elaine said, "come to London?"

Nathalie paused.

"Yes," she said doubtfully.

"And your brother?"

"Maybe—"

There was another pause. Nathalie had pulled her knees up hard against her chest and put her forehead down against them.

"Nathalie," Elaine said, "I think you had better come and see me. Or I'll come and see you."

"No," Nathalie said.

"Then you come—"

"Yes."

"And we'll take your brother from there."

And now here she was, in the coffee shop of a supermarket in West London, waiting for Elaine Price. She was early. She'd caught a train well before the train she'd needed to catch and had let one cappuccino get cold and depressing already. Ordering another seemed not just futile but artificial, as if she was pretending there was something, anything, ordinary about sitting waiting for a complete stranger next to a plate-glass window overlooking the West Cromwell Road. Why fake any more normality, anyway? Why delude yourself that there is anything remotely, conceivably *normal*, as David had angrily said the night before, about any sane woman giving her own baby away? Why kid yourself that having to go and *find* the woman who gave birth to you and then gave you away is the kind of thing that normal people ever have to contemplate in a million years?

Nathalie pushed the coffee cup away. The foam on the surface had subsided into a thin sludge. Nathalie tipped the pot of paper tubes of sugar out onto the table and began to arrange them in categories.

"Nobody regrets making this journey," Elaine had said. She'd said it just before the call ended, just after she'd said that every child has a right to know where they come from, a right to try and make sense of themselves. "I can promise you that."

"Really?"

"It'll stop you defining yourself by loss. It'll help you move on."

Nathalie shifted the sugars. Was that what it was? Was that what had dogged her all these years, made her insist that, if she was indeed an outsider, then she was an outsider by choice? She began to balance the blue paper tubes of white sugar carefully against one another, as if she was building a miniature bonfire.

A woman paused beside her, and waited. She was younger than Nathalie had expected, with long pale hair and a denim jacket.

"Hello," the woman said.

Nathalie tried, clumsily, to get up.

"I'm Elaine," the woman said. She put a large patchwork suede bag down on the chair next to Nathalie's. "Don't get up." She smiled and glanced at the cold cappuccino. "I'll get us some more of those."

"No, I'll—"

Elaine put a hand briefly on Nathalie's shoulder. She had a ring on her wedding finger with a big turquoise in it.

"You stay there."

Nathalie watched her walk over to the self-service counter. Besides the denim jacket she wore cutoff trousers and trainers without socks and her bare ankles were brown. Nathalie wasn't, now, quite sure what she had been expecting sartorially, but a suit possibly, certainly a skirt, and a briefcase rather than a kind of bag she'd taken herself on long-ago weekends to the music festival at Glastonbury. She also hadn't been expecting long hair. Elaine Price, Nathalie had decided, would be like the woman from social services, with a wash-and-wear haircut that was no trouble—or signal—to anyone. She let out a breath. The denim jacket and bare ankles and unofficial hair were all a surprise and a comfort.

"There," Elaine said.

She put two big coffee cups down on the table and transferred Nathalie's discarded one to an empty table nearby. Then she moved her bag from the chair next to Nathalie's and sat down in it herself.

"Dark hair," she said to Nathalie, "white top. Leather jacket. Just like you said."

Nathalie looked round the coffee shop.

"Plenty of those in here—"

"But not waiting for me. You had waiting written all over you."

Nathalie said shyly, "I've been here ages—"

"Most people do that. The other habit is to be late, really late. Sometimes that's how I sort out who wants to do this search and who needs to."

Nathalie drew a spoon through the foam on her coffee and made a soft furrow.

"Does it matter?"

"Well," Elaine said, "it's better to *want* to, if you can. Otherwise there's a likelihood of wanting to punish your mother."

Nathalie stared at her coffee.

"I can't imagine that," she said. "I can't even see she's real."

Elaine picked up her coffee cup and held it balanced between the tips of her fingers.

"Let's start at the beginning."

Nathalie nodded.

"Don't you want to know about me?"

"I hadn't really thought—"

"Well, why are you here and not with an official agency?"

"Because—because you aren't official—"

"But I'm trained."

"Yes."

Elaine put her coffee cup down again. She pushed her hair behind her shoulders.

"Go on."

"My brother wanted to know about your training. My brother David."

"It was intensive," Elaine said. "I did it at the Post Adoption Center. There were modules on searching, on infertility, on genetic sexual attraction. I do a retraining course every year."

"I'll tell him."

"Nathalie," Elaine said. "Relax."

Nathalie took a spoonful of coffee foam.

"I've upset so many people, wanting to do this. I can't tell you. Everyone seems to feel let down, as if I'm doing something unnecessary, something deliberately destructive. My partner, my sister-in-law, my mother—"

"Your mother?"

"Yes. My mother."

"I'm afraid," Elaine said, "that your adoptive mother has to stay out of this. This isn't her journey."

"Really?"

"Really."

"You mean—"

"I mean," Elaine said, looking straight at Nathalie, "that you are entitled to do this. People who are adopted are damaged by adoption and are looking for healing. You are entitled to look for healing."

"Thank you," Nathalie whispered.

"Don't thank me. I'm not a benefactor, I'm a service. You're going to pay me to find your mother. To find your brother's mother."

"Yes—"

"It won't take long."

"No—"

"You said you had your birth certificate. That's a start. It will probably take less than three weeks. It'll cost between two and three hundred pounds per person. I'll need a deposit of a hundred and fifty from each of you."

"Of course."

"And I'll need to know why you want to do this now."

"Now?"

"Yes, now."

"It's hard to describe—"

"With a lot of people, it's something quite specific that's the trigger, like having your own child."

"Polly's five."

"Does she look like you?"

"More like her father."

"Nathalie," Elaine said, "I have some responsibility too, for your birth mother. I have to know something about your thinking."

Nathalie looked up.

"I want to *know*," she said, "I want to know where I come from. I want to know if I'm like her or not. I want to know about my father. I want to stop—*not* knowing. I don't know exactly what set me off, but I'd suddenly had enough of pretending, and now that I've started, I can hardly stand not knowing anymore. Even—" She paused, and then she said, "Even if I don't like what I discover."

"You might not. She might not. She might refuse you."

"I don't want a *meeting*—"

"You don't now. Wait and see. You might feel like exchanging letters and photographs."

"Photographs—"

"Don't forget, in theory you have a position on two family trees."

Nathalie said slowly, "If you find my mother—"

"When, more likely."

"What will you do?"

"Tell you. Immediately."

"And then?"

"Write to her."

"Write a letter—"

"She'll read it, from me. If it was from social services,

107

she'd throw it away. Especially if she's married. If she's got other children."

Nathalie's head came up.

"Other children!"

"Oh yes."

"I didn't think—"

"There mayn't be any. Up to forty percent of women who give up a baby for adoption don't conceive again."

Nathalie picked up her coffee cup and took a swallow. It tasted warm and silky and synthetic.

"My dad taught me a word once. I think it's Spanish. It's—I'm not sure if I'm saying it right—it's *duende*. It means kind of a spirit of the earth, something roused in the very cells of the blood."

"Sounds a good kind of dad."

Nathalie nodded.

"He is. He's the only one not making a fuss over all this."

"Not threatened, then."

Nathalie said angrily, "*Nobody's* threatened."

"You hang on to that. That, and these instincts you're obeying."

"Yes."

"I think," Elaine said, "that our instincts play a big part in all this. I think that instinctively we know whether we were wanted or not."

"Do I know?"

"I think you do."

"And David—"

"Yes?"

"Maybe," Nathalie said, "he isn't so certain. Maybe that's what he's frightened of." She glanced at Elaine. "What are you going to do now?"

"I'm going looking for your mother's birth certificate. I'll get on the Internet."

Nathalie swallowed.

"She was called Cora. Cora Wilson."

"I know. You told me on the phone."

"And—and what do I do?"

Elaine smiled. She picked up her suede bag and plumped it on to her lap.

"You wait to hear from me," she said.

In Paddington Station, Nathalie bought a cup of tea and a bar of chocolate and an apple. Eating the chocolate, she found herself automatically justifying herself silently to Polly, who declined to understand that if chocolate was a food and therefore nourishing—as opposed to sweets which were purely chemical concoctions and therefore harmful—she couldn't eat it whenever she felt like it, and especially as a substitute for meals she didn't care for, like breakfast. After the chocolate, the apple tasted metallic and empty, and had a hard, wet texture that hurt her teeth. She drank half the tea from its plastic cup and dumped the rest in a litter bin. There were times, she thought, when you simply should not eat or drink, times when you were so agitated and consumed by something happening in your mind or spirit that basic functions like digestion were best ignored. If you didn't, they only declined to function properly anyway, and added to the turmoil. She threw the chocolate wrapper and the half-eaten apple into the bin after the tea, and went in search of her train.

It was waiting at one of the more obscure platforms, a short train of small carriages with uncompromisingly upright seats. There was almost nobody on board yet except a boy eating a filled baguette out of a long paper bag and a couple of women with bulging plastic carriers crammed defensively behind their legs. Nathalie went down the carriage to the far end and chose a seat in a corner by a window. The window was dappled with dirty dried raindrops, and in the grime outside somebody had written the word "fuck", backwards, with a finger, so that it was legible from inside. Nathalie sat down and took out her mobile phone.

"Hi," David said, from somewhere windy.

"Where are you?"

"At Fernley. About to pull out some tree roots."

"Can't someone else do that?"

"I like doing it."

"Dave," Nathalie said, "I saw her."

"Yes," he said. His voice was flat.

"She's cool. I liked her. She made it all sound quite easy."

"Um."

"She'll do it all for us. She'll find our mothers and then she'll write to them. She said—"

"Yes?"

"She said nobody regrets doing this."

"You told me already."

Nathalie turned herself sideways so that she couldn't see the word on the window.

"Dave, I thought you were with me, that you were coming with me—"

"I am."

"But—"

"It isn't easy. I can't go back and it's hard going on. I'm just not finding it *easy*."

"Nor me."

"But you're excited."

"And frightened."

"Oh yes. Frightened."

Nathalie said, "Do you want to stay as you are?"

David said nothing. She could hear a whine which might have been wind or might have been a mechanical saw.

"If you want to hang on to how you're feeling," Nathalie said, "then fine. Nobody can help you. You stay right there and nurse yourself."

There was another pause. Nathalie took the phone from her ear and then put it back again.

"Bye, David," she said.
His voice came hesitantly.
"Nat?"
"Yes?"
"Help," David said.

CHAPTER EIGHT

Connor Latimer went into the sitting room to tell his wife that he was going down to the Hurlingham Club to play tennis, and found that she was fast asleep. He stood looking at her, weighing up how much his tennis would be spoiled by not being certain that Carole knew precisely where he was. He was used to her knowing his movements, after all. They'd had close on thirty years of running a business together and, in the course of those years, had needed to know each other's exact whereabouts with the result that Connor had become dependent upon this knowledge. It made him frankly uneasy to be out of Carole's radar now, because if she didn't know where he was, and how long he would be, how could she be thinking about him, visualizing him, in the way he, well, *liked* her to?

He leaned forward a little. Carole was sleeping very trimly, her head balanced on a small brocade cushion wedged into the angle of a wing chair. Her hands were folded in her lap, her ankles were crossed and her mouth was not open. Her hair, a kind of creamy, tawny color which was elegantly reminiscent of the blonde she'd been when they met, was hardly disarranged. Looking at her, Connor wondered if he had actually mentioned his tennis game already, over breakfast, and whether he could re-member Carole saying, "Oh good. With Benny?" in reply.

But perhaps he hadn't. Perhaps he just thought he had. Carole had, after all, been reading the *Financial Times*, which she still read, out of habit, and this might have prevented her from completely taking in the information about the tennis game. Connor leaned a little closer and put a hand on Carole's arm.

She opened her eyes. She smiled.

"I'm sorry to wake you," Connor said, "but I'm just off to the Hurlingham."

She still smiled.

"I know, darling."

"I'll be back about six. We might have a drink after the game."

"Lovely."

He gave her arm a pat.

"Have a nice sleep—"

"Mmm," she said. She closed her eyes again.

"About six," Connor said.

He straightened up and felt in his pocket for his car keys. He wondered whether, before he left and Carole slid back down into afternoon oblivion, he should also remind her that Martin had said he was coming round later. He opened his mouth.

"Goodbye, darling," Carole said with surprising distinctness. "Have a lovely game. Love to Benny."

"Yes," Connor said. He rattled his keys. "Yes."

He took a step away. Carole's face was now serenely, conclusively shuttered. He thought of asking her whether she would like the French windows open since the sun was now coming out, and decided against it. He took another step away and sighed. Then he gave himself a little shake and left the room with as decisive a tread as he could manage in his tennis shoes.

His Mercedes was parked in the basement garage below the flat. The garage had been one of the elements that had attracted him to the flat in the first place, the others being that its location in this part of West London was central enough for civilized life, and that the bay windows of its sitting room and main bedroom opened into spectacular communal gardens containing established trees and shrubs, and maintained by a team of nicely mannered gardeners in green overalls.

"All the pleasure of the countryside," Connor would say to guests, exclaiming at the seclusion and charm of the gardens, only a mile or two from Marble Arch, "and none of the labor or inconvenience."

Carole had made a delightful place to sit, too, on the patio outside the sitting-room windows, surrounded by Italian pots and urns, and a wisteria trained up a trellis painted a dull shade of bluish-gray which Connor would never have chosen but which, when he saw it, he had to acknowledge was absolutely spot-on. It was always like that, with Carole. She'd make these decisions, these choices, and he'd be full of doubts and hesitations, but then he'd see, in the end, that her instinct, her—her flair, was justified. He always thought that was why they'd been so good in business together, the contrast between his caution and steadiness—well, what else would you expect from a man who'd got top marks in all his accountancy exams?—and her nerve and imagination. Between them, over the years, they'd built the business up into something that had been *very* well worth selling when Connor had reached sixty and declared himself due a bit of rest, due time to devote himself to his hobbies, to his tennis and his sailing and his print collection. And Carole was due something, too. He was very aware of that, very conscious of what he owed her, his wife, his business partner, the mother of his children. Indeed, he had been careful to pay tribute to her publicly, to make sure that, at the dinner given to celebrate the final sale of the company, his speech had made emphatic reference to Carole's contribution.

"I would like to make it plain," he had said, standing up at the table in the private room of an expensive Chelsea restaurant amid the handsome detritus of a good dinner, "that none of this—and I mean *none* of it—would have been possible without Carole. I have no hesitation in saying I owe her everything, and so does this company."

Carole had cried on the way home. She had sat beside him in the Mercedes on the way home to this new and wonderful garden flat and wept decorously into his white-linen breast-pocket handkerchief. At the time, he had been flooded with gratification, expansively convinced that she had been so moved by his heartfelt acknowledgment of all she had done for him as both a woman and a colleague that she had been unable to express herself in anything other than tears. It was only later, when she had been incomprehensibly reluctant to let him make love to her—and he was longing to make love to her—that a small disquieting doubt began to tiptoe round the edges of his mind. If she wasn't weeping out of gratitude and emotion, what was she weeping for? Surely it couldn't be for the company. Surely, after all those decades of work and sacrifice and anxiety, she couldn't possibly be grieving to see the company go? Not when such freedom beckoned. *Surely* not.

Connor put the key into the ignition now, and reversed the Mercedes smoothly up the ramp and into the street. Carole of course didn't drive the Mercedes, she had her own little town car which she said she preferred because you could park it on a playing card. He'd indulged her about that as he'd indulged her about so many things. Damn it, he *liked* indulging her, he *liked* her to have what she wanted. And mostly, he thought, turning the car into Ladbroke Grove, she had got what she wanted, he'd seen to that, he'd made sure that he'd compensated her for all the rotten things that had happened to her in her early life, all the troubles with men, with insecurity. He'd rescued her, really, he knew he had. He'd rescued her and given her all the things a woman needs to make her happy—a good marriage, a comfortable life, satisfying work (Connor prided himself on that, prided himself on believing that a clever woman needs work) and—children.

Children. Connor took his sunglasses out of the pocket of the driver's door and, even though the sun was shining only fitfully, put them on. He'd been convinced, certain, that Carole needed children. He wanted them himself, of course, always had, was known for his way with them, with his nieces, with the children of friends, but Carole needed them even more because Carole was a special case. Carole, after all, was, when he met her, a woman with a past, an almost tragic young woman from a disturbingly unsupportive home who'd been disowned by her parents after a feckless boyfriend—whom she'd adored in the way girls persist in adoring attractive shits—had insisted she had an abortion. Carole's parents were Catholic, devoutly Catholic, with views on sex and abortion which even Connor, whose friends teased him about his social orthodoxy, thought came out of the Ark. Carole had had her abortion to try and placate her boyfriend, and then of course both the boyfriend and her parents turned their backs on her, simply refused to have anything more whatever to do with her. So Connor had picked up the pieces. He'd met this gorgeous, bruised-looking blonde at a private view in some gallery in Cork Street, and he'd scooped her up, almost literally, out of all the confusion and hopelessness and near poverty she was stumbling along in.

He had to admit that after the first glory of love and gallantry was over it wasn't easy. He'd thought he didn't mind about the abortion, about her desperate passion for the boyfriend, but he found it was harder to come to terms with than he expected. He'd really had to struggle with himself, he'd had to speak to himself very severely about behaving in a mature and compassionate manner, and it was in the course of these stern internal lectures that it had occurred to him that a baby might be, if not the answer to their difficulties, at least a significant part of the answer. A baby would give Carole something to love that was her own, that would—wouldn't it?—replace the aborted baby. A baby, *his* baby, would tie Carole to him more firmly and, at the same time, would help expunge for him the painfully present jealousy he found he still suffered thinking about another man's potent penetration of the woman who was now Connor's wife.

And so Martin was born. Blond, blue-eyed, charming Martin, the first grandson for Connor's parents, the right and proper obliterator of that previous lost baby. Except—well, Connor thought, blowing the car's horn imperiously at a black boy in a Vauxhall Vectra, that wasn't how it worked out, that wasn't how it happened. In modern terms, Connor supposed, Carole had failed to bond with Martin. She hadn't wanted to feed him, had hardly wanted to hold him. Everyone had told Connor about post-baby blues, but he wasn't prepared for Carole to cry hardest when the monthly nurse left. He shook his head, as if to get a kind of ringing out of his ears. He couldn't think about that time, really, never had been able to. He couldn't think about it because the fact was, the unpleasant, disagreeable, uncomfortable fact, that things hadn't got better. Ever. Martin was now twenty-eight and you couldn't kid yourself for a moment that he and Carole saw eye to eye about anything much. And however much Connor admired Carole, was grateful to Carole, tried to be supportive of Carole, he couldn't help feeling—*knowing*—that Carole was hard on Martin, hard sometimes to the point of unkindness; hard and critical and unencouraging. And Martin couldn't take it, he wasn't an easygoing laid-back character like his younger brother Euan. Martin was thin-skinned and defensive, and every time he made a mess of something, which was distressingly often, he'd lash out, almost as if he wanted to deflect any criticism before it got within a hundred miles of him.

The heartbreaking thing was that Martin wanted Carole's approval, longed for it, longed for her to tell him that she was proud of him, that even when he cocked things up she would stand by him. Even now, as Martin approached the supposedly adult age of thirty, Connor would catch him looking at his mother like a spaniel not knowing whether to expect a kick or a chocolate. And Connor would see Carole suppressing something, contriving something in her responses, not aware, seemingly, that everything she did was as transparent as glass. She was easier with Euan, but then Euan was easier as a person, less needy, less chippy.

Connor sighed. He had a sinking feeling about the reason for Martin's wanting to come round that evening. The way the boy had asked hadn't boded well: too brash, too casual. He sighed again, and swung the Mercedes into the car park of the club. Thirty feet away he noticed, at once, the comfortingly bulky figure of Benny Nolan lifting his tennis bag out of the boot of his BMW. Connor's heart lifted with it. Good old Benny. Good old familiar, cheerful, *normal* Benny.

When Carole Latimer woke, the room was dusky. Through the French windows she could see a glimmer of pale evening spring sky behind the black outlines of roofs and chimneys and trees. When she was working, she'd had a view from her office window of roofs and chimneys and trees, looking west. She'd watched thousands of sunsets from that window, thousands and thousands. She sat up a little and took the pillow away from behind her neck and laid it on her knee. No good thinking about those sunsets now. No good thinking about that window or room or office either. No good thinking about lovely, blessed work. No good *thinking*.

She leaned forward and put her elbows on the brocade pillow. She must have been asleep for more than two hours, almost three. Awful, really. She'd never done this in the past, never wasted whole afternoons just sleeping them away in this depressing elderly fashion. But then, she'd never felt about sleep as she did now, she'd never sought it, fled to it, as she had the last few weeks and months. She'd never seen it before as a refuge.

She stood up slowly and stretched, letting the pillow fall to the floor. People said, didn't they, that when you were stressed or unhappy you either stuffed your face or stopped eating altogether. Presumably the same thing could happen with sleep, that you either binged on it or couldn't capture it for a second. She'd never seen herself as a binge person, someone who can't ever quite let themselves off the lead for fear of what boiling cauldron of self-indulgence or self-abuse they might fall into. Apart from those long-ago feelings for Rory—and she'd never known anything in her life which had even begun to approach the madness and intensity and seductiveness of those feelings—she had been able to manage herself, had been able to arrange and dispose of her desires and needs and fears in such a way that they did not stalk her, or haunt her, or wait in dark places to spring out on her. No—her life with Connor, her work with Connor, had been something satisfying and control-lable and without menace.

Until it stopped. Carole bent and picked up the cushion and threw it inaccurately towards the sofa. Of course life with Connor hadn't stopped, but work had. She wouldn't have believed what work meant to her, until it stopped. She'd always thought, had always said, that men identify themselves by what they do, and women by their relation-ships. But what had happened to her? Work had stopped when Connor was sixty and she was two years younger and she had gone, almost overnight it seemed, from a place of great security and certainty to a howling wilderness where all kinds of events and people she had vowed not to think about again—indeed had largely succeeded in hardly thinking about again—had come swooping down at her like bats out of a cave. That was when the sleeping began, the longing and capacity for oblivion, for the mind to be freed and stilled and soothed. Some days, meticulously making their bed in the mornings in the way she had always done, Carole had to fight herself, almost physically, to prevent herself from just climbing hungrily back in, back into the embrace of the pillows and the fat American comforter and the thick, sweet forgetfulness.

She hoped that, apart from the sleeping, she'd given Connor, especially, no sign of how she was feeling. She hoped that she'd been as pleasant and placid as he liked her to be, as—as he *deserved* her to be. That was the trouble really, Carole thought, this matter of her obligation to Connor, this elusive kind of emotional debt to him that she seemed to have contracted so long ago, almost without knowing it, and which she had wearily come to see would never be quite paid off. Sometimes she'd had moments of resentment about it, flashes of pure, exhilarating, blinding rage about the unfairness of some kinds of emotional liability conditioned so powerfully by social convention, social expectation. Sometimes, she thought she'd be punished forever, for every day that she lived, for something that had been at base and quite simply a powerful, natural, human instinct of the heart.

She went out of the sitting room and across the hall with its polished pale floor and interesting modern rugs to the kitchen. She would put the kettle on. She didn't, she reflected, much want a cup of tea, but she felt she ought to want it, that it was a respectable thing to want, just as a proper gratitude for her life and comforts was only respectable. She laid a hand on the kettle and lifted it off its base. Respectable. Her hand shook. If only they knew, all those people who recognized and judged Carole Latimer by what they saw and heard. She almost let the kettle drop. If only they knew about the letter which was lying in her stocking drawer, under the lining paper, out of sight, the letter which had been lying there for ten days now and about which she hadn't breathed a syllable to a single soul.

A key turned in the lock of the front door across the hall. Carole grasped the kettle firmly and took a brisk step or two towards the sink.

She called out cheerfully, "Hello, darling! Good game?"

"It's me," Martin said.

Carole spun round. Martin was coming across the hall wearing jeans and a leather bomber jacket. His hair needed cutting.

"Hello, darling—"

"Sorry I'm a bit early."

"Early?"

"I told Dad," Martin said. "I told Dad I'd be here around seven."

Carole lifted her cheek for a kiss.

"Dad never told me. He didn't say you were coming—"

"Does that matter?"

"No," Carole said. "No, of course not."

"Look," Martin said, "I'll go away. I'll go out and come in again, later. Would that suit you better?"

Carole said tiredly, "Don't be silly, darling."

Martin took the kettle out of her hands and ran water messily into it at the sink.

"It shouldn't matter, should it, *what* time I come? This is my home, isn't it?"

"Of course—"

"Or am I going to get another lecture about my complete failure to get my act together and leave home and be independent?"

"Stop it," Carole said.

Martin carried the kettle across the kitchen and banged it down on its base.

"I could do with a bit of *support* sometimes."

"Darling," Carole said, "I went to sleep by mistake and I've only just woken up and I wasn't expecting you. That's all."

Martin grunted.

"I don't really feel like tea," Carole said. "I don't know why I was filling the kettle. Shall we have a drink?"

"I'm not drinking."

"Good for you."

"What's that supposed to mean?"

"It means," Carole said tightly, opening the cupboard to find a whiskey tumbler, "that I admire you for your restraint."

"Sorry," Martin said. He took the tumbler out of her hand. "I'll do it for you."

"That's OK—"

"I'll *do* it," Martin said. He crossed the kitchen to where the spirit bottles stood on a lacquer tray. Carole watched him splash whiskey into the glass. And down its side.

"Water or soda?"

"Water, please," Carole said. She tried to smile. "You should know that by now."

Martin picked up a mineral-water bottle.

"I should know a lot of things. Shouldn't I?"

"Darling," Carole said, "please try and forget that I didn't know you were coming. Please forgive me. You know you're welcome any time. Why else would you still have a key?"

Martin's shoulders drooped a little. He handed her the whiskey tumbler without looking at her.

"Sorry."

"There's some juice in the fridge," Carole said. "Bring it into the sitting room." She reached past Martin to tear off a paper towel from the roll on the wall. Martin watched her wrap it round her wet whiskey glass.

"When'll Dad be back?"

"Any minute."

"I might wait then—"

"Wait for what?"

"Well, wait to say what I've got to say."

Carole looked at him. She took a swallow of her whiskey. "Oh."

Martin shrugged. He went over to the fridge and swung the door open.

"Is it important?" Carole said.

Martin didn't turn round.

"You could say so."

"If it's important, darling," Carole said, "then it's going to be a bit difficult to talk about anything else while we wait for Dad, isn't it?"

Martin put a carton of juice on the counter, lifted it to drink out of directly, remembered, and opened a cupboard for a glass.

"I guess so."

"Well, then."

Martin turned round slowly and leaned against the counter. He crossed his ankles and stared at his feet. He was wearing peculiar modern trainers, black canvas with wavy soles and elastic gussets. Carole found herself wondering how much they had cost.

"Mum," Martin said, "it didn't work out."

Carole rearranged the paper towel round her whiskey glass.

"What didn't?"

"Danny's company."

Carole went very still.

"Your friend Danny? The one you invested in?"

"Yup."

"It didn't work out. You mean it's failed?"

"He did his best. He worked all hours. But it's been the stock market and September 11th and stuff. It was all against him."

"So you've lost your investment?"

Martin nodded. His head was still bent.

"Was—was it much?"

Martin nodded again.

"How much?"

There was a pause. Martin crossed his ankles the other way.

"Everything."

"What do you mean, everything?"

Martin sighed. Carole put her glass down.

She said again, "What do you mean, everything?"

He mumbled something.

"What?"

"My flat. Everything."

"Your *flat?*"

"I re-mortgaged it to give him the money."

"You *didn't!*" Carole said.

Martin shouted suddenly, his head jerking up, "Mum, Danny is a *friend!*"

"Sorry," Carole said. She turned and picked her glass up again. "Sorry."

"I know it's a bit of a shock. It's a shock to me."

"Yes."

"I've known for a week. For a whole week. I've known I've got nothing left except my job and you know what I feel about *that*."

"Yes," Carole said. Her hands were shaking again.

"Sorry, Mum."

She shook her head. She put a hand out to him.

"It's all right, darling, it's all right. It's just—"

"I know."

Carole let her hand fall. She took a swallow of whiskey.

"What a pity."

"What a waste is what you really mean," Martin said.

"That too."

"Don't you want to start on all that stuff about my education and your hopes and investment in me?"

"No," Carole said.

"Well, thanks for that anyway."

Carole closed her eyes.

"You say everything's gone. Or going."

"Yes."

"Well." She took a huge breath and opened her eyes again. "Well, darling, is there anything Dad and I can do to help?"

Martin said sourly, "Sound as if you mean it, for a start."

"I *do* mean it."

"There—is, actually."

Carole waited.

"And?"

"You won't like this."

She smiled. She felt her lips tight against her teeth.

"Try me."

"Can I move back in?" Martin said. He raised his head and looked straight at her, straight at her tight small smile. "Just until I get myself a bit sorted, can I come back home?"

Through a tapering chink in the curtains, Connor could see the reddish London night sky. Every so often, there was a tiny light across it, maybe a star, or a plane. Or his imagination. He didn't like what his imagination did when he couldn't sleep, didn't like how disproportionate it got, how it played tricks and tried to frighten him. His usual comfort on these occasions was to focus on Carole, warm and steady and sleeping beside him, a palpable reminder of the reality and reliability of things. But tonight was different. It was different because Carole wasn't asleep either and because she wasn't her body exuded tension and unhappy preoccupation, instead of repose and reassurance, and these silent agitations conveyed themselves to Connor in a way he found very hard to bear indeed.

It had been an awful evening. Heaven knows, over the last twenty-eight years they'd had too many awful evenings either with Martin or on his account, but this one had been unusually upsetting. And it had been so horrible because— Connor couldn't pretend otherwise—Carole herself had been out of control, out of her senses, out of—what was the phrase?—out of *order*. Connor had got back from the Hurlingham full of the satisfaction of having narrowly beaten Benny Nolan in three sets to find Carole and Martin propped up in the kitchen glaring at each other in an atmosphere of indescribable disharmony. He'd taken a deep breath and ushered them both into the sitting room and re-filled Carole's glass and got himself a gin and tonic and made Martin go through the whole pathetic, inevitable saga of Danny's failure and Martin's involvement in it. And then he'd heard Martin out, on his pitifully threadbare plans for the future, which included—even Connor's heart sank here—the proposal to return to live at home for six months, and he'd just been about to reply in as measured and calm a way as he could when Carole lost it, just lost it, went from a standing start of self-control to a hundred miles an hour of pure fury in a single second.

They'd just gaped at her, her husband and son. They'd sat there, eyes and mouths open, and watched her while she screamed and gestured and spilled her whiskey. Connor had never seen anything like it in his life before, never seen anyone lose it like that, and certainly not Carole. And what made it worse was that it was extremely difficult to know exactly why she was going on like this, exactly what her deep, furious, unhappy trouble was. Of course it was irritating to think of Martin returning to disturb the civilized order of their lives, and of course it was worrying that he'd lost so much money and in a venture anyone with half an eye could have told him was doomed from the outset, but neither his hopelessness nor his lack of judgment justified an outburst quite like the one they were witnessing. It was terrible, horrifying. There was something about it, Connor thought now, staring at the chink of reddish light, that was unacceptably *primitive*.

He turned his head on the pillow to look, apprehensively, at Carole. She was lying stiff and straight on her back, and he could see in the dimness that her eyes were open: he could just see the glint of her eyeballs. He wondered if she'd been crying again. She'd wept bitterly that evening, wept until her face was raw and shiny and she could hardly speak for the paroxysms that gripped her throat. After Martin had gone—he'd clung to his father, briefly, in the hall, with a fierceness that he hadn't shown since he was seven—she'd shut herself in the bathroom and Connor, miserably pacing outside, could hear that she was crying still, crying and crying with an intensity that Connor supposed meant she had no words left to express the depth of whatever it was she was feeling. When she came out of the bathroom at last, he didn't try to speak to her, he merely guided her, as if she were ill, to their bedroom and left her there, with a nightcap and Radio 3, while he went to restore some order to the sitting room and his own mind.

But the latter proved impossible. Here he was, three and a half hours later, as awake and agitated as he'd been since he got home. Playing tennis with Benny seemed to have happened at another time, in another life. He took a breath.

"Can I ask you something?"

"Of course," she said. Her voice was still thick, after all those tears.

He hesitated.

Then he said, "I don't want to upset you any more, and I know Martin is a great disappointment to you—indeed, he is to me, in many ways—but don't you think you were a bit hard on him this evening?"

There was a silence. Carole rubbed at her nose with a tissue.

Then she said, with surprising clearness, "Yes."

Connor raised himself on one elbow. He smiled at her in the dimness.

"*That's* my girl."

Carole rubbed her nose again. She didn't look at him.

She said, "It's not about Martin."

"What's not about Martin?"

"Why I got in such a state tonight. I mean, frankly I don't much want him back here, and I don't think you do either, and it's typical of him to risk everything for someone unreliable, but that—well, I can bear that. I mean, it isn't as if there's anything new there, it's just more of the sad same."

Connor stopped smiling.

He said, more tensely, "Well, if it isn't Martin, what is it? What on *earth* could induce you to behave like that?"

Carole laid her arms straight down by her sides, like a figure on a tomb.

"The past," she said.

"The past? What in heaven's name could there be in our past—"

"Not our past. My past."

Connor sat up straighter. He found himself consciously reaching for his dignity, as he used to do in his working days when it became necessary to issue a reprimand.

He said, in a voice he hoped was more relaxed than it sounded, "Perhaps you'd better tell me. Perhaps you had better explain."

"Yes," she said, "I better had. In fact I should have told you years ago."

"But I thought you had," he said, his voice shaking now with something very close to fright. "I thought you'd told me everything, about Rory, about the abortion—"

"There wasn't an abortion," Carole said.

Connor stared into the dark room, across Carole, across what had always seemed entirely secure into something he didn't want to look at, at all. He wanted to say something, to speak in a way that brought things back to the familiar, but he couldn't. He couldn't utter, he couldn't do anything but wait, wait entirely helplessly, unacceptably, at Carole's mercy. She stirred a little and gave a tiny sigh.

"There wasn't an abortion," Carole said again. "There was a baby."

CHAPTER NINE

Betty and Don had run their bed and breakfast for twenty years. They'd started it after Don had his accident in the factory and was registered disabled, and Betty said that if she was going to have to give up work to look after him, they might as well think of something they could do together, instead of moping about at home, drawing the dole and wanting to cut each other's throats.

"I'm not having your bad back turning into the family pet," Betty said. "I'm not having you thinking about it and talking about it all the time. It's bad enough we've both got to live with it."

Don, who was in considerable pain at the time, having been half crushed by a forklift truck driven by a boy so hungover he could barely see straight, thought of pointing out that his back was hardly his fault, and decided against it. It was hard on Betty, after all, hard to leave the retail trade which she loved, hard to have to come home and play nursemaid. He hitched the elastic corset belt he was now supposed to wear even in bed a notch tighter, and said with only mild sarcasm that he'd do his best to remember that he was actually as fit as the days he'd played scrum half for Northsea Rugby Club.

It was Cora who'd suggested doing bed and breakfast; Cora, Betty's younger sister, who was eking out a living teaching adult-education classes in pottery and ceramics.

Cora was the artistic one in the family, with an eye for color and no head whatsoever for figures or practicalities. Betty used to despair, and disapprove of the hand-to-mouth way Cora led her life, with no money put by for the future, and no insurance, and an inclination to spend what might have fed her for a month on a piece of arty rubbish that wasn't fit for more than the bric-a-brac stall at a jumble sale. But Cora could come up with ideas, now and then, ideas of surprising inventiveness, and when she said why not turn Number 9, Woodside (not a tree in sight) into a bed and breakfast, and call it Balmoral because of Betty's passion for royalty, and Don's fondness for Scotland, they knew she was onto something.

Over the years, Balmoral had been a respectable little earner. It had given them a modest living and, more importantly, an occupation. Quite a lot of their guests, mostly businessmen, were regulars and Betty found she could adapt the patience she had needed for customers in shops to an obligingness about the way guests liked their eggs or their pillows. The lift they installed on the stairs for Don proved rather a draw, even a source of mild fun and games. The whole enterprise became more difficult, of course, when Mother needed a home, and looking after, but at least that had been a question of adapting rather than changing outright. Mother had, too, been infinitely more civil to the guests than she ever managed to be to her own family, so in her own way she'd become rather an asset, a kind of crochety fixture, whose presence lent a small air of stability, and therefore of home, to the place. When Mother finally died—it took her six years and three false alarms— Betty found it strangely hard to do anything commercial about her room which was, you had to face it, the least prepossessing room in the house, being small and narrow and ground-floor and next to the kitchen. Whatever you did, the smell of frying seeped through the wall to cling immovably to the curtains and carpet. Mother, of course, had liked it. That was typical of Mother, to like only the element in her living conditions that nobody else would have put up with. But then, perverse should have been Mother's middle name.

It was all this really, Mother's being gone, and the room being full of drawbacks and memories, and Betty missing that sense of family that Mother had provided, despite herself, that made Betty offer the room to Cora. She'd always felt protective of Cora, not just as a younger sister, but because Mother bullied her so, especially after the baby, and because Cora couldn't seem to stand up to Mother, couldn't stand up to anyone much. But that was Cora really, sweet-natured and soft and always inclined to blame herself, even when things weren't really her fault. She'd always been sympathetic, too, able to imagine herself into someone else's shoes. In fact, if Betty hadn't had Cora there when she'd realized, after four miscarriages, that this baby thing just wasn't going to happen, she wondered what she would have done. She couldn't believe how good Cora was to her then, how strong, how understanding. And when you thought about what Cora had been through herself, it made her conduct all the more extraordinary. Betty had never forgotten that. She might have inherited Mother's sharp tongue, but she wasn't going to harbor the same hard heart. She would offer Cora Mother's room because, despite her funny clothes, her funny ways, her uselessness with money and form-filling, Cora was her sister, Cora was *family*.

At the back of her mind, too, there was something else, something uneasy. She had a feeling—no, more than that, a nasty little knowledge—that when Cora had really needed her, over that business with her own baby, Betty hadn't helped. It wasn't that Betty hadn't sympathized, hadn't felt for her, hadn't tried, in a way, to stand up to Mother on Cora's behalf, but she knew, in her heart of hearts, that she hadn't done *enough*. It was only later, when she knew she was never going to have a baby of her own, that she even began to see what it had been like for Cora at sixteen, dominated by other people, shouted at, reprimanded, cajoled, persuaded, threatened, until, at last, she'd agreed to give the baby away. And Betty hadn't been with her then, hadn't really tried to be with her. Cora had gone off to Scarborough, and got a job in a hotel as a chambermaid, and Betty hadn't tried to follow her, to see her. Not for three years. Not until Cora wrote and told her she was doing pottery classes in night school and beginning to feel better.

All this had weighed on Betty down the years. Because of it, she'd never asked Cora to lift a finger to help her with Mother and never felt a morsel of resentment about it. In fact, she did her best to keep Mother away from Cora and, when Mother began on one of her tirades about Cora, all based on the assumption that someone who falls pregnant out of wedlock is automatically pathological, Betty refused to listen. It wasn't possible to shut Mother up, but Betty could, and did, leave the room, sometimes slamming the door behind her. As time went on, the basis of Mother's grievance became baldly plain, which was that her daughters, for one reason or another, had failed to make her a grandmother. When Betty shouted she'd had enough of this, Mother would shout back, "Girls should be good, women should be wives, and wives should be *mothers*!" and Betty would want to hit her in the face.

So Cora came to Balmoral shyly and gratefully, and hung Indian bedspreads on the bacon-scented walls and made a little shrine in one corner with joss sticks and a tea light and a cross-legged god with his eyes shut. She brought with her, too, items that Betty found quite hard to bear, bed linen in burnt orange, a Mexican rug in brilliant colors, peculiar lamps she had made herself out of bits of driftwood or car parts, paintings of nudes.

"Grit your teeth," Don said. "Not a word."

He'd got very thin lately, especially in the face, worn down by years and years of never being quite free of pain.

"The joss sticks—"

"Better than drains," Don said. "Better than kippers. And she's quiet. Most days you'd never know she was there."

She was quiet. She played no music in her bizarrely appointed room and if she turned her television on—you could almost have covered the screen with your hand, it was so small—she must have had the sound down almost to off. If Betty went in—she always knocked, family or no family—Cora would be embroidering something in primary-colored wools or doing some of her pen-and-ink drawings (not to Betty's taste) or reading, curled up on her bed under a striped blanket thing it gave you a headache to look at. When she went out to work, to teach her evening classes or the supplementary art classes she taught at neighboring schools for children with learning difficulties, Betty almost never heard her go. Sometimes she'd hear the front-door latch but mostly she'd just be conscious, with the kind of antennae she supposed mothers had, that Cora wasn't there. She ate with them at teatime but that was only because Betty told her she had to, that she had to have one proper meal a day, and once a month, at the kitchen table, Don made her go through her accounts. He'd made her buy an account book, and make lists of incomings and out-goings, and every month he explained to her, very patiently, that paying more out than you have coming in means debt. Cora would gladly have turned all her earnings over to him and had him dole it back to her, like pocket money, but he wouldn't let her do that.

"I won't be here forever," Don said. "I won't be here to do your thinking for you."

"She's like a child," he said to Betty afterwards. "Get her onto money and you'd do better with a quick five-year-old."

"But she's clever," Betty said, thinking of the books in

Cora's room, the way she could fashion and invent things, her talent for explaining how you use your hands to make a pot, stitch a buttonhole.

"Not for figures," Don said. "And you need figures."

In some ways, she supposed, Betty thought of Cora as a child still, as someone who couldn't be expected to shoulder the full burden of adult life. And maybe something had happened long ago, in that traumatic year when she was sixteen, that had arrested her, that had made her, at some profound level, either unable or unwilling to develop any further, to venture deeper into a world of expectation and feeling that might only bring more pain. She'd never had any real relationships, for example, no boyfriends, not even the kind of undemanding male companions some of Betty's friends had, who went with them to the pub, or Bingo, or outings to the Dales. It wasn't that Cora seemed anti-man, but more that she didn't seem to see them, let alone need them. Sometimes Betty would catch one of her guests eyeing Cora, speculating, puzzled but slightly fired up by Cora's indifference, Cora's faded but still distinctly present prettiness. She'd want to say, "You leave her alone. You'll only upset her." And they would, if they persisted. Betty didn't want Cora upset, ever again, and as long as she'd got Cora safe, among her gods and her blankets, in the little room next to the kitchen, she would see to it that it never happened.

Cora sat in the doctor's waiting room. It was a new waiting room, tacked on to the old surgery, decorated with a false, childish brightness and hung with posters about nutrition and sexually transmitted diseases. Cora didn't look at them. Food didn't interest her, and sex, having led her down into the darkest pit of her whole life, was something she didn't even think about. Why should she? After all, nuns presumably didn't either, and it didn't kill them, did it?

She shifted her hands in her lap. Her hands were why she was here, really, her hands and arms and now, if she was honest, her hips and knees too. Dad had had arthritis, after all, he'd been crippled with it, his poor old hands like a throbbing bunch of roots. Cora knew about the throbbing. There were some nights when the bones and joints in her hands hurt so much she'd have given anything just to slip them out of her skin and lay them on the Mexican rug to go on hurting all by themselves, far away from her. She didn't like to think—couldn't think—what she would do if her hands got too stiff and painful to use. She looked down at them. They looked perfectly normal still but they belonged to someone in their mid-fifties, and Dad had begun to be crippled up with arthritis earlier than that. But then Dad had been a miner, and working all those years deep underground had to be one of the least natural, most body-challenging ways that anyone could spend their life. He'd have agreed with that. He always saw his arthritis as a punishment for obeying his father in going down the mines instead of working on the land as he'd wanted to. Dad was very puritanical, very keen on punishment. Cora looked at her hands. Maybe her arthritis was a punishment too.

She looked at the clock. The doctor was already twenty minutes late in seeing her and there were a lot of people in the waiting room who'd been there when she arrived. She leaned forward and picked up the nearest magazine, a battered copy of one of those women's magazines that try and persuade their readers that, despite the emphasis on eyebrow-shaping and sex, their hearts are actually in important social issues. Cora flicked idly. Girls gazed out, flawless, improbably arranged girls, girls of a kind never seen on any high street, in any supermarket aisle. Cora sighed. There was a piece on aphrodisiac food, a piece on seductive lighting, a piece on getaway weekends with the emphasis on romance. Cora thought she would rather stare into space than glance on. She turned one more page.

"Roughly," said a headline in bold black type, "one woman in twenty-five has had a child adopted."

"Think," the article went on in slightly less emphatic type, "Just think. We have no word for the mother who surrenders her child for adoption, do we? Is this because she is expected to disappear? It wasn't always like this. The medieval world saw no stigma in illegitimacy, after all. It was capitalism that made a child a dependent, a liability, because it couldn't support itself. That's all! So what's gone wrong?"

Cora closed the magazine. Her mouth was dry. She could now see, on its cover, in purple capitals, the words "UN-MARRIED MOTHER?—CAN'T WIN!" She put the magazine down very carefully on the pile she had taken it from and stood up. She couldn't stay, she couldn't wait. At this precise moment, it didn't seem to matter how much her hands hurt: it didn't seem to matter, actually, if they simply fell off.

She found a bench in the park with, blessedly, no one slumped moodily on it already. Northsea Park, instituted by civic-minded Victorians, occupied some high ground above the lower part of the town, thus giving both a view out to the gray sea above the uneven lines of rain-washed slate roofs and a healthy dose of sea air. The wind from the sea had blown most of the carefully planted trees back against the slope, making them look as if they were painfully trying to ascend it, and thus also removing any shelter they might have given to the seats placed thoughtfully in front of them.

Cora sat down and shrank herself back inside her coat. Trust her to pick up that magazine of all magazines, trust her to go on looking at worthless rubbish just one page too many. So much of her life had been dedicated to making sure that these accidents didn't happen, that she didn't get into situations where she would be reminded, and in consequence dragged back to a place she could hardly bear to remember, let alone revisit. There'd been a colleague at work once, a woman with a social-science degree who taught classes in citizenship, who'd been very keen that Cora should unburden herself, should recall every last word and deed from that dark time, so that she could do more than just limp along through the years, getting by, and really start to live again.

"Denial," she said to Cora, "is only ever a coping mechanism. It's no more than that, believe you me."

But Cora wasn't in denial. Cora was instead in a place of privacy, where all the things she knew had happened, had been felt, had been said, were to be kept safe and not spread out for someone else to pick over, like rubbish at a car-boot sale. It was acutely painful going back to the private—private, not secret—place where all these memories were stored, which was why Cora had chosen to do it as seldom as possible, but that didn't mean Cora was remotely pretending that what had happened hadn't happened. She wasn't denying anything, she finally told the citizenship teacher with the energy that was the closest to anger Cora ever got, but she was guarding something, and she had a right to guard it, thank you very much, because it was hers and it was precious, however much heartache it meant. And, she added as an afterthought, her personal growth was her business, and if she chose to stop growing that was her business too, and hers alone.

"You haven't lived my life," Cora said. "Nobody's lived it but me."

Yet, she thought now, sunk down inside the collar of her coat and staring over the dark gray roofs to the paler gray sea and sky and the wheeling gulls, you couldn't blame the woman for trying. She taught citizenship, after all, her mind was geared to the communal, to the collective, it wasn't the kind of mind that could understand the safety of living your life on your own without manipulation or disturbance. If she was honest, Cora had felt like that—separate, contained—even before the baby and all those horrors. Perhaps it was that extra sense of self and distance that had caused her to allow Craig Thomas to take her to that party where they put something in her cider, and where the sailor was. Perhaps she thought, somehow, that she wasn't touchable, that she was far enough away in her inner self not to be affected by the cider or the sailor. When Mother had, among all the other accusations, screamed at her that she was such a slut she didn't even know the sailor's name, it had seemed to Cora that this was just part of her pattern, part of her not belonging—not needing to belong—to a world where everything had to have names and labels. Why on earth should it matter knowing someone's name, when you could hardly remember what he'd done to you? Or, to be fair, and Cora wanted to be fair on account of the baby that came after, what you'd done together? Cora had never blamed the sailor, never wanted to, had never blamed Craig Thomas or the spiked cider. If she'd blamed them, the baby would have known it, wouldn't it? The baby would have known, she was sure, that it wasn't wanted, and Cora wasn't having that. Oh no. Cora was, had always been, very clear about that—she'd wanted that baby from the moment she knew it was coming, and she'd never stopped. Ever.

It was other things that were less clear, things that happened after her baby was born, things that were said, things she was told. She remembered them all talking at her, social workers, the adoption people, her parents, and they said to her that if she was selfish enough to keep the baby that showed she was immature and an unfit mother. When she said that maybe if she had enough support she could manage with the baby, even finish her schooling, they said her feelings were not now of consequence, that she had used up her share of indulgence in that department with her

139

promiscuity and her fertility. When she said what about bad luck, what about all those millions of women who have sex outside marriage and don't get pregnant, they told her that if she wanted to get away without a stain on her mental-health record she would do well to accept that there was a wonderful social mechanism in place—adoption— which would give her baby the chances that she, having given birth outside marriage too young, in poverty and in the wrong class, would be totally unable to do. Did she want to be that deviant? Did she want to be that destruct- ive? If she wanted to repair the damage she'd done to an innocent baby, she should let it go.

"If you really love that baby," the social worker said, sitting there with Mother beside her, their eyes like jet beads, "you should give her up to a *proper* home and parents."

Cora gave in. Worn down she was, worn out, nothing left to fight with, powerless. Looking back, she realized that there hadn't even been someone to rehearse the options with, not even Betty, despite hearing Mother and Betty screaming at each other like fishwives in the kitchen, and Dad going coughing off to the pub where the talk could be relied upon never to touch on women's things. Alone in her bedroom, disgraced, guilty, dirty, broken-hearted, Cora told herself that nothing would ever hurt this much again, that in order to stay alive for—Samantha (only whisper her name, whisper it in private), even if she never saw her again, she must live life in such a way that she never need plunge in again, never be in that seething mess of things where other people could tell her what to do.

It was getting cold. Cora's hands in her coat pockets, tense with the tension of her thoughts, were beginning to stiffen and throb. Someone at work said stay off cheese and chocolate; someone else said try extract of green-lipped mussels. They came from New Zealand or somewhere and you could get them in the health-food shop behind the

Parade. Sounded disgusting. Cora stood up, painfully flex-
ing her fingers. She'd make another appointment to see the
doctor, she'd go round to the surgery on the way home, and
make it now. What was arthritis anyway, compared? When
did pain, however acute, in your body ever hold a candle to
pain in your mind and heart? Yet that other pain—well,
Cora wouldn't have been without it now, not for a moment. If it went away, if her mind and heart were cleared
and calmed, she'd be scared that her love had gone, and
that was the most unthinkable thought of all.

"She never gets letters," Betty said. She had propped the
envelope against the china cottage in which she kept sugar,
just as Mother had always done.

Don was reading the paper, the editorial page where all
the rabid opinions expressed consoled him in his own
abiding moderation.

"Perhaps it's a job offer—"

"From London?"

"Why not? Why shouldn't they need art teachers in
London?"

"Not Cora—"

Don shook the paper.

"You don't know."

"Of course I don't know. But I'm wondering." Betty
looked at the clock. "She should be back by now. Her
appointment was two-thirty."

"They're never on time—"

"It worries me," Betty said. "She'll never have said how
bad it is. You can tell, just by looking at her, how bad it is,
but she won't say. She never does. She's never said how bad
anything is, ever."

"Makes a nice change then," Don said, "from the rest of
us."

Betty picked the envelope up again.

"Not typed," she said. "Handwritten."

"Boyfriend."

"Don't be daft."

Don looked up from his papers.

"Betty," he said, "as it's for Cora, whatever it is, it won't stop the clocks. OK?"

CHAPTER TEN

Polly had decided that, when her uncle David came round, as her mother had said he was going to, she would sit on his knee. She had taken to doing this lately, capturing all the men who came to the house—Titus from Daddy's office, Grandpa Ray from the Royal Oak, even her father if he looked as if he might be paying attention to her mother—by hitching herself into their laps and staking her claim on them. Her uncle David always said he liked her on his knee. He said Ellen was too old for it now, and Petey was too wriggly and Daniel was a boy, so that only left Polly. Polly, safe inside the clamp of his forearm, could then survey her mother from her citadel, with a cool and appraising gaze which left Nathalie in no doubt that, as a mother, she was somehow currently being found wanting.

"You're getting quite heavy," David said.

He was wearing a green jersey and the sleeve round Polly was speckled with little twiggy and grassy bits that had got caught in the wool. Polly began to pull some of them out, with elaborate concentration. Nathalie, across the kitchen table, was wearing the kind of expression that usually led to Polly's being asked to go and play in her room for a while. Polly didn't want to play in her room. There was something about the atmosphere in the kitchen, and David's being there, and her mother having poured some wine out even though it wasn't nearly dark—grown-up drink, in Polly's view, should only begin after her bedtime—that made her feel she didn't want to leave, that she didn't want to be left out of anything that might be happening. When her mother looked as she was looking now, as if there was something secret inside her that was longing to burst out, Polly had no intention of missing the bursting. She began to lay the tiny pieces of twig from her uncle's sweater sleeve in an elaborately neat pile on the table.

"Polly," Nathalie said, leaning forward, "would you go and play with your Barbies for a while?"

"No," Polly said politely. She balanced a fragment of feather on her pile.

"Polly—"

"I am very comfortable," Polly said, leaning closer to David's sleeve to examine a shred of grass very minutely.

"Polly," Nathalie said in an extremely level voice, "I want you to go and play in your room for just five minutes and then you can come back and have a bag of your special crisps."

"*Or*," Polly said, "I could have them now. Here."

David's arm moved a little, loosening his hold on her. She felt his mouth come down against her hair, near the ear that wasn't very good at hearing things.

"Polly—"

Her eyes slid sideways.

"Mmm?"

"Do as you're asked," David's voice said, close to her ear.

She wriggled. She pushed her lower lip out and hung her head. It occurred to her that tears might be coming on account of losing, on account of not wishing to displease her Uncle David. She sniffed.

"Good girl," David said.

She felt his arm move away some more and then his hands were on her sides, under her arms. Next thing, she was on the floor. She leaned against David and pushed her face into his sleeve.

"Five minutes, Poll—"

She tore her face away from David's sleeve and charged out of the room, slamming the door so hard that the wine on the table jumped in the glasses.

"No flies on Polly," Nathalie said. "She knows there's something going on."

"She's right."

"It's just that I can't explain about this extra granny thing yet. Not until I've sorted it myself a bit."

David moved his wine glass an inch to the left.

"It isn't an extra granny anyway—"

"It is!"

"It isn't, Nat. Not yet. It's about mothers."

Nathalie said in a whisper, "I know. Really, I know."

David moved his glass again.

She said shyly, "I feel kind of thrilled. I didn't think I'd feel like this, I didn't think it would be—exciting—"

"And frightening."

He looked at her.

"Yes."

She said, "I keep thinking about that saying that you must be careful what you wish for in case you get it."

He slid one hand across the table towards her.

"Don't chicken out on me now, Nat."

She smiled.

"Wouldn't dream of it."

He said wonderingly, "She's called Carole. I didn't even know her name."

"But she knew yours."

He smiled, an inward, private, pleased smile.

"She *gave* me mine."

Nathalie put her hand on his.

"Yes," she said, "she did."

"And there she is, in London, in her posh flat. And—I've got two brothers. Two brothers—"

"Never any substitute for a sister—"

He turned his hand over to grasp hers.

"*Never* that."

Nathalie said, "Cora hasn't married. She never did."

"Are you pleased?"

She nodded. She was coloring a little.

"Yes. Yes, I am. And she had her own name for me."

He gave her hand a squeeze.

He said, "Samantha."

"Mum called me Nathalie. After her sister that died."

"That's nice, though—"

"Yes. Yes, but it's nice to have mattered enough—"

"Of course we *mattered*!"

She gave him a sharp glance.

"You didn't used to think like that."

He smiled again.

"I didn't know about Carole. Did I?"

She pulled her hand gently out of his.

"Don't get carried away."

"I rather like it—"

"Dave, the next bit might be much harder."

"Disappointing?"

"Maybe—"

"I don't think so," David said. "It's exhilarating."

"So far," Nathalie said carefully, "it's been easy. And we haven't had to do any of the work."

David picked his glass up and held it so that the light shone through the wine.

"I have a fifty-nine-year-old mother who was a company director!"

The door burst open. Polly stood there wearing her pajamas and a defiant expression.

"Heavens, Poll. Is it bedtime?"

She glowered.

"What were you talking about?"

David smiled at her. He moved slightly sideways and patted his knee.

"Mothers."

Polly came forward to be lifted on to his lap.

She said carelessly, "I don't want one."

"Don't you?"

Polly glared at Nathalie.

"Don't *laugh*."

"Why not?"

"It's rude," Polly said. "It's rude to laugh when there's no joke."

David said, "But you're quite funny."

She considered this. She looked at her mother again.

"You're a rude laugher."

"I'm happy," Nathalie said.

Polly rolled her eyes to the ceiling.

"Can't I laugh when I'm happy?" Nathalie said. "Can't we both laugh?"

"I'm not laughing," Polly said stonily. She pointed to her mouth. "Look."

"No, darling. Not you. David and me. We're laughing because we're happy." She glanced at him across the table. "Aren't we?"

"*Yes*," he said.

Steve had tried to persuade his mother-in-law to stay and have coffee after lunch.

"No," Lynne had said, gathering up her bags and her scarf. "No, dear. Thank you, but no. I've taken up too much of your time already."

"You haven't," Steve said patiently. "You haven't. I've liked it. I'm glad you rang."

She glanced away from him.

"It took a bit of courage—"

"To ring your own son-in-law and ask to have lunch with him?"

"You're so busy—"

"Not that busy," Steve said. "And certainly not when we're in the same boat."

She'd put down her bags again then.

"Are we?"

"Aren't we," Steve said, "somehow being made to feel that we've failed where we thought we'd succeeded?"

She gazed at him. He looked back at her face, at the slightly pleading quality in her eyes that must have seemed so appealing to Ralph once, like the eyes of a young deer.

"I always felt I had to be pitied," Lynne said. "Because I couldn't have children. And I hated that, I *hated* being pitied. And I don't want to go back there, I *don't*."

"Nobody can take away what you've done, what I've done—"

Lynne dropped her gaze to the table, to the remains of her chicken salad.

"It wasn't just that I wanted a baby, you know," she said. "It wasn't just going on and on wanting that. It was that I was scared of the future, too—I was scared of my private life just thinning out without children, without grandchildren, thinning out until there wasn't anything there, really, and I was just left with the wanting." She stopped and took a breath and then she said, "It's so terrible, that wanting."

Steve put his hand over her nearest one for a moment.

"But you *have* got children. And grandchildren. You've got all that."

Lynne began to gather herself up again.

"Not with all this. Not with all these—discoveries. I feel—" She stopped again.

"What?"

"I feel I've gone from being the goodie to being the baddie."

"Lynne—"

"Nathalie told me this wasn't my journey."

Steve said, almost bitterly, "If it's any consolation, she's made it pretty plain it isn't mine either."

"That's what you mean about being in the same boat—"

"Yes."

Lynne stood up finally, struggling to arrange her burdens.

"Ralph says there's nothing I can do but wait. He always says things like that. Present Ralph with a problem and he says well, the only way to the other side is *through*. Drives me mad."

"He isn't the same person as you. He isn't the same person as me. Maybe his emotions don't trouble him so much."

She gave him a quick smile.

"No."

Steve stood too.

"You take care."

She reached up to give him a quick little kiss on the cheek.

"Thank you, dear. Thank you for listening. It—it isn't that Ralph doesn't understand—"

"No."

She took a step away.

"Give my love to Nathalie. And a kiss to Polly."

"Course."

He watched her go out of the lunch place, bumping her bags against other tables and chairs as she went. She was like someone who'd had a sad, fearful secret that had been forgotten for years but which had now somehow surfaced in all its old misery. She'd always been someone Steve saw as vulnerable, someone you'd take care not to be careless with, but today her back view, moving awkwardly away from him, looked defeated, as if some long, brave struggle had finally come to nothing. He sighed. Beyond sympathy, there was nothing he could do for her, nothing he could give her to restore Nathalie to her as her child and hers alone.

"Don't you go being selfish," his own mother had said to him. "Don't you go behaving like your dad and just riding roughshod. We've all got our feelings about what Nathalie's doing, we're all affected, but I've got my own children, same as you have, and Lynne hasn't, and don't you forget that."

Steve paused by the cash desk and paid the bill. The girl handing him his change had a bluebird tattooed on her cheekbone and fine blonde hair cut so short that it merely lay on her skull like a dusting of icing sugar. Steve had never really liked short hair on girls, had always loved the luxuriance of, say, Nathalie's hair, but recently he'd begun to see something edgy and attractive in short hair, something almost challenging. It was as if short-haired girls were daring him to think of them as boys. Steve grinned. He put three pound coins in the plastic pot by the till with "Tips thank you!" crudely inked on it with magic marker.

"So long," Steve said to the bluebird girl, and went out into the street.

From across the office, Justine could see that Titus was doodling. Instead of being crouched intently in front of his computer, as if coiled to spring right into it, he was slouched against the back of his chair, one hand in his trouser pocket, the other stretched out across his desk making the easy looping movements that people who can really draw make when they're not trying. It looked as if he was scowling, too, not because she could see his face, but because his whole demeanor looked gloomily, angrily slumped from behind, a sort of scowl of the neck and shoulders.

She glanced around the office. Steve wasn't back from lunch yet, and Meera was sorting invoices with an intensity of concentration that made her look almost spiritual. She got up and smoothed down the hair at the base of her skull, hoping it was lying in funky little straight strands and not curling up babyishly as it had seemed to want to do ever since she cut it. She yanked her jeans down half an inch so that the ring in her bare navel showed, and sauntered over.

"It's like trying to work with the lights out," she said. "You in that mood."

Titus was drawing a fanciful elephant with an elongated trunk and ears like wings.

"Sorry."

Justine hitched one thigh across a corner of his desk.

"What's up?"

Titus heaved an enormous, fed-up sigh.

"I just feel—that the *energy's* gone out of things—"

Justine swung her leg.

"Happens to everyone."

"Not to me," Titus said. "I *invented* energy."

"Come to think of it," Justine said, "I can't imagine a *languid* small man."

"I am not small."

"Aren't you?"

"No. I am short but I am not *small*."

She grinned.

"Quite right. Nor you are."

"I am short," Titus said, "and square. And fed up."

"With what?"

"Every bloody thing."

"Like Sasha, you mean."

Titus threw his drawing pencil so that it spun in an arc away from him and landed neatly in Steve's waste bin.

"Why do girls *always* think it must be love?"

"Because," Justine said, "it mostly is."

"What about the atmosphere in this office, then? What about Steve being in a permanent mood so we all have to tiptoe round him in case we step on the fuse and all get blown to perdition?"

"What's perdition?"

"Look it up," Titus said.

Justine leaned forward.

"You don't have to take it out on me, you know."

"No," he said.

"So don't."

Titus picked up another pencil and began to add angel wings to his elephant.

"Why does Sasha have to be so fascinated by this Nathalie adoption business? Why does she have to think she's the only person Steve can talk to?"

"Maybe it's her thesis thing—"

"Bloody hell," Titus said, "we don't all have to *live* our thesis, do we? Thesis is work, life is play. Steve gets a little hiccup in his perfect work/play balance and we all suffer. He's such a fucking control freak."

"You don't *have* to be controlled—"

Titus regarded her. He looked at her jeaned thigh on the desk, at the slice of flesh between her jeans and her top where the navel ring glinted, at the zip in her top that ran right up to her chin which somehow looked quite a different shape now that her hair was shorter.

"Thing is," Titus said, his eyes on Justine's chin, "that I *like* feeling cheerful. Cheerful is how I'm *meant* to feel, how I'm programmed, and when I'm not cheerful it totally does my head in."

Justine let a beat fall, and then she said, "You are *such* a tosser."

"That's a boy's word."

"You're a boy—"

"You're not. It's a word for boys to use."

"You're not just a tosser," Justine said, "but a pathetic has-been toff tosser at that."

He grinned at her.

"I like a bit of abuse. Cheers me up. Keep going."

"I can take all kinds of things," Justine said, "but I can't take self-pity."

Titus pointed his pencil at her, one eye closed.

"I'm pretty sick of it, too."

From across the office Meera called out sweetly, "Shouldn't you two be working?"

Titus swiveled in his chair.

"Shut it, my little Bombay dream."

"It's such a shame," Meera said, her eyes never leaving her work, "to see an expensive English education so completely wasted."

"That's the whole *point* of it," Titus said, "my sweet and stupid little pakora."

Justine stood up.

"I don't know why she puts up with you. I don't know why anyone does."

"Including you?"

"Including me."

Titus swiveled his chair back and leaned forward, gazing up at Justine.

"You've made me feel one ton better."

She said nothing. Her hand went to the nape of her neck.

"Have a drink with me," Titus said. "Or would you rather have a nice bunch of flowers?"

Justine looked across at Meera. She had put her head-phones back on and was typing up dictation. Justine took a step away from Titus and put her chin up. Her voice was as bored as she could make it.

"Both," she said.

From the kitchen window, Ellen could see straight down the sloping garden to the hedge with the green gate in it which led to the golf course. Halfway down the garden on the left-hand side was an immense old apple tree, the random relic of an ancient orchard when this part of Westerham had all been fruit farms, in which David had built Ellen a tree house, when she was six, with a rope ladder which could be pulled up after her to prevent Daniel's following her. Beside the rope ladder, to placate Daniel, David had hung two old car tires at different levels, and in the left-hand one of these, hunched into its cramped circle, Marnie was sitting. Her back was to

Ellen and she was swinging very slightly, one deck-shoe-clad foot pushing rhythmically against the worn turf underneath.

She'd been there for ages. Ellen glanced at the kitchen clock. It was after three and Petey had been asleep for nearly an hour now, worn out by his own paroxysmic rage. He was on the kitchen sofa, tossed among the cushions like a rag doll, his pale hair fanned out, his mouth slightly open. Ellen had come back from the tennis club in a bad mood, having failed to elicit an invitation to lunch from anyone there, and found Marnie and Petey in the kitchen and the kitchen floor a mess of squashed broccoli and spaghetti hoops. Petey was screaming and Marnie was crying, not just quiet grown-up crying with a lot of tidy nose-blowing, but real out-of-it crying, with her head in her hands and her breath coming in heaving gasps. Ellen had put her tennis racket down on the table, stepped carefully through the mess, picked Petey up off the floor and put him, to his amazement, in the sink. Then she had filled a glass of water from the filter jug, handed it to her mother, and turned on Radio One so that Atomic Kitten could drown out the noise.

Well, that must now have been an hour and a half ago, an hour and a half since Marnie, pausing to give Ellen a brief, wordless hug, had drained her water and walked out of the garden door and down to the swinging car tire. Ellen expected her to sit there for a while, and then to go on down the garden to the gate and out onto the golf course. But she hadn't. She just stayed there, hunched and slightly swinging, her pigtail hanging dejectedly down her back. In the meantime, Ellen had picked Petey, quietly sobbing now, out of the sink, carried him upstairs, changed his nappy—he was devoted to his nappies still—and then brought him back down to the kitchen and laid him, not unkindly but decidedly, on the sofa with his sleepy rag. Throughout this procedure, she had not said one word to him, and he, hiccuping with subsiding sobs, had fixed his huge blue gaze on her as if he knew, in his sinking two-year-old heart, what she was thinking. When he was asleep, Ellen went across the kitchen and took up her station by the window.

In three days, thank goodness, it would be school again. And it would be safely school all the rest of April and May and June and then it would be Canada. In July and August it was always, thankfully, Canada, *always*, first a couple of weeks in Winnipeg with Gran and Lal and then the cottage which was complete perfection in every way except the blackfly which you kind of accepted as the price to be paid for everything else. Perhaps when Marnie got to Winnipeg, Ellen thought, she'd be OK again, she'd go back to being the person you could rely on not to go mental, not to give up on Petey and getting supper and making Daniel read something other than Wisden. The thing about Winnipeg too was that Dad wouldn't be coming. Or at least, he would, to the cottage for a couple of weeks or so, but he wouldn't come for the whole time, he never did, because of work. And maybe, because it was obviously something about Dad that was making Marnie behave like someone who needed Prozac—Ellen knew about Prozac because both Zadie and Fizz in her class had mothers who swallowed Prozac, Zadie and Fizz said, like M&M's—it would help Marnie to have a little holiday from him. Perhaps they all needed a holiday from him, from being English, from the unevenness of family life when some members put in so much more, in Ellen's view, than others.

Personally, Ellen blamed chess. She understood Daniel's passion for cricket, in a way, because Daniel was the age he was, and a boy, and all his weird boy energies had to go *somewhere*, however boring. But Dad was different. Dad was a grown man, a grown-up father, and to spend two nights a week playing chess and all those hours and hours on the computer in his office playing it too was not on. It wasn't normal, it wasn't what other fathers did, it wasn't *fair*. She'd asked Marnie about it once and Marnie had said all kinds of stuff she didn't quite understand about chess, as a game, rescuing people from their own sense of powerlessness, but Marnie had sounded remote while she was speaking, as if she didn't quite believe herself, as if, even if what she was saying was true, it kind of exhausted her to think about because it meant a struggle. Ellen had then got Zadie, who was brilliant at IT, to go on the Internet with her and they found a whole load on the psychology of chess, about players who weren't anarchic by nature and had no desire to subvert their worlds but still couldn't cope with life, and who retreated from it, even from their families, into the consistently resolvable world of chess. Ellen hadn't grasped all this, but she'd got a gist, got enough to develop a suspicion—quite a big suspicion— that chess was actually a rival to his children in her father's eyes, that David in some way *preferred* chess to his children, because it was easier.

Zadie thought it was all crap, but then Zadie's father didn't play anything except card tricks so Zadie didn't have to deal with a rival like chess. This was annoying because on most subjects Zadie was good to talk to, and had plenty of ideas and energy and made you think in ways you hadn't thought of thinking before. But the whole chess thing bored her, in the way that Ellen's Canadian life bored her because Canada hadn't caught Zadie's imagination the way all things American had.

Ellen leaned her elbows on the window ledge and made herself look past Marnie's slowly swinging figure, past and down the green carpet of grass to the hedge. Now she came to think of it, it occurred to her that Daniel probably felt as she did about their father and chess, otherwise why would he, who loved all sport, all competitiveness, be so completely stubborn about learning the one game their father had set his heart on teaching him? Of course, Ellen couldn't talk to Daniel about it. It wasn't possible to *talk* to Daniel in any except the most undemanding and factual way, but just because he couldn't speak didn't mean he couldn't feel things. In fact—Ellen and Zadie and Fizz discussed this a lot—one of the difficulties, the many difficulties, with boys was this very impossibility of letting anything out so that they got absolutely blocked with stuff until they went mental and smashed up a greenhouse. Maybe it was the same with men. Maybe playing chess was a way of stopping yourself from smashing up greenhouses.

Ellen sighed. A huge tiredness was beginning to creep over her, like the tiredness you have after a major row or being ticked off about something. She didn't mind sorting Petey because it wasn't honestly a big deal, sorting Petey. But she wasn't sure she could cope much more with Marnie, and with Dad pretending he didn't have to join in, and Daniel lying on his bed like a goof chanting the names of the New Zealand first cricket eleven. It wasn't, she thought, the way someone of twelve should have to live, all this stifled stuff and not saying, and everyone living as if they were in different houses instead of five members of a family in the same one. But it didn't look as if anyone was going to notice the unfairness just now, it didn't look as if anyone was going to do anything, and if there was any kind of person Ellen couldn't stand, it was someone who never did anything about things they didn't like, but just sat about moaning.

From behind her, Petey stirred. She turned to look at him. He had raised his head a little from the sofa cushions and was regarding her sleepily with the kind of look that was gratifying despite his previous behavior. He gave a little wave with his sleepy rag.

"Bic?" he said hopefully.

Ellen went across to the sofa and sat beside him. Maybe what she had to do was to confront her father, ask him about this chess stuff, tell him what it was doing to Marnie. Whatever that was. She poked Petey's stomach.

"Fatty pig."

He giggled. She put her face down next to his. He smelled of sleep and damp stickiness. Yes, she thought, that's what she'd do, she'd talk to her father.

"Bic!" Petey said again, still giggling.

CHAPTER ELEVEN

David parked his car where he always left it outside his parents' house, with two wheels on the sloping verge to get it out of the roadway. Lynne had never liked him to do this because of the marks his tires left, in wet weather, but Ralph didn't mind. Ralph, David reflected gratefully, climbing out and locking the doors, didn't usually mind anything if the reasons for it were practical.

He looked across the roof of his car at the façade of the house, at the metal-framed windows that Ralph had always said he'd only change when it became necessary, at the brick porch where Lynne left a little daily crate of washed empty bottles for the milkman, at the frothing clematis which David remembered Ralph planting, remembered Ralph giving a slug of gin to, out of a cut-glass tumbler. "Clematis like gin," Ralph had said, "even more than me."

He moved round the car and across the verge to open the gate. Nathalie used to swing on that gate, doubled over, her knickers showing, until she was good and dizzy. His own version of dizzy had been taking his bike up to the top of the steep cul-de-sac a hundred yards away and freewheeling madly down it, forbidding himself even to touch the brakes. It was a pity that getting older made it so much harder to access such pure sensation, made him bring his mind to bear on the external senses, with all the attendant doubts and questions. He put his hand involuntarily to his mouth. If he freewheeled down Mortimer Close now, he'd be fretting about breaking his teeth.

The light was on in the workshop that lay to one side of the house. Ralph had built it himself, the year after he and Lynne moved in, the year they began on the long, slow, rigorous process of adopting Nathalie. For months and months Ralph had been out in most weathers, in his boiler suit, building his workshop, while inside Lynne sewed curtains and planned fantasy nurseries. All David's life, Ralph's workshop had been a place of sanctuary, a place where every dilemma gave the impression of being solvable with the turn of a screwdriver, the planing of rough edges. He went quickly now across the grass in front of the house—Lynne might be watching out for him—and opened the workshop door.

Ralph was sitting at his workbench under the central glaring strip light, with his spectacles on. In front of him lay an open manual displaying diagrams of the position of a cam belt in a car engine.

"Hi, Dad."

Ralph smiled down at his manual.

"Daylight robbery."

"What is?"

"What garages charge for fitting these things."

David moved to look down over Ralph's shoulder.

"Look at that," Ralph said. "Piece of cake, to fit a thing like that."

"Only if you have the right tools."

"Exactly," Ralph said. He stood up and took off his spectacles. "And would Peugeot sell me precisely the right tools? Not bloody likely." He put an arm round David's shoulders. "How are you, son?"

David looked down.

"I have no idea."

"And the children?"

"Mmm—"

"Marnie?"

"Dad," David said, "we're not exactly pulling together. None of us."

Ralph took his arm away. He folded his spectacles and tucked them into the breast pocket of his shirt.

"Funny what we can't help being threatened by—"

"There's no threat."

"It's not what is, you know. It's what's perceived. And you can't know what that is till it hits you."

David sighed.

"The way I see it, I'm just on a fact-finding mission."

Ralph gave him a quick glance.

"Oh?"

"My adoption is part of my life that's always been missing. I just need to know certain things."

Ralph looked at the ceiling of the workshop, where his saws hung like a jagged row of dragon's teeth.

"Simple, eh?"

"Yes."

"Except, son, it isn't. It isn't just facts, is it? It's feelings."

David's shoulders drooped. He turned away and bent over the drawing of the cam belt.

"Dad, you don't want this to bust on you unexpectedly. It would smash the engine."

"I'm not a complete idiot," Ralph said gently.

David gave the manual an angry little shove.

"Nor am I. And what really does my head in is everyone thinking my feelings for them will change just because I know who my birth mother is."

"Everyone?"

"Mum," David said, "Marnie." He paused and then he said again with miserable emphasis, "*Marnie*."

"Marnie," Ralph said slowly. He turned and looked at David. "I wonder what's rattled *her* cage? I thought she was egging you on."

"She was. And now she doesn't like it. It's—it's as if it was some kind of betrayal, as if I was choosing someone who wasn't her."

"Mmm," Ralph said.

David looked at him sharply.

"You *agree* with her?"

"No," Ralph said, "but I understand. We all have our insecurities, don't we? We all have areas that send us into a blue funk."

"*You* don't—"

"Don't you be so sure."

"Well, Dad, you're the only person in this whole business who, as far as I can see, hasn't taken it personally—"

"I don't *feel* it personally. I mean, I care very much it all turns out well for you, but I'm not afraid you won't be my son anymore."

"Well, there you are."

"No," Ralph said, "no. This is OK for me because this is not my funk department."

"Dad?"

Ralph took his spectacles out of his shirt pocket and began to buff them slowly on his sleeve.

"If your mother ever left me," Ralph said uncertainly, "I'd be leaving Marnie *standing*."

"But, Dad—"

"OK," Ralph said, "OK. Tell me there's as much chance of that as cows over the moon and I'll *still* tell you that's what I couldn't handle."

David put a hand on Ralph's arm.

"Dad—"

"Dull old sod like me," Ralph said, "pottering about, mending things, never getting worked up, never surprising her."

"You're not dull—"

"You try being me," Ralph said.

David said awkwardly, "Nat and I think you're great."

"I don't frustrate you," Ralph said, "I don't disappoint you. A dull dad is fine, a dull dad is supposed to be a very benign and formative force in a boy's life."

David moved his arm to put it across Ralph's shoulders.

"But Mum can be so bloody maddening."

"Yes."

"I mean," David said, "the main reason I'm here now is because I feel so guilty about her, about going to find Carole. I feel so guilty."

"Join the club," Ralph said. He moved a little, out of David's embrace. "You're a good lad. You're a good son. You didn't come here to have me do a big-girl breakdown on you."

"You haven't—"

"It's good of you to come. It's good of you to think of your mother."

David hesitated.

"Has Nat been?"

"She's tried."

"Oh."

"Mum isn't—well, always quite as fair to Nathalie. She's a bit harder on Nathalie."

"Dad," David said, "do you think we're doing the wrong thing, Nathalie and me?"

Ralph put his spectacles on.

"No."

"Do you think we're doing the *right* thing?"

"Yes."

"Then why do I feel so guilty about Mum?"

Ralph sighed.

"You've been the center of her life, you and Nathalie. All she ever wanted was children, all she ever wanted was to give you back what she thought you'd lost." He glanced at David and shrugged. Then he said, almost under his breath, "It's a lot to make a child grateful for."

"So not my fault?"

"No," Ralph said. "You'll have to deal with it, but it's not your fault."

David looked at the workshop door.

"Will you come into the house with me?"

Ralph looked at his car manual.

"Five minutes."

"Only five—"

Ralph moved to put his hands on the workbench, either side of the manual. He leaned on them, looking down.

"When you're talking to your mother, lad, try and remember what you mean to Marnie."

"*Marnie?*"

"Yes," Ralph said, not looking up. "Marnie."

"I'm sorry I'm late," Steve said from the sitting-room doorway. Nathalie was sitting on the floor in front of the fake-log gas-fueled fire she wouldn't let him take out, holding her knees. "Is Polly asleep?"

Nathalie nodded. She was half turned away from him and he could only see part of her cheekbone and her forehead beyond the tangled bulk of her hair.

"You never sit in here," Steve said, too heartily, "do you? You always call this the front parlor. Why are you in here?"

"I felt like it," Nathalie said.

"Is something wrong?"

"I felt like it. I felt like the fire."

Steve ran his tongue round his teeth. He no doubt smelled of wine so a kiss might be risking things.

"Sorry I'm late," he said again.

"You said."

"I meant to read to Polly. It was the Gardentime contract. I told you." He paused. It wasn't exactly a lie but it wasn't the whole truth either. The Gardentime contract had segued somehow and—Steve was very sure of this—without intention, into a glass of wine with Sasha. The glass of wine, and Sasha, had made Steve feel briefly that he was handling everything in his life, both personal and professional, pretty well, all complicated things considered.

"I'm impressed," Sasha had said. "*Very* impressed. It's a lot to deal with." She was wearing black fingerless gloves which obscured her thumb rings and made her exposed fingers look weirdly seductive, like miniature stockinged legs. "And you're dealing. You really are."

Nathalie let go of her knees.

"Polly didn't want a story."

"Oh?"

"She isn't letting me do anything for her just now if she thinks it's something I like doing."

Steve hesitated. He put a hand up to the scarf he had wound round his neck for the cycle journey home. He had taken to wearing scarves just lately, bulking them up round his ears in the manner, he hoped, of French movie stars.

"Oh, such imitation," Titus had said. "*Oh*, such flattery."

"Shall I start supper?" Steve said.

Nathalie began to scramble to her feet. She had no shoes on and Steve could see there was a hole in the toe of one of her socks. It was not like Nathalie to have a hole in anything.

"I meant to—"

"It's OK," Steve said, relaxing. "It doesn't matter. We'll do it together."

Nathalie was standing now. She looked suddenly rather small and defenceless in her holey sock on the hearthrug.

She said in a rush, "I rang her."

Steve stopped unwinding his scarf.

Nathalie said, "I didn't mean to, I wasn't going to, I was going to take my time and you were going to be there, and I was going to think about it, and do it in a measured, mature way, but I didn't, I just rang her."

Steve pulled off his scarf and dropped it on the back of the sofa.

"Well?"

Nathalie said shyly, "She sounded northern."

"Did she?"

"Sort of—Newcastle. Geordie."

"Yes. Well."

Nathalie brought her hands together almost in a gesture of prayer.

"She cried."

Steve was startled.

"Did she?"

"She cried and cried. She said she'd thought about me every day. She said she'd called me Samantha."

"You knew that."

"It was different," Nathalie said, "when she said it."

"Oh Nathalie," Steve said.

Nathalie was shaking slightly. She gripped her hands together.

"She kept crying. She was crying and crying. She asked me if I was angry with her."

"What did you say?"

"I said no."

"Aren't you? Weren't you?"

"No," Nathalie said. "Not at her."

"I see."

"She was only sixteen when she had me. Can you imagine?"

Steve gave a little shrug.

"Must have been hard—"

"Yes," Nathalie said, "Yes."

She unlocked her hands and moved around the sofa to stand in front of him. He looked down at her.

He said, "How did you feel?"

"Don't know—"

"Better? Better at all?"

She gave a tiny nod. She leaned forward and put her cheek against his chest, against the rough wool of his donkey jacket. He put his arms around her.

"I'm glad."

She nodded again.

"First step—"

"Yes."

"All that crying," Nathalie said. "I've been sitting here thinking how it would be if it had been Polly, if I'd had to give Polly up."

Steve tightened his grasp.

"And I was thinking, too," Nathalie said, "that for women especially, love is somehow all we know but we still don't really trust it."

Steve swallowed.

He said, again in his too hearty voice, "You could *try*."

"Is it something to do," Nathalie said, "with wanting to be wanted?"

Steve hesitated. He had told Sasha about his awkward and touching lunch appointment with Lynne, and Sasha had taken Lynne's side.

"The myth *is*," Sasha had said, dipping her mittened finger in her glass of red wine, "that adoptive parents get what they want. But look at the reality. The reality is no pregnancy, no preparation and a lifetime of fears and pretense and expectation. Is that getting what you want? Is that actually what you want in the first place? Why does Lynne have to go through all this when she's been through all that already?"

"It sounds," Steve said carefully now, "as if *she* wanted *you*."

"I'm—beginning to dare to think so."

"Good."

"And now I'm hungry."

"Good again."

Nathalie took her cheek away from his chest and looked up at him. She was smiling.

"Thank you," she said.

"What for?"

"Putting up with me."

He said uncomfortably, "But I haven't really—"

"I didn't make it easy."

"Nat," Steve said, "none of this." He dropped his arms. "Supper. Time for supper."

He stood back to allow Nathalie to leave the room ahead of him. She went past him slowly, as if she was still deeply absorbed in something else.

"I can't believe it," she said, pausing in the passage, "I really can't. She was *crying*." Her voice was awed.

The hairdresser, folding neat little packets of aluminum foil over strands of Carole Latimer's newly tinted hair, told her she had lost weight. She looked at herself in the mirror, absurd in her frill of tinfoil, and thought that if she had it was a) only in her face and b) not becoming. She looked in fact, she thought, old and tired and wrung out, which was not surprising as it was precisely how she felt.

Caspar, who came from Klagenfurt in Austria, and was the middle child of seven and his mother's favorite, said that he was trying to eat just a little every three hours so that his body never got in a panic that it was never going to be fed again and started storing fat.

"Is that what it does?" Carole asked, not interested. It wasn't her body panicking that alarmed her, but her mind, the mind that she had so confidently, stupidly supposed she had learned to manage.

"Almost no carbs," Caspar said, deftly painting and folding. "Lots of protein."

Carole knew her cue.

"The Atkins diet."

"It works for everyone. *Every*one. They've all tried it." He glanced at Carole in the mirror, his young-old face hardened by a cruelly short haircut. "No fruit, though. Too many carbs in fruit."

Carole sighed.

"Not for me, then."

"You learn your own metabolism, don't you?"

"I suppose so," Carole said. "*If* you're interested."

Caspar looked faintly shocked. He tucked the last strand of hair into its square of foil and stood back.

"Time for the heat machine!"

Carole closed her eyes.

"Thank you."

"Twenty minutes, darling," Caspar said. He patted her shoulder. "No distractions."

Carole winced. When she had first started coming to this salon almost twenty years ago, time in the chair had been a complete luxury, time without telephones or questions, time that was somehow sanctioned as her time, even by Connor, the sort of time women with proper self-respect should be regularly allotted, no questions asked. But now—well, now was so different, and so frighteningly familiar at the same time, from the two distinct worlds of her past that three hours in the salon being transformed—for what purpose, beyond habit?— from dark dirty blonde to pale dirty blonde seemed to represent not so much a blessed and restorative escape as an attempt to hold on to all the flimsy little rituals that gave her the illusion she wasn't drowning. Drowning women do not, after all, have their hair carefully colored, and grade the towels in their linen cupboards according to size, and never run out of oranges to squeeze for breakfast juice—do they?

She felt the pleasant semicircle of warmth round the back of her skull from the heat machine.

"Thank you," she said, without opening her eyes.

Caspar's hand rested for a fleeting moment on her shoulder.

"Enjoy, darling."

She nodded, clattering her foils.

"Shall I come and pick you up?" Connor had said as she

169

left the flat. "Why don't you take a taxi there, and then I'll pick you up?"

"Thank you," she said, "thank you, but no. I never know how long it will be with color, but thank you."

Thank you. It was all she seemed able to say to him now, thank you, and sorry. Sorry for having loved someone else, for having had sex with someone else, for having had someone else's baby. Sorry for lying about having that baby aborted, for actually having had that baby, for never telling you that that baby was alive. Thank you for taking me in when Rory dumped me, thank you for marrying me and making me respectable, for making me a wife and mother. Thank you for giving me a career opportunity, for encouraging me, for praising me to other people. Sorry I couldn't love you a tenth as well as I loved Rory, thank you for not probing so I didn't have to tell you how I resented that baby for driving Rory away, sorry for not loving Martin, thank you for being able to love Martin, sorry for all these recent scenes, thank you for not throwing me out, sorry, thank you, sorry—oh *God*, Carole thought, pressing her eyelids so tightly shut that she could almost feel her separate lashes, is there one single tiny corner of my life to hide in where there isn't a price to pay?

Connor had, since that awful night when she had finally told the truth about Rory's baby, been—well, *majestic* was the word that came to mind. He'd been appalled, of course, and stunned and horrified, sitting there in the wing chair in his cashmere dressing gown holding the letter from this Elaine Price woman which told Carole that her son, David, would, if she was willing, like to get in touch with her. He sat there, holding the letter by its edge, his eyes full of tears, shaking his head. It was like watching someone slowly taking in the news of a death, rather than that of a life. She had crouched on the edge of the sofa, watching him, wondering what he would do, and what she would do when he decided. It felt to her just as it had felt when Rory

170

told her he didn't want to be saddled with a baby, as if, despite all her efforts to gain control of her life, to decline any kind of victimhood, some great arbitrary force could always come swinging over the horizon and knock her flat. But of course, it wasn't an arbitrary force. It was love, the kind of passionate, vulnerable, craving love that nobody in their right minds would ever seek but that, once you had known it, successfully drained the color out of all other more manageable loves. She could see Rory as some kind of monster now, she could see his self-absorbed destructiveness, his terrible carelessness with other people, his almost criminal changeableness; but she could never feel indifferent to him, or to remembering him. When she remembered him, great lumps of intensity—she didn't care, any longer, to define them—choked her mind and her breathing. She would never have been able, she knew, to be in the same room with him again. She would never have dared. She would never, even with all her unhappy knowledge of the sort of man he was, the sort of man he perhaps couldn't help being, have been able to trust herself.

And with Connor? Well, Connor was trustworthy, in the sense that he didn't eternally let her down, eternally play games with her feelings, eternally exploit her. But even Connor required her to acknowledge that, because of what had happened to her, because of what she had *done*, he was in a moral position to call the shots. After what seemed like an eternity of watching him sitting there gazing at Elaine Price's letter, like some aghast character in a Victorian melodrama, he had risen from his chair and come to sit beside her on the sofa. She had stared at her knees under the blue wool of her dressing gown, stared and stared at them as if they represented proof of her existence when everything else was so out of control that existence was hard to discern.

Connor hadn't touched her. He'd laid the letter—respectfully and without obvious anger—on the coffee table in front of the sofa, and then he'd said gravely, "I shan't reproach you."

There had been, then, a small, appalled silence. Now glaring rather than staring at the knees, Carole fought down waves of both fury and laughter. Not reproach her! Not reproach her for something that had happened long before they even knew each other, something that was part of a life that he could not—should not—lay claim to! How dare he . . .

"Did you hear me?"

She'd nodded.

"I think," Connor said, adjusting the tie belt on his dressing gown, "I think I understand why you didn't tell me the truth."

She bit her lip. Whatever the truth was now—whatever the truth ever is—the truth *then* had been that she hadn't told anyone about the baby for the raw and unacceptable reason that she hadn't wanted the baby. She had wanted his father. With the help of a friend, she had gone away to a strange little nunnery in East Anglia to have the baby, a place where it was hardly necessary even to have a name; a place where common humanity in humans was unquestioningly accepted as very, very common. She remembered the duney beach beyond the convent, and the cloudy, ginger-beer North Sea, and the gulls, and her terror of looking at her baby, in case, in case . . .

She fought with her feeling.

"I did hear," she said to Connor. "I did. Thank you."

He'd brought them brandy then, cognac in old-fashioned balloon glasses, and urged her to drink hers as if it was a medicinal tonic. He'd become, as the cognac went down, increasingly solicitous, almost possessive, talking to her in the way she recalled he'd talked to her when they first met, in the deep and thrilled voice of the acknowledged savior of the bruised and fallen angel.

"Will you see this boy?" he'd said, his hand on hers.

"I don't know."

"I think you should."

"I'm not sure I want to—"

"I think you should."

"I can't think—" Carole said.

"No, no. Of course not. Of course not now. But when you can, I think you should."

And then, of course, there followed what always followed when Connor felt a renewed affirmation of control, a sweet sense of his true power delivered in great grace. Carole had always liked sex, had enjoyed the physical possession of looks and health and appetite. But that night, lying on the marital bed, staring up at the ceiling from beneath Connor's energetic and triumphant shoulder, she had wondered if she would ever be able to see the point of sex again.

The timer on the heat machine gave a small, polite ping and the warmth on Carole's neck began, inhospitably, to subside. She opened her eyes and, in the mirror, saw Caspar four mirrors away talking animatedly to a girl in leather trousers whose long copper-colored hair he was meticulously, almost reverently, smoothing. She sighed, bending her head forward, and feeling the cooling foils rattling against her neck. In the bag by her feet, her mobile telephone began to ring. It occurred to her to ignore it because it would only be Connor, planning to have the Mercedes purring at the curb outside the salon for her, planning a surprise glass of champagne at the Ritz or a visit to the gallery in St. James' to look at yet another of the maritime prints he seemed able to see such charm in. Then it struck her that to ignore Connor would only mean subsequent explanation, subsequent justification, and apology. She scrabbled in her bag and found the phone.

"Hello?"

A man's voice said, "Is that Carole Latimer?"

She straightened a little in the chair.

"Yes—"

"I don't want to startle you," the man said, "but Elaine said it would be all right to ring. She told me you had said it would be all right to ring." There was a tiny pause, and then he said, "I'm David."

Carole gripped the phone. She couldn't look at herself, she couldn't look at that grotesque in the mirror, that distorted face and person. She opened her mouth to stall him, to say some anodyne thing that would give her a moment, seconds even, and heard herself saying, in a tone she hardly recognized, "What do you want?"

There was silence the other end. Carole swallowed. She couldn't immediately say sorry; she couldn't start all this fatal sorry business off again, all over again, not now, not with this adult male person, this grown-up—*son*, on the other end of the line.

"I don't want to frighten you," David said. "Elaine said you'd said—"

"Yes," Carole said.

"Do you really think," Elaine Price had said on the telephone in that tone of firm kindness that Carole had always found hard to resist, "do you really think this son of yours is going to go away? Don't you think he has a right to know where he comes from?"

"Sorry," Carole said to David.

"It's OK," he said.

"Oh—"

"I've been getting my courage up for ages. I don't know why, but I could suddenly do it. I'm a contract gardener, you see, and I'm in the middle of planting a hornbeam hedge and I'd been thinking about you. So I rang."

"Yes."

"I've always," David said shyly, "wondered who you were."

The copper-haired girl rose to her feet and offered a cheek for Caspar to kiss. They said goodbye, laughing, and then Caspar began to walk down the salon towards Carole, brushing his cropped head with the flat of his hand.

"I'm afraid I can't talk now—"

"Can I call again?" David said.

"Perhaps—"

"Look," David said, "this is on your terms. I mean, I know I can't just walk into someone else's life and take what I want and walk out again."

"No."

"I don't know your circumstances, after all. I don't know what your life is like."

"Lovely," Caspar said, moving the heat machine backwards. "Lovely. Done to a turn."

"Another time," Carole said to David, "another time—" She snapped the phone shut and smiled at Caspar in the mirror.

"You all right, darling?" Caspar said. "You look ever so pale."

CHAPTER TWELVE

Meera liked her position in Steve Ross's studio. She liked it professionally—being both indispensable and able to keep order suited her—and she liked her desk in the corner, away from the noise of the street below the front windows, and with a comfortable view down the length of the room. From where she sat, with a wall behind and to the left of her desk, she had a direct sightline to the door to the stairs, and another both to Justine and to Titus. Steve's desk was partly obscured by Titus's computer, but not so much that it prevented Meera from seeing, from the angle of his head, whether Steve was working, or on the telephone, or thinking, gazing up at those ancient and twisted ceiling beams that seemed to Meera little short of barbaric.

Meera had learned this art of quiet watchfulness at home. She had learned, in the noisy and crowded little house behind her parents' thriving corner shop, that the way to progress in life was not to join in. The fourth child—and third girl—in a family of five, she had watched her brother and older sisters clamoring and elbowing their way into positions of advantage, into the narrow parental focus left over from managing a business that employed relations as well as immediate family, and which was open for sixteen hours a day. Meera, who favored her maternal grandmother in her composed and slender looks, elected at an early age to withdraw from this rowdy battleground.

She wasn't particularly bookish, but she had an aptitude for organization and holding her tongue.

"My God," her father said to her when she was twelve, in possibly the only compliment he ever had time to pay her, "you are the only person in this family who doesn't drive me crazy."

When she was fourteen, she told her parents—it was not an announcement, merely something more than a remark—that she wasn't going to work in the business. She wanted to work in an office, she said, and to that end she was going to concentrate on her IT skills. She'd be very happy to help with the accounts but she wasn't going to stack shelves or fight with her sisters about doing the weekend evening shifts. She expected a row. There wasn't one. She looked at her parents' faces, bruised with fatigue, and saw something like relief there, something straying reluctantly towards admiration. Her father leaned towards her. He put a hand out in her direction, forefinger pointing.

"Just no crazy ideas about who you marry, huh?"

"Of course not," Meera said.

Of course not was what she still thought, ten years later. She was independent now, sharing a flat in Westerham with a girlfriend who was a solicitor, and going home on Saturdays so that her mother could describe, and relive, the dramas of the week to her. She would marry, of course, and she would marry as her parents expected, but not a shopkeeper. When Meera married, she would choose a professional, a professional man of her own race and religion who could help her continue with the kind of life she had chosen. She would like to like him, of course, but she didn't need him to sweep her off her feet and out of her senses. That kind of love, that kind of knock-you-sideways love, was something Meera found not simply incomprehensible, but also almost distasteful. How could such loss of self to emotion ever lead to anything but wretchedness and humiliation?

She raised her head and looked down the length of the studio. Steve was out—never good for the firm's productivity, in Meera's view—and Titus and Justine were, it was perfectly evident, conducting an e-mail flirtation from desks at most eight feet apart. Titus had his back to Meera, but his back was quite animated enough to convey to Meera what was going on. As for Justine, she wasn't even pretending to cover what she was doing. Her face was alight, bent towards the screen, the fronds of hair at her neck curling up as if in response to her delight.

Meera clicked her tongue. It wasn't disapproval she felt so much as a profound exasperation. Even if you set aside the fact that this was paid work time, it pained her to see that Justine was so obtuse about Titus, that she seemed unable or unwilling to see that Titus was doing no more than having a bit of fun. Titus wasn't a bad man, after all, but he was the kind of overly straightforward man, Meera knew from her years of watchfulness, who when thwarted in one area of his male desires and energies took the easiest route to gratifying them elsewhere. It was plain that that great tall girl—big blondes looked almost androgynous to Meera—was playing hard to get, and therefore Titus, in frustration, was in his turn playing with something more amenable. And Justine, for all her vaunted contempt for men like Titus, was being very amenable indeed.

If it was just a game, Meera considered, and the players were equally matched, it wouldn't matter, except for the principle of not playing at work. But watching Justine over the last few weeks had made Meera feel that this was not a game for Justine, any more than whatever was preoccupying Steve at the moment was a game for him. Justine was being drawn into this love thing, this in-love thing, and Titus, while not cruel, could very easily be careless. Perhaps for Justine, from her rather angry and underprivileged background, Titus's nonchalance and over-privilege represented the attraction of opposites. Perhaps Justine just liked something that Meera most disliked, which was danger. Perhaps—and Meera had come across many, many girls like this—Justine just needed that power of being openly fancied.

She stood up. Neither of them took any notice. She picked up her handbag and moved quietly out onto the floor, and across it until she was standing behind Titus. Justine was staring at her, excited and guilty.

"Not clever," Meera said to Titus.

He didn't turn round. He went very still.

"And don't accuse me of spying," Meera said. "This is an open-plan office."

"I wouldn't dare," Titus muttered.

"And you wouldn't dare behave like this if Steve was here."

Justine ducked her head. Titus turned his head slightly.

"Try not to be priggish, passion flower."

"Shut it," Justine hissed.

Meera turned and walked steadily across the floor and through the door to the stairway. Titus didn't look at Justine.

He said, staring ahead of himself, his jaw tight, "If Steve was here. If Steve was ever bloody here—"

Justine's shoulders drooped.

"Where is he?"

"You don't want to know," Titus said furiously. "And neither do I."

Lynne sat on the edge of the cream leather sofa in the upstairs sitting room of the Royal Oak, holding a teacup and a triangle of shortbread.

"Only packet, I'm afraid," Evie said. "I don't seem to get round to much baking nowadays."

Lynne took a bite of shortbread and looked hastily down at the carpet for crumbs. The flowers and trellises around

179

her feet bore the sweeping signs of having been freshly hoovered.

"I shouldn't think I've baked a cake since the children left home—"

"If I baked one," Evie said, "Ray'd only eat it and he's eighteen stone already. Don't you mind about crumbs. I should have given you a plate."

Lynne put her shortbread in her saucer.

"It's nice enough of you to see me."

Evie regarded her. She'd been much surprised when Lynne telephoned, and even more surprised when Lynne had asked to come round. It wasn't so much that she and Lynne didn't get on, but more that she was aware that Lynne couldn't quite forget the difference between living in the Royal Oak and living in a detached house on Ashmore Road. Also—and Evie's antennae were even more sharply attuned to this distinction than the social one—Lynne had always allowed Evie to know that, as the mother of the mother of the grandchild, she was unquestionably, in the subtle ranking of these things, the *first* grandmother.

But the sight of Lynne now on the edge of her sofa worrying about crumbs on her carpet—who else, of Evie's rare visitors, ever had the grace to concern themselves with such details—inspired in Evie nothing but pity. Never mind the past, never mind the unsubtle jockeying for precedence over Polly, never mind any kind of insecurity-induced silliness, the woman sitting on Evie's sofa looked both lost and unhappy, and it smote at Evie's heart. She leaned forward.

"Make yourself comfortable, dear."

Lynne looked doubtfully at the sofa.

"Once you get yourself back into it," Evie said, "it's ever so much better."

Gingerly, Lynne inched herself backwards across the leather surface. Evie watched her, with the indulgence she used to watch Polly with, when Polly attempted her first climbs up the ladder to the slide in the children's playground behind the Royal Oak.

"There now."

"I expect," Lynne said, allowing herself to half relax against the sofa's unyielding gleaming cushions, "I expect you wonder why I've come."

"Well," Evie said, "I've a *bit* of an idea—"

"I'm not sure myself, really," Lynne said. "I mean, I knew I needed to talk, I knew I needed to talk to someone who knows the situation. But I don't really know what I'm after."

"We're all a bit on edge," Evie said. She lifted the lid on the teapot on the tray beside her and peered inside. "Well, when I say all, I'd have to exclude Ray. Ray's never on edge, not really, not unless it's to do with the business. Ray does good mood, bad mood, finish. It depends on the day's trade."

Lynne leaned across the sofa and put her cup down on the seat two feet away.

She said suddenly, "Ralph hasn't a clue."

"No."

"He can't see it—"

"No."

"He can't," Lynne said, her voice abruptly loud, "he can't see how I feel having both my children do this, together, at once. He can't see what it does to me, seeing them so excited. Evie," Lynne said, turning towards her, "I can't remember when I saw them so happy. *Happy*."

Evie put the teapot lid back on.

"It's early days—"

"What for?"

"For being happy," Evie said. "They haven't met these mothers yet."

"Mothers," Lynne said. "*Mothers*. How am I supposed to compete with *two mothers*?"

Evie got up. She walked across her hoovered carpet to the leather sofa and removed Lynne's teacup. Then she sat down.

"It's not a competition, dear," Evie said.

Lynne sighed.

"You brought those two up," Evie said. "You took them into your home and you looked after them and schooled them and taught them how to live in the world. You *mothered* them. No one can take that away from you."

"But I didn't give birth to them. I didn't give birth to *anyone*."

"That's only the beginning," Evie said. "It counts, but it doesn't count for everything. It's the going on afterwards that counts, the going on you did for Nathalie and David."

Lynne fished in her pocket for a tissue.

"It isn't the same as belonging. Nothing will make them belong to me like they belong to *them*."

"Nonsense," Evie said.

"All very well—"

"Don't you start on that," Evie said. "Don't you even *begin*. Take my Verena. Just take Verena. I gave birth to her all right, but if you asked her now if she thought she belonged to me she'd laugh in your face. We don't belong to nobody in the end. Nobody but ourselves."

Lynne bent her head.

"It just all reminds me—"

"Course it does."

"And I find it hard to see them so excited—"

"Well," Evie said, "try being just irritated about that. You try seeing it as childish. Don't let it upset you."

"No."

"They're not halfway there yet. Not even a quarter of the way."

"No."

"They know their names. They've heard them on the telephone. It's like a Lonely Hearts column, if you ask me."

"One's an art teacher," Lynne said. "The other's a retired company director. In London."

Evie sniffed.

"Could mean anything—"

"It means, in both cases, something utterly different to what they've known. I'm not artistic. I couldn't run a business to save my life."

"I told you," Evie said, "this isn't a competition." She looked straight at Lynne. "You're their mother, you brought them up, and that's *that*."

"But, Polly—"

"Polly lives here. We live here. We've known Polly since she was four hours old."

"Yes."

"I tell you," Evie said, leaning forward, "if there's any funny business with Polly, they'll have Ray to deal with and they won't like that. Nobody does."

Lynne smiled again, faintly.

"Heavens—"

"You're to stop worrying."

"I know—"

"It'll all pass," Evie said. She put out a hand and patted Lynne's nearest one. "They'll go haring off and fill in all these blanks they're so obsessed by and then it'll all pass. You'll see."

Lynne looked up. She turned her hand over so that she could grasp Evie's.

"Thank you," she said. "*Thank* you."

Evie smiled at her. She returned the pressure of Lynne's hand. It was good to see her looking better, but it was also time for a tiny triumph.

"I've got Polly coming Saturday," she said. "That's two Saturdays running. Two on the trot."

Petey sat in his bath, slowly filling an empty shampoo bottle with bathwater and then squirting it dangerously close to the edge of the bath so that sometimes, thrillingly, the water arced out onto the bathroom floor. There was, after all, no one there to supervise him for the moment. Daniel had been sent to watch him, and had begun by being quite participatory, kneeling on the floor beside the bath and aiming the shampoo bottle directly at Petey's tummy button and making him squeal. But then Petey had found three of Ellen's glitter hairclips lying in the soap dish, and had wanted to put them in his own hair and Daniel, for some reason neither comprehensible nor acceptable to Petey, had wanted to prevent him. Petey had insisted, Daniel had objected, Petey had screamed, Daniel had shouted and then stamped out of the bathroom. When he had gone, Petey arranged the clips in a clumsy clump above his forehead and resumed the water game with the shampoo bottle.

"Where's Daniel?" Ellen said. She was standing in the doorway in jeans and a pink sweatshirt top, which Petey much admired, with a hood and "Sugababes" printed on the front, in sequins.

Petey crossed his eyes and put the neck of the shampoo bottle in his mouth.

"Don't drink the *bathwater*," Ellen said, swooping.

Petey beamed up at her. He put a coy hand up, to finger the hairclips.

"You look ridiculous," Ellen said. She turned and yelled over her shoulder, "*Daniel!*"

David said, from further down the landing, "He's in the kitchen."

"He's supposed to be watching Petey."

"Isn't it simpler to do it yourself?"

Ellen sighed.

"That isn't the *point*—"

David came into the bathroom. He stooped to kiss Petey's head.

"You look a right little fairy."

Petey lowered his eyelashes.

"The floor's *soaking*—"

"I'll mop it," David said.

Ellen began to soap a flannel vigorously.

184

She said, in a voice strongly reminiscent of her mother's, "There's a cloth under the basin."

"I know."

"Only reminding you—"

"I *know*," David said.

Ellen picked up Petey's nearest hand. It was covered with green and purple slashes from coloring pens.

"It's always me," Ellen said. "I don't mind, because I can do it, but I do mind the assumption that I *will* do it."

David knelt beside her on the floor, holding the cloth.

"Do you mean looking after Petey?"

"Petey!" Petey shouted, rattling his hairclips.

Ellen picked up his other hand.

"Well, yes. But it's other stuff too."

David began to sweep the cloth across the pools of water on the floor.

He said carefully, "What other stuff—"

"You know," Ellen said, rubbing Petey's hand. "You know what I mean. At least, you'd know if you could think about *any*thing except chess, *ever*."

David got up, and wrung the floorcloth out over the basin.

He said, his back towards Ellen, "You mean Mum."

"Yes."

"In what—way exactly?"

Ellen lifted Petey to his feet in order to soap his body.

She said crossly, "Do I have to spell it out to you?"

"No," David said. "But nor do you have to be rude."

Ellen turned to look at him, one hand still steadying Petey in the bath.

"I'm fed up!" she shouted. "I'm fed up with nobody paying attention to us, with you so obsessed with chess you can't think about another thing and Mum so out of it because of you that she goes from being so much of a mother we can't breathe to absolutely no mother at all! I'm sick of having to pick up the pieces!"

Petey dropped the shampoo bottle and began to cry. Ellen gave an exasperated sigh and let go of his hand. He sat down abruptly in the bath, sobbing.

David came across the bathroom holding a towel—not Petey's—and bent to lift his son out of the bath.

"That isn't his towel."

"It doesn't matter."

"Mum—"

"It doesn't bloody *matter*," David said. He straightened up, holding Petey clumsily wrapped in the towel.

Ellen said into her chest, "I didn't mean to be rude but I did *mean* it."

"I know."

She looked up at her father.

She said, in a suddenly much less confident voice, "What's the matter with Mum?"

David sat down on the closed lid of the toilet with Petey on his knee. Petey was whimpering now, his fingers in his mouth.

"He needs his sleepy rag," Ellen said.

"He can wait—"

"He can't," Ellen said. "You don't want him screaming. I'll get it."

"Thank you," David said. He began to unclip the plastic bows in Petey's hair. Petey's eyes widened for a second, ready for piercing protest, but then he remembered whose knee he was sitting on and merely went on whimpering round his fingers.

"There," Ellen said. She held out the sleepy rag. "Dad?"

"Yes."

"What about Mum?"

David wrapped Petey close in his towel and held him hard.

"I meant to tell you. I was going to tell you—"

"What?" Ellen said sharply.

"It isn't chess."

"Oh no?"

"No," David said. "I know I play far too much and you all get fed up with me, but it isn't that."

Ellen leaned against the wall. She reached behind her head and pulled up the hood of her sweatshirt, yanking it forward until it covered her hair and shadowed her face.

"What then?"

David had his face against the top of Petey's head.

"You know I'm adopted. You've always known I was adopted."

"So?"

"And you are quite sure you know what being adopted means?"

Ellen sighed.

"Course."

"Tell me then."

"It means," Ellen said with elaborate boredom, "that your mother couldn't keep you so she had to give you away and she gave you away to Mr. and Mrs. King and they got killed in a bus crash in France so you got given to Granny Lynne and Grandpa, who brought you up and are your parents, end of story."

David closed his eyes.

"Not quite."

Ellen flicked the sequins on her front.

"Well, there was Nathalie, too."

"Yes, but that isn't everything. There's something else. My mother, the mother who gave birth to me, is still alive."

Ellen stopped flicking.

"She's called Carole," David said holding on to Petey, "and she lives in London."

There was a pause.

Then Ellen said, "How do you know?"

David opened his eyes.

"I've talked to her."

"You've *talked* to her?"

"Yes," David said, "on the telephone."

Ellen turned slowly until her back was against the wall, and then she slid down until she was sitting on the floor.

"Why?"

"Why what?"

"Why did you talk to her?"

"I wanted to," David said.

Ellen put her hooded head against her bent knees so that her voice was muffled.

"But she gave you away."

"I know."

"I wouldn't talk to someone who'd given me away."

"I wanted to know the reasons," David said. He reached down and began to rub Petey's toes, through the towel. "There have to be reasons for doing something as big as that. Think of"—his tone became jocular—"giving Petey away."

"Not funny," Ellen said.

"No. Not funny."

"Who gave you her number?"

"Someone called Elaine Price. Someone who specializes in helping adopted people find their mothers—their parents—if they want to."

Ellen turned her head a little.

"Why did you want to?"

"I just wanted to know."

"Know what?"

"Where I'd been born, what had happened, who my father was."

"Why?"

David lifted Petey's rag-holding arm to dry beneath it.

"Wouldn't you?"

"I do know," Ellen said.

"Exactly. And if you didn't, wouldn't you want to?"

Ellen tipped herself slowly sideways until she was curled on the floor on her side.

She said babyishly, "But you've got us."

David sighed.

"El, this was *before* you. Before you were even thought of. When I was smaller than even Petey is now. This is my baby story."

Ellen tugged at her hood.

"What was your father called?"

"I don't know."

"Doesn't your mother know?"

"I've talked to her for two minutes on the telephone. We didn't get as far as that."

"What did she sound like?"

"Nervous," David said.

"Why?"

"I expect she didn't know what I wanted."

Ellen rolled towards him. She put up a hand and took hold of one of Petey's feet. He gazed down at her, sucking.

"What did you want?"

"I told you," David said, "I want to know my story."

Ellen sat up slowly. Her hood was slipping backwards, pulling her hair off her face.

"What'll happen?"

"I don't know."

She said uncertainly, "Will you tell us?"

"Of course. I should have told you this much before, probably. Maybe I should have told you when Nathalie first thought of it."

Ellen's head came up. She let go of Petey's foot.

"Nathalie—"

"Yes. The search lady has found Nathalie's mother too."

"Oh."

"Do you want to know her name?"

"No," Ellen said. She stood up. She said unsteadily, "I wish it *had* been chess."

He looked down at Petey.

"Sorry."

Ellen took a step away. She looked suddenly very young, very truly like the child of twelve she actually was rather than the one of fourteen or fifteen she usually chose to present to the world.

"I'm going to find Mum," she said.

Daniel withdrew his right leg from under Ellen's sleeping weight, and arranged it, awkwardly, across his left. He'd been amazed when she'd come into his bedroom, when all the house lights were off, and he was listening to Test Match Special from Adelaide, on long wave, under the bedclothes, and then even more amazed when she'd wanted to get right into bed with him and he could see, by the light of the torch he kept by his bed, that she'd been crying.

It had admittedly been a pretty dire evening, with all this stuff about Dad's real mother, stuff that made Daniel want to go out of the room until it was all over and they could talk about normal things again. It wasn't so much the fact of Dad having a mother that upset him—even Daniel could see that everything, including hamsters, had to have had a mother to give birth to them at some point—but rather the look on Dad's face when he talked about it, over supper. And the look on Mum's face, which didn't match Dad's, and Ellen saying nothing and jabbing her fork into her baked potato until it was a flat, floury mess which you wouldn't want to eat unless you were so starving you'd eat anything. It was just that there was something wrong— badly wrong—about Dad's being all turned on by some- thing they couldn't share in, something that was just his, and important to him. Daniel wasn't in the least keen on his mother's lectures on the importance of loyalty and com- munal concern in family life, but she had got it through to him that families do things together, that a family is a club you can always go home to. Dad, at supper, had looked, quite frankly, like a pretty happy little club of one.

They'd all gone to bed early. Daniel didn't think anyone

was particularly tired—he certainly wasn't—but there didn't seem to be anything else much to do or say. And he'd only been in bed an hour or so, waiting for it to be Jonathan Agnew's turn to commentate on the cricket from Australia, when the door had opened and Ellen had come in and, without a word, climbed over him to the wall side of his bed and slithered down beside him under his duvet.

"Ow," he'd said, and, "Your feet are freezing."

"I've been in Petey's room," Ellen said, "sitting on the floor."

"Why didn't you take your duvet?"

"Didn't want to."

"Didn't *think*."

"Didn't *want* to."

Ellen humped herself sideways until she was facing Daniel. He shone his torch in her face.

"You've been crying."

Ellen shut her eyes. She took a breath and then she said fiercely, "I don't *want* her."

"*Who?*"

"This Dad-mother-granny person."

Daniel shone the torch on the ceiling, on the rusty stain where he'd once successfully flicked a melted piece of chocolate, on a hot day, with a plastic ruler.

"We don't have to."

"What?"

"She's nothing to do with us," Daniel said. "She's nothing to do with us at *all*."

"But she *is*," Ellen said, "because of Dad. It'll *make* her be something."

Daniel said stoutly, "I shan't."

"You'll have to."

"I shan't. I'll go to Canada."

"Oh," Ellen said sarcastically, "wave a little Harry Potter wand and zoom off to Canada."

"You could come too. And Petey."

"And Mum."

"Course."

"But," Ellen said, "I don't want to be without Dad. And I don't want Dad to be like *this*."

Daniel turned the torch off. It occurred to him to ask Ellen why their father should want to do this, to do something that they didn't want to join in, couldn't join in, and then it struck him that Ellen couldn't answer him any more than he could answer himself, and that the reason she was in his bed, and taking up too much space, was precisely *because* she didn't know the answer. And, like him, didn't like the question.

After a while, Ellen began to snuffle. At first Daniel thought she was crying again, but then he realized that she was actually snoring faintly, that she had fallen asleep with her mouth open, taking up most of his pillow and with his right leg imprisoned under hers. He sighed. He supposed he couldn't even turn the radio on again now, because Ellen, sad but asleep, was more manageable than Ellen sad and awake, and anyway, if he was honest, there was a peculiar comfort in having her there, snoring or not, and in a frame of mind in which contempt for him and his pitiful gender was not uppermost.

He gave his leg an experimental twitch. Ellen grunted and muttered something, moving just enough for Daniel to ease himself free. He assessed the position. He was more comfortable, but not quite comfortable enough. He gave Ellen a nudge with his right shoulder.

"Shove over," he said.

CHAPTER THIRTEEN

When the photograph came Cora rearranged the shrine in the corner of her bedroom. She didn't move the little Buddha from his central position—there was something about gods that required the limelight—but she moved him back a little, back among the candles, and the black lacquer vase of incense sticks, and the silk orchid rooted in its waterlike block of resin, in order to be able to put the photograph in front, where she could see it. At first, she just propped it against the Buddha, but that seemed disrespectful to both of them, so she put the photograph in a frame she had made herself, years ago, from scraps of Oriental brocade glued round cardboard and stood it independently in front of the flames and the flowers and the Buddha's removed and timeless smile.

Samantha—Nathalie—had sent her the photograph. It showed a dark-haired woman and a curly-haired child in an armchair together, looking at a book. It wasn't a very big picture but it had enough detail in it for Cora to devour with her eyes: Nathalie's earrings and Polly's red cardigan with buttons shaped like ladybirds and the outlines of their cheeks and noses.

"She's the image of you," Betty had said, "the image."

"Yes," Cora said, delighted and disbelieving. "Yes."

Betty put the picture down.

"But that's enough."

"What d'you mean, that's enough?"

"That picture's enough," Betty said. She turned away and began to rummage in the vegetable rack. "You've seen this photo of her, you know she's got a little girl, you know she's well. Just let that be enough."

Cora looked at the picture, at the stylish modern armchair, at Nathalie's hand holding the book open for Polly to see.

"What d'you mean?" she said again.

Betty dumped a double handful of carrots on the draining board.

She said, her back to Cora, "You'll only get hurt."

"Hurt?"

"Yes," Betty said, clattering in the drawer for the peeler. "If you go any further with this, you'll only get hurt again."

"Why will I?"

"Because," Betty said, spinning round, "that's what will *happen*. She may be a lovely girl but you've gone your different ways, you've lived your different lives and nothing but hurt'll come out of trying to go back *any*where."

"But I'm not—"

"Of course you are," Betty said. "What else are you trying to do but make what went wrong go all right instead? I don't blame you, Cora, but you can't. She's not baby Samantha. You're not schoolgirl Cora. I wish she'd never rung you."

Cora said quietly, "I liked it."

Betty pulled a chair out from the table and sat down opposite her sister.

"She's not angry with me," Cora said, gazing at the picture. "She said so."

"Why should she be angry, for Christ's sake?"

"I was careless," Cora said, "wasn't I? I was careless enough to let myself get pregnant, and it was her life I was being careless about."

Betty gave an exasperated sigh.

"You were drugged. You were raped—"

"I wasn't raped," Cora said. "Don't ever say that. Don't ever say that baby was forced on me. Don't ever say I didn't want that baby."

Betty leaned across the table.

"I'm just not having you hurt again. You're a single woman, Cora, and we all know that whatever might be good for a married woman isn't so good for a single one."

Cora put the photograph down flat on the table and covered it with one of her painful hands.

"All my life," she said, without particular resentment, "I've been on the receiving end of other people's views."

"Yes. Well?"

"You all describe me. You always have. It's as if I've got a whole lot of labels stuck on me, as if I've got to be explained away."

"Not *away*, dear—"

"You've been good to me," Cora said. "You've been better to me than anyone, but even you haven't let me express my feelings."

Betty sat up straight.

"I'm protecting you—"

"Yes, but sometimes it's support I need, not protection. It was support I needed in that Salvation Army home for unmarried mothers, it was support I needed when they took Samantha away, when they told me that I wasn't fit to keep her, I wasn't fit to be a mother. I tell you," Cora said, leaning forward over her photograph, "what they meant was that it was wicked to be fertile. It was wicked to be poor and working-class and fertile."

Betty sniffed. She bent her head towards her folded hands on the tabletop.

"So, right or wrong," Cora said, "this photo isn't enough for me. If Sam—Nathalie wants to meet me, I'm meeting her. It may throw me back where I started, but I'm taking the chance. All these years, I've been in agony that she'd hate me.

It's all I've worried about, all that's really haunted me. Would she be angry, would she hate me. Well, she didn't sound angry. Not at all. In fact, she sounded quite surprised I'd asked her. So if I want to meet her to make sure she isn't angry, if I need to do this to put myself out of all the misery I've been through all these years, then I'm going to do it, risk or no risk. I can't be in more pain than I've been already, Betty, I can't. But if I'm going to do this, and I am, if she'll let me, then I'd rather do it with your *support* than without it. Not protection, Betty, not that. Support."

There was a pause. Betty raised her head and looked at Cora. Her eyes were red.

"I'll support you," she said, "but don't say I didn't warn you either."

From the street outside her flat, David could see that Nathalie was in the kitchen. He stood there on the pavement and watched her for a while, watched her as, propped against the table and quite unaware of being watched, she read something in the local newspaper, her arms spread wide to hold out the pages. She had her hair pulled back behind her head with some kind of red scarf or band and there was music playing. He couldn't hear the melody, but he could hear the beat.

He looked at the gap the basement created between the pavement and Nathalie's kitchen window. It was just too wide to lean across, just too far to touch the glass and alert her. He considered. He could do the conventional thing, of course, and ring the doorbell, but that didn't seem to him quite to chime with the mood of the moment, the mood that had impelled him to make a detour through this part of Westerham and surprise Nathalie at eleven o'clock in the morning. He took a deep breath and sprang in the air. Nathalie went on reading her paper. David took another breath and sprang again and again, shouting. Nathalie looked up from her paper and saw him.

"You're crackers," she said through the window glass.

He nodded, beaming.

"Let me in—"

She vanished from the window and reappeared at the street door, still holding the newspaper.

"What are you doing?"

"What are *you* doing," David said, "reading the paper during working hours?"

She reached up, the newsprint crackling, and put her arms round his neck. He held her.

"I can't settle to much."

"Me neither."

"How's Marnie?"

David released his hold a little.

"Um. Calmer. Very reasonable. *Very* reasonable. Buying tickets for Canada for the summer. And Steve?"

"Fine," Nathalie said. She stepped out of his embrace. "Lovely, actually. Kind."

"Right," David said, "so, good or bad?"

Nathalie led the way into the kitchen.

"Just—just, well—*better*. Nicer."

"Marnie's always nice. It's just that she can easily make me feel I'm not being nice at all."

Nathalie opened the fridge.

"Define nice."

"Good family man."

"Is it too early for a drink?"

"Yes."

Nathalie put a bottle of wine on the kitchen table.

"Perhaps we aren't very good at family."

"What?" David said. "You and me?"

Nathalie took two wine glasses off a shelf.

"Yes. Perhaps we have problems with intimacy."

"Oh, give me a break."

"It's a phrase of Sasha's."

"Who's Sasha?"

"Titus's girlfriend. She's doing a thesis or something. She's got a phrase for everything. Psycho stuff."

"Sounds a bit wacky—"

Nathalie poured wine into the glasses and pushed one towards David. He picked it up.

"I'm driving—"

Nathalie said, "D'you know what I've been thinking? About this intimacy stuff?"

"Tell me."

She folded her arms.

"Perhaps we *are* a bit removed. Perhaps we *do* make it difficult for people to get close to us. Perhaps that has always been our sort of defense mechanism."

David took a tiny sip of wine.

"And?"

Nathalie looked down.

"You know this feeling—"

"What feeling?"

"Well, this feeling we've always had, however kind people are, however much they love us, however much they say we're just the same as everyone else—" She stopped.

David waited. He waited for several moments and then he put a hand out and touched her shoulder.

She said slowly, "There's always this unspoken thing, isn't there, if you don't know who your parents are, if you don't know where you come from. There's always this little kind of whisper, this echo, as if society is saying, 'Let's just disappear you.' "

"Rubbish."

She looked up at him.

"Not *literally*. Not, let's let you starve. But more, let's forget who you really are, let's rub out your real name, and start again, on *our* pattern."

"Real name," David said.

She nodded.

He said, "You know yours."

She nodded again. "And you know yours."

"But not," David said, "my father's name. Not that name."

Nathalie picked up a glass of wine and looked at it and put it down again.

"So, if we discover these things, if we discover these names and things, these histories, then maybe we'll be able to join in. Properly."

"Is that what you've been thinking?"

"Yes."

"I wish," David said, "that I could think like that."

"You've got me to do it for you."

He put his hands in his pockets.

"I wish you could come and see Carole with me."

Her eyes widened.

"You're seeing her!"

"Yes. That's what I came to tell you."

"Oh my God."

"I know."

"Did she ask you?"

"No. I asked her. I had to ask her several times."

"Didn't she want to?"

David shook the change in his pockets.

"She sounds frightened."

"Aren't you?"

"Oh yes," David said. He took his hands out of his pockets and put his arms round Nathalie. He said, his face against her hair, "I don't think I've ever been so nervous about anything."

Carole had imagined meeting David in a bar, a bar somewhere perhaps like the Portobello Road. She had visualized somewhere trendy, somewhere where David's age would pass unnoticed in a crowd of similar ages, a place where she would be the oddity and therefore un-likely to be spotted by anyone she knew. She had been, covertly, on a small mission or two to find such a place, and thought she had found one, near the old cinema, with a smart restaurant upstairs and downstairs something much more relaxed and casual, a kind of brasserie cum bar, with sharp young waiting staff dressed entirely in black. It seemed to Carole that in such a place David would pass without comment, and she would be invisible. When he next telephoned—and he was telephoning with a quiet regularity that threw her into a turmoil every time it happened—she was going to say to him that this was the place where they should meet, and that she would be wearing a brown suede jacket and carrying a copy of the *Financial Times*.

But then Connor intervened. His superb and stately response to her revelation had continued almost without a hitch, as if, she sometimes thought spitefully, looking at his well-shaven face, his well-ironed shirt front, he had at last found a role in which he could see himself as he had always wanted to, calm and majesterial, possessed of the kindest, most reasonable of powers.

"Where do you propose to see the boy?" Connor said, his eyes on the crossword on his knee.

"He's called David," Carole said.

Connor raised his glance and looked steadily, significantly at her.

"I think you heard me."

"I haven't decided," Carole said. She ran a hand through her hair. If she told him the truth, he would try and change her mind. "I haven't really thought."

Connor took his reading glasses off and laid them on the folded paper.

"May I make a suggestion?"

Carole waited. Two weeks ago, a week even, she might have said appeasingly, "I'd be so glad if you did." Now, newly stubborn in the face of her conflicting hopes and apprehensions, she waited.

"Carole," Connor said, "darling, I think you should see him here."

She stared at him.

"Here!"

"Yes," he said. "Why not?"

"But we live here!"

"And so that's where he should see you."

She pushed herself back into the cushions of her chair. "No."

"Why not?"

"Because—because it's got to be somewhere impersonal, somewhere neither of us belongs—"

"Why?"

"Because," Carole said, almost shouting, "I don't know how it will be!"

Connor cleared his throat. He put the newspaper and his spectacles down on the low table beside him.

Then he said, in a much less portentous voice, "He's your son, Carole, and nothing's going to change that. He ought to see you in your home, the place that reflects your life, and who you are. He'll be pretty at sea as it is, coming to meet you. Why make it worse by inflicting a hotel lounge on him?"

Carole said stupidly, "I wasn't thinking of a hotel."

"You should see him here," Connor said. "You should invite him here and give him a whiskey." He paused, and then he said, "Don't you want to help put him at his ease?"

Carole looked down. She looked at her hands in her lap, at her well-shaped nails, at her wedding ring.

She said faintly, "What about the boys?"

"I'll talk to them," Connor said, "I'll explain why David is coming here."

"Martin won't like it—"

Connor said, "Martin doesn't like anything much at the moment."

"But this is his home just now—"

"Just now."

"Connor—"

Connor looked steadily at her.

He said, with decision, "You see him here. For a couple of hours. Then I'll bring the boys in."

"I can't!" Carole cried, almost shrieking.

Connor picked up his paper again. His voice was lofty again.

"You have to, darling," he said.

And now, here she was, waiting. Here she was alone, abandoned by Connor and Martin and Euan—Martin in a smoldering rage, Euan in a characteristic state of cheerful curiosity. It was to Euan she had said foolishly, gesturing at her clothes, "Do I look all right?"

He'd glanced at her, grinning. He had all the comfortable confidence in the world, all the happy assurance of personal acceptability that had been entirely left out of Martin. He'd given her a quick kiss.

"Why'd it matter, Mum?" And then he'd said teasingly, "What were you wearing last time?"

He'd made her laugh. He could usually make her laugh. She watched the three of them go down the steps to the basement garage as if she would never see them again, as if everything that held her world together was going off to certain death. She waited in the front doorway until the Mercedes came gliding up the ramp and turned towards Ladbroke Grove, and it nearly broke her heart—the heart she had always supposed to be so unsentimental—that none of them thought to turn and wave to her.

And now she was waiting. She was crossing from the wooden floor of the hall to the carpeted floor of the sitting room, and listening, with idiotic concentration, to the way the sound of her footsteps changed. She was looking out of the sitting-room windows, looking at the white lilac and not seeing it, and then she was turning and walking back again, past Connor's favorite chair, past the sofa, past the television, past the bookcase of all those unread books, and back into the hall and the sharp sound of her heels on the pale-wood veneer. When the doorbell rang, it briefly stopped her breath. She stood on the rug in the middle of the hall and looked at the bland back of the front door and thought, I'm not breathing, I can't breathe.

The doorbell rang again.

"One," Carole said. "Two. Three."

She felt her legs move stiffly as if they had no joints, she saw her hand on the heavy gilt handle of the lock, she saw it turn, and the door swung smoothly inward and there on the step a man was standing, a tall man, older than she remembered and fairer somehow, but still Rory. Rory . . . She swallowed. No, not Rory. Of course not Rory. The man seemed to sway a little, or perhaps she did, and then he leaned in through the doorway and kissed her cheek, rather clumsily, and said, "Hello, Carole."

"I don't usually drink whiskey," David said. He looked down into his glass, at the silky tea-colored liquid sliding about at the bottom.

"No," Carole said, "but this isn't a usually occasion."

She was sitting across the room from him, not far away, but not exactly close either, not where he could look at her properly, examine her. And it was difficult, he found, to look anywhere else, to avoid looking at this person, this woman, this Carole Latimer in her elegant clothes, in her elegant and adult sitting room with its careful lighting, its subdued colors, its absence of child or dog or clutter. They had lived here for just a few years, she'd said, it wasn't where her—other sons had been brought up, it wasn't where family life, in the accepted sense, had ever happened. David had glanced at the carpet.

"I hope," he said, "my shoes are clean."

It was the first time she'd looked at him. She'd looked at him quite directly, and he'd seen how remarkable her eyes were, greenish, clear, almost speckled, and his stomach had given an involuntary little lurch.

"I shouldn't," she said with a warmth she hadn't yet displayed, "care at *all* if they aren't." And then she said, in a lower tone, "You're not on trial, you know."

He tilted his whiskey now, slipping the liquid round the glass.

He said, not looking at her, but at the whiskey, "Did you think about me?"

She turned to gaze out of the window.

"No."

"Never?"

"I told you," Carole said.

David tipped the glass so that the whiskey in it crept to the very rim.

"I can't quite get my head round the fact that nobody knew about me."

"I went away," Carole said. "I went away quite deliberately. I said I needed to convalesce, so nobody took account of the time."

"Who's nobody?"

"My parents."

A little whiskey splashed on to David's thigh.

Carole said nothing. She went on gazing out of the window.

"My father?" David persisted.

There was another pause and then Carole said, "He didn't know."

"He didn't know I'd been born?"

"No."

"Why not?"

Carole's head whipped round.

She said furiously, "Because he didn't *want* to."

"Didn't—"

"No. Didn't *want* to. What right have you to ask me questions like this?"

David put his whiskey glass down with elaborate care.

"Because," he said, "he is my father and you are my mother and without the two of you, I wouldn't be here."

Carole bent her head. It was hard to tell if she was angry or distressed or if she was crying.

"I meant what I said," David said. "I meant what I said on the telephone. All this is on your terms. I don't want to upset anything you've got now, your family. I just want a few answers."

She nodded. She reached a hand out blindly for her own drink and took a big swallow.

"Like what?"

"Do I look like my father?"

She nodded again, violently.

"Exactly?"

Carole looked up slowly.

"Fairer," she said faintly. "His features. My coloring. Maybe—maybe you're taller."

David leaned forward a little.

"Did you love him?"

"Oh my God!" Carole cried. "What kind of question is that?"

"So you did—"

"Yes."

"So you loved the man you had me by?"

"I told you," Carole said again. "I told you, didn't I?"

"But you didn't want me."

"I never said—"

"He didn't want me."

"He didn't want a baby," Carole said. She pushed her hands through her hair. "We were too young. He was just starting. We weren't ready for a baby."

"But if there wasn't a baby, I mean, if nobody but those nuns in Suffolk and your friend whatsername knew there'd been a baby, why didn't you stay with him, why didn't you stay until you *were* both ready for a baby?"

"He'd gone," Carole said.

"Gone—"

"He went when I knew I was pregnant. He said I had to have an abortion and—I did think about it, I did, but then he went anyway. I think—I think now," Carole said loudly, "that he wanted to go. That my being pregnant was a kind of excuse, the excuse he was actually looking for."

David shifted in his chair.

"He sounds a complete shit."

"No," Carole said.

"No?"

She looked up.

"I didn't have an abortion, because I wanted his baby. Or at least, I did then. I wanted something of him, of his. I thought—" She stopped, and then she said, "I thought he'd change."

"And he didn't."

"I don't know. I couldn't find him. I tried, but I couldn't. I've never found him. I don't want to find him."

"Perhaps he went abroad—"

"Quite likely."

"Perhaps he died—"

An expression of intense pain crossed Carole's face.

"No—"

"I only said perhaps," David said. "But would it be easier?"

"Nothing to do with him has ever been easy. That's not the point."

David leaned forward more and put his elbows on his knees.

"What's his name?"

"It doesn't matter."

"It does. It matters to me."

"I never say it," Carole said almost desperately, "I never say it out loud."

David said quietly, "It's one of the things I came to ask you. It's one of the things I need to know. It's—it's something I don't *have*."

206

She said, almost in a whisper, "Rory."

"Rory. Rory what?"

"Ecclestone."

David thought. He bent his head and considered for a moment. Then he said, "So I am David Ecclestone?"

"No," Carole said. "You were born David Hanley. Hanley was my maiden name."

"But Ecclestone was my father's name."

"Yes."

"And David?"

"Your father's second name."

"Right. Rory David Ecclestone. R. D. Ecclestone."

"Yes. But it's not your name. Ecclestone isn't your name. You were registered as David Hanley."

David said, with the first small show of anger he had displayed all afternoon, "Don't you think that's for me to decide?"

She was startled.

"What?"

"Isn't it for *me* to decide, now? Haven't I been handed round all these names belonging to other people long enough? Haven't I worn these labels that aren't mine for years and years without complaint? Isn't it about *time* I was allowed to be who I really am?"

"Sorry," Carole said. "Sorry—"

"And suppose, whatever he was like, whatever you *say* he was like, I'd rather go the accepted route and carry my father's name? Why shouldn't I?"

Carole stood up abruptly.

"Don't you take your anger out on me."

"I'm not angry—"

"No."

"But you have been."

David stood too, slowly.

"Yes."

"For having you adopted—"

"It's hard," David said, sighing, "to get over the fact that you were given away."

Carole took a few steps closer. She looked up at him. He could see her green eyes and smell scent and whiskey.

"I had to."

He said nothing.

"I'd lost everything."

"You'd lost him, you mean—"

"And ever since," Carole said, and he could see a faint glitter of tears, "ever since, all those years, I've had no one to talk to about this. No one."

"You must have had friends, girlfriends—"

She shook her head.

"I hadn't done something very easily—acceptable. I'd fallen for the wrong person, fallen pregnant, betrayed my upbringing. I'd put myself beyond the pale."

David glanced round the room. He gave a small snort of laughter.

"Hardly—"

"It *looks* all right," Carole said. "It all looks fine, doesn't it?"

"What?" David said. "Your marriage? Your sons?"

Carole took a step forward. She was very close to David now. She put up her hands and grasped at the lapels of his jacket.

"I can't take hostility," Carole said. "I can't. Not in any form."

He put his own hands up and covered hers. The skin on her hands felt light and smooth and thin.

"No—"

"You are so like him! You look so like him!"

David took hold of Carole's hands and gently detached them.

He said, "I'll try and think about that. About what you said."

She took an unsteady step or two backwards.

"Well," she said, with regained composure. "Have you filled in some blanks?"

He said uncertainly, "I think so."

"Another whiskey—"

"No. No thank you."

"There's actually some more blanks to fill in."

"Oh?"

"My husband," Carole said, "my sons. Your—half brothers."

"Oh. Yes. Well, one day—"

"Today," Carole said.

"Now!"

"Soon."

"Coming here—"

"They live here," Carole said. "They're coming back." She glanced at him. She had retrieved her distance, her self-control. She gave a fleeting smile. "They want to meet you."

CHAPTER FOURTEEN

Sasha told Steve she had once lived in a squat. He rather suspected that she had told a lot of people this, especially men; that it was the kind of achievement she took out and polished publicly every so often, to impress. Steve was impressed. He was, himself, the kind of person for whom radical, even anarchic, behavior was at best pitiful and at worst downright destructive. The very thought, at sixteen or seventeen, of exchanging the dubious advantages of the back bedroom at the Royal Oak for something spectacularly worse would have seemed to him completely lunatic. Even freedom had its proper price, not any old one.

After the squat, it seemed, Sasha's living arrangements had always remained fluid. There'd been a spell at home helping her mother nurse her dying stepfather; a spell living with a Turk—relationship heavily unspecified—in a decaying wooden house on the Bosphorus; a spell training—unfinished—as a mental-health nurse; a spell looking after a penthouse flat in the Canal Street district of Manchester; a spell in a caravan in a wood in Northumberland with two retired greyhounds and a boy with learning difficulties. Now, in her view, Sasha had washed up somewhere very secure. Now, on a mysterious mixture of grants and subsidies and part-time jobs in shops and bars, Sasha had achieved her own room, with a lockable door, in a house occupied by a divorced mother of three who needed the rent from a lodger. The room was good, Sasha said, biggish with a wide window, and Della downstairs was so fanatical about her own unquestioned independence that she wasn't about to cramp anyone else's. That's why she was divorced, really, Sasha said: Della just couldn't compromise, not to the smallest degree.

Trying to get a picture of the exact nature of Sasha's life, Steve thought, was like trying to sculpture water. He didn't think she lied to him, or invented things, but her priorities were so different from his, and her view of essentials so other, that she presented a picture to him that was, at its clearest, elusive. She was loosely attached to Westerham University—until recently Westerham Technical College— where she was working, equally loosely it seemed, on a thesis. Where this would lead, Sasha couldn't say, and couldn't seem to see that it mattered. When she wasn't in the university's new and impressive computer room, she was working in a small health-food store with vegan principles (not even gelatin permitted), or in a bar called Rouge Noir, or in a second-hand book and music store specializing in early rock, or babysitting Della's three children. She seemed, at the same time, always to be busy and always to be free if the mood took her. Her list of commitments—which included yoga and a salsa class—appeared to be consistently ongoing and yet never to have a pattern.

"I don't know," Steve said, "how you don't drive yourself barmy."

She smiled at him.

"Practice," she said. "Attitude. Particularly attitude."

It was the attitude that drew Steve back and back. It was her ease with the looseness of arrangements, her acceptance of the unconventional, her capacity to achieve a somehow approvable distance from human responsibility that made him feel, in a strange and exhilarated way, liberated from all the exhausting burdens and preoccupations of his present life. It had nothing to do with love, he told himself. In no way could his desire to be with Sasha even begin to impinge on the unshakable *love* he felt for Nathalie and Polly, but being with Sasha was not only exciting and intriguing, but also gave him a holiday from himself, a holiday from Steve Ross who was currently caught in an emotional thicket from which he had no means of extricating himself. When it occurred to him—as it did quite often—that he should not see Sasha again, he felt a small panic rise inside him, as if there was a real threat of a vital conduit being cut off. And when he saw her—the long coat, the boots, the seal-pelt hair—he felt a surge of pure relief.

When she asked him if he'd like to see her room, in Della's terraced house looking on to the railway line, he'd said no.

"Why not?"

He shrugged. He didn't want to say that he was afraid, afraid of what might happen in Sasha's room, and nor did he want to examine that fear too closely and discover that it contained some more urgent elements as well.

"Are you afraid?"

He shrugged again.

"I've almost never," Sasha said, "had a room to show anyone before. I've never had a place that I felt reflected me. But this is a beginning. I'd like to show it to you."

Steve put his hands in his pockets.

"Does Titus—"

"Of course," Sasha said. "Of course Titus comes. He thinks it's awful." She smiled. "But then, he likes disliking what I like. He likes that a lot."

"Perverse—"

"More about control," Sasha said. "Titus is very into control."

"Really?"

She glanced at him.

"Very," she said, and then she leaned towards him a little. "Come and see my room," she said.

She let him into the house through an Edwardian door painted purple with stained-glass panels. Inside, it was everything Steve deplored, a cluttered cave of fabrics and objects. He knocked immediately against a cascade of wind chimes.

"Ignore," Sasha said. "Up here."

She went ahead of him up the staircase, past paintings on mirrors and a birdcage full of dolls and a vase of peacock feathers. He watched her put a key into a door on the landing and then she turned and looked at him.

"Deep breath," she said.

The room was almost empty. It was painted red, with a black floor and white blinds at the window. It contained almost nothing except a futon.

Steve said, "Where's your life?"

She pointed at the futon.

"There."

He swallowed.

"*Every*thing?"

"Why not? Don't you work in bed?"

"No." He looked about him. "Clothes. Books—"

She pointed at a stack of canvas boxes.

"There."

"Do you recognize me? Do you recognize me here?"

He took a step or two further into the room. He looked at the single Japanese print—a woman, in a kimono, looking over her shoulder—on the red walls, at the futon, at the pair of running shoes on the floor, precisely side by side, and he said, "It figures."

"Sit down," she said.

"On that?"

"Where else do you suggest?"

"Sasha—"

"Never stand if you can sit. Never sit if you can lie."

"I can't lie on a futon in the middle of the afternoon—"

Sasha went past him and knelt to unlace her boots. Inside

them, her feet were clad in black socks with scarlet toes. Then she turned herself and slid gracefully on to the futon and lay looking at him.

"I'm not up for this," Steve said.

"For what?"

"I'm not lying on your bed with you."

"We can talk very well here," Sasha said. "This is an admirable place to talk."

"I shouldn't be here."

Sasha sighed.

"Possibly," she said, "you are unaware of what is due in relationships. How the balance works."

"What do you mean?"

"I listen to you," Sasha said. "I am happy to listen to you, I am interested. I listen to you while you tell me about your problems, your difficulties, the things you can't understand about Nathalie wanting to find her mother. I listen to you and I tell you that you are coping very well, that Nathalie is asking a lot of you while telling you very little, that I admire you for your tolerance and, sometimes, stoicism." She paused and shifted her body a fraction, as if she were making room on the futon beside her, as if she were creating an inviting space. "But possibly," Sasha said, "it hasn't occurred to you that we have been driving down a one-way street. Your street." She paused again and then she gave him a smile, a direct, clear, open smile. "My turn now."

In his bedroom—furnished by his mother for guests who almost never came—Martin sat in front of his laptop. Or rather, he sat squashed at an angle because the only surface in the room suitable for a laptop was a small chest of drawers. Carole had put a lamp on the chest of drawers, and added an extra chair to the room, and cleared out all the drawers and hanging space to accommodate some of Martin's possessions, but she hadn't, he felt, tried to make the room his, she hadn't given any indication that this comfortable, light room was in any way anything more than briefly on loan to him. And the fact that he had angrily, aggressively, filled it with things, piled the second bed with his clothes, stacked boxes, and bags of sports equipment, on all the available surfaces and floor space only, it seemed, served to underline her unspoken assumption that he would soon, somehow, be gone again. He'd made the room a shambles, and she was quite serene about it because, as her serenity indicated calmly, the situation was only temporary. Very temporary.

He stared at the screen of his laptop. He'd called work that morning, pleading a migraine—he'd been susceptible to them ever since adolescence—and his boss, who appeared immune to any kind of headache, said that that was too bad but that Martin had better finish up those figures at home because he needed them for a five o'clock meeting. It was now ten past three and Martin had been sitting at the chest of drawers since noon, one knee pressed against a drawer handle, and his mind roaring in his skull like a swarm of bees.

From beyond the closed bedroom door, he'd heard his parents' movements. He'd heard his father go out, and then his mother unloading the dishwasher in the kitchen, and the telephone ringing a couple of times, and then the front door closing again with a kind of studied quietness, as if the person going out was anxious that their departure should be unremarked. That had been about eleven-thirty. Before that time, Carole had been nowhere near Martin's bedroom door. She had not asked him if he would like coffee, she had not told him she was going out, she had made no mention of what he might find in the fridge to make himself lunch. She had simply tidied the kitchen, spoken briefly to two people he didn't know about, and gone. He typed three words with angry inaccuracy, and swore.

There'd been nothing, either, on his mobile all morning, not even a text message. His brother Euan had taken to texting him recently, sending him idiotic facts and filthy jokes. He was grateful for these, but simultaneously resentful too, resentful that he needed them, resentful that his need was so evident, resentful that Euan, who was technically in exactly the same position as he was, appeared to be coping with it with extraordinary ease. They'd had a session about it, of course, a session with Dad, and then another, and then a session together in some awful pub in Chelsea after they'd met David where Martin had drunk several vodka chasers after his beer, and had ended up on the sofa in Euan's flat, much to the distaste of Euan's girlfriend, Chloe, who had seemed unable to grasp that Martin's plight was worse than her sofa's. He remembered Euan saying things like, "We've got to accept it, Mart, we can't put the clock back," and, "Seemed a nice guy. Didn't you think? A nice guy," and himself raging back, incoherent and muddled, raging about everything he could think of, everything relevant and irrelevant, but mostly, raging about Carole.

"I'm not the first-born," he said, his fingers white around his shot glass. "I'm not, am I? I never have been. She let me think I was, and I wasn't. It explains everything, it explains how she's always been to me—"

"Crap," Euan said. He was yawning. "Bollocks. Bullshit." He glanced at his watch. He'd told Chloe they'd be an hour and they'd been three. "Nothing changes except we have David to factor in."

Euan had talked to Carole, too. He'd asked Martin to join in, but something in Martin wouldn't let him, wouldn't allow himself the possibility of being reconciled, even comforted. They'd gone into the sitting room, leaving the door ajar for him to join them, and he'd found himself flinging out of the front door instead, slamming it so that they could be in no doubt as to his feelings, his outrage. He'd just wandered that evening, miles and miles, amazed and insulted that the people in the streets could be so callously going home or into bars and cinemas, just like usual. When he finally got back, Euan had gone and Carole was in the kitchen with his father, making an omelette. She'd looked up at him and he could see she'd been crying again. She balanced the spatula on the edge of the omelette pan and came towards him.

"Sorry," she'd said. "Oh Martin, sorry, sorry—"

She'd tried to touch him then, tried to put her arms round him, to put her drained, red-eyed face against his, against his offended, injured one. But he hadn't let her, he couldn't. He stood there, his arms by his sides, his chin raised so that she couldn't reach his cheek.

"Martin," his father had said. "Come on, come on—"

He shook his head. He'd stepped backwards then, and turned and headed off across the hall to his bedroom, pursued by the smell of burning butter. How was he to know that the sweet thrill of triumph wouldn't last more than a minute or two?

She hadn't tried again. Or at least—Martin tried to push Euan's remonstrations out of his mind—she hadn't tried in any way acceptable to Martin. She'd done quiet domestic things, ironing, cooking, asking the watchful Romanian maid to clean Martin's bedroom and the guest bathroom, but she hadn't come near him again, she hadn't tried to touch him. She had been, in fact, rather weird with him, not angry, not punishing, but behaving more as if she was afraid of him, and her fear had made her withdraw. There'd been moments, even, when he'd almost expected her to slip apologetically out of a room when he entered it, like an Edwardian housemaid. He wasn't at all sure what he wanted from her—utter abasement sometimes seemed alluringly to fit the bill—but he knew it wasn't this, he knew he didn't want this kind of control, this kind of power which seemed, so subtly, so horribly familiarly, to put him in the wrong.

He hit the shut-down keys on his laptop and stood up.

There was a sharp pain in his knee and his shoulders ached from sitting crookedly. He caught sight of himself in the framed mirror hanging above the chest of drawers. He looked tired, out of sorts, old. His hair was beginning to recede. He touched his forehead gingerly, apprehensively. His hair had begun to recede when he was twenty-two; he remembered noticing it in a changing room after a game of squash, suddenly being aware of the peak of hair on his forehead and the shadowy triangles either side where the hair was thinning. David's wasn't receding. David was taller than he was and broader than he was and his hair had a thick permanence about it that had been one of the first things Martin had noticed, one of the first things to go on the list of rivalries. Martin turned away from the mirror and crashed out of his room and across the hall to the kitchen.

It was as tidy as the kitchens of his childhood had always been, as tidy as the kitchens of women whose primary preoccupation is not culinary so often seem to be. On the table a place had been laid, a knife and a water glass, and next to the fruit bowl, a sandwich on a plate under a skin of clingfilm. Martin picked the sandwich up and peered at it sideways through the film. It appeared to be cheese and tomato, the sandwich filling he had always chosen in childhood, the sandwich filling you could only get now, on account of its simplicity, in old-fashioned places.

Martin peeled the film off the sandwich and sniffed it. Then he crossed the kitchen, trod on the pedal of the chrome Italian waste bin, and tipped the contents of the plate inside.

"Tell me," Nathalie said. "*Tell* me!"

She was holding the door open for him, gripping it almost, and her eyes were shining. He bent and kissed her.

"What was it like? What was she like? What happened?"

"Everything," David said. "Nothing."

218

"What do you *mean*—"

"I'm so tired," David said. "I feel absolutely sandbagged. I haven't *done* anything, physically, and I'm worn out."

Nathalie took his arm and propelled him into the kitchen. There was a basket of mixed polyanthus on the table, as brilliantly colored as a Mexican mural. David gestured towards them.

"Nice—"

"Never mind them," Nathalie said, pushing him towards a chair. "Never mind. Tell me. Tell me what happened. What did she look like?"

David stared ahead.

"She looked great."

"What kind of great?"

"Quite tall, blondish. Sort of expensive-looking—"

"Did she cry? Did she hug you?"

"No—"

"Dave—"

"She's in quite a mess," David said. "She's got this husband. And boys. Two sons."

"Did you meet them?"

"Yes."

"And? David, *and?*"

David shut his eyes.

"Nat, I got what I went for. I got that and more. Rather a lot more."

Nathalie was hovering over him. She had her hands clasped in front of her, almost as if she was praying.

"Like what?"

He opened his eyes and looked up at her.

"I know who my father was. I know where I was born. I know why she gave me away—or at least, I know why she says she gave me away. I know that nobody knew about me, not even this Connor guy she married. I know that seeing me threw her back somewhere she never thought she'd have to go again."

Nathalie loosened her hands. She put one on David's shoulder.

"You OK?"

"I don't know."

"Did you—did you like her?"

"If you mean," David said, "did she feel like my mother, the answer is no."

Nathalie felt for a chair, still looking at David, and sat down.

"Was she kind to you?"

"Not really."

"You mean *hostile*?"

David's eyes widened.

"She used that word."

"Hostile?"

"Yes. She said she couldn't take hostility. She couldn't take it from anyone. It was the one thing, she said, that she couldn't take."

"Did you tell her you were angry with her?"

"I said I had been. But I wasn't when I was with her. I wasn't angry then."

Nathalie leaned forward.

"How *did* you feel? I can't imagine it, I can't imagine how I'm going to feel—"

David frowned.

"I was kind of—fascinated. And fearful. I wanted to know the answers but of course having them means I have to deal with them. When you just imagine, you don't have to face anything, in the end."

Nathalie swallowed.

"No."

"My father was called Rory David Ecclestone. He buggered off. Before I was born. She said I looked like him."

Nathalie attempted a small smile.

"Lucky her—"

"I don't think so."

"And her husband? Connor?"

"Oh," David said, "you know. I work for hundreds of them. Well-set-up guy in his sixties, perfectly pleasant, prosperous. Probably reads the *Telegraph*. Collects maritime prints. When he shook my hand, he looked me straight in the eye and said, 'Welcome, my boy.'"

"Nice of him—"

"I don't know. Or establishing something, making sure I knew—" He stopped.

"Knew what?"

"Where I stood," David said. "Where I'd be, in relation to his sons. I felt he was making sure I knew he was doing the right thing." He leaned forward and touched a polyanthus petal. "She changed when he came in."

"Did she?"

"A kind of frankness went. She hadn't been very generous to me before he came, but at least I felt she wasn't pretending. But when he came in, a kind of mask went on. She was more polite to me, but I didn't feel she was being so honest. I felt she knew her family were watching her."

"I can't imagine it—"

"The younger son was fine. He's going to be like his father, minus the pomposity. He just behaved like this was bloody awkward, but it was bloody awkward for everyone so let's just make it as pleasant as we can. The older one looked like he wanted to kill me. He hardly said a word. He wouldn't sit down, he just stood there by the door, glaring."

"For God's sake," Nathalie cried, "what are you taking that's his?"

"Nothing. And maybe I could have asked him the same question. I don't want anything of his, I don't even want his *mother*—"

"David!"

He turned to look at her.

"I don't."

221

"You can't say that. You can't know that after one meeting—"

"I can."

Nathalie was silent. She gazed at him with huge, troubled eyes.

"Remember what Elaine said?" David said.

"What—"

"Something she said to you. Something you told me. That—that we all know, deep down, if we're wanted."

"Didn't Carole love your father?"

"Oh yes," David said. "That's the trouble. It was my father she *did* love."

Nathalie gave a little shiver.

"Oh."

"If she hadn't been pregnant, she might have kept him."

"But you look like him—"

"That just confuses things. It confused her. Perhaps I'm a kind of travesty of him, to her." He put a hand out and laid it on top of Nathalie's. "I'm OK, Nat. Really. I'm exhausted, but I'm OK." He took his hand away and got slowly to his feet. "Better get home."

"Haven't you told Marnie?"

"Not yet."

"Dave—"

He bent and kissed her forehead.

"Now, would I? First?"

Nathalie had her eyes tight shut.

"David, go home, *go*."

"I'm going," he said. "Now I've seen you, I'm going." He took a step towards the door, and then he stopped. "Marnie wanted to meet her. Before I went to London, she reminded me that she wanted to meet her. What am I going to do about that?"

CHAPTER FIFTEEN

Titus's kitchen looked, he told himself with a kind of swagger, hideous. It usually looked pretty awful; it was not uncommon, after all, he thought, tiptoeing gingerly across it, to stick to the floor, but this aftermath of cooking on top of its usual carefree squalor was award-winning. There were even violently colored smears—turmeric? chili? blood?—down the fronts of the cupboards and the sink was so full it was impossible to wedge the kettle in, to fill it. It was a prime case, in fact, for that television program where a couple of presenters swoop down for the weekend, and whip all your crap away, and sell it to some sad other-people's-crap-hunters at a car-boot sale.

Gingerly, he moved the stack of crockery and pans in the sink to one side and inserted the kettle under the cold tap. The kettle was interestingly full of flakes of limescale, floating about like chunks of coral in a tropical sea. Sasha had once bought a sachet of descaler to deal with the kettle, but as she declined, on principle, to take on the burden of Titus's living conditions, and as Titus himself didn't give a monkey's about the state of his kettle, the sachet lay where she had left it, now obscured by a moldering bag of bagels.

Plugging the kettle in, Titus remembered Sasha commenting on the extreme contrast between the meticulous fastidiousness of Titus's approach to his work and the boastful slovenliness of his attitude to his domestic arrangements. She'd said it as she said all these things, as an observation rather than as a criticism, and with a lack of personal engagement which indicated that she wasn't going to lift a finger to change things. She was wonderfully unfeminine in that way, miraculously unmaternal, and to Titus, consequently extremely attractive. It was therefore, he thought, looking at the mess in the sink, a bit odd that not only had he noticed when Justine had made no move to clear up after their drunken cooking session the night before, but also it had irritated him. He'd almost, he thought he remembered, asked her if she wasn't going to wash up. Or, at least, he'd noted the enquiry somewhere in his mind, in amongst all the other possibly more pervading thoughts about sex. He sighed. Sex. Amazing how much you wanted it when you wanted it. And conversely, even if this feeling only lasted an hour or two—how much, if standing in a revolting kitchen with a headache and the distinct possibility of being late for work, you didn't want it when you didn't.

Titus picked two mugs out of the chaos on the counter and rinsed them cursorily under the cold tap. His mother had always been scornful about hygiene, claiming that germs only invaded those who were afraid of them and that anyway too much sanitary preoccupation was bourgeois. He fished about in a cupboard and found a handful of teabags squashed into the top of an open box of rice. "Rice with Lime Leaves and Ginger," it said on the label. Titus looked at it for a moment. It must have come from Sasha's health-food shop. He dropped the teabags into the mugs and reached for the kettle. He hadn't seen Sasha in almost three weeks and when he left her messages she just sent little laconic texts back saying "Busy" and "Back soon." Part of him burned to know what was going on and part of him shrank from the knowledge. When you knew, after all, you had to deal, and Titus didn't want to deal. He just wanted to be back in a place where he was carrying two mugs of tea—milkless, as the milk had settled into a rank lump in its plastic bottle—back to a bed which contained Sasha, rather than Justine.

He picked up the mugs and kicked the kitchen door open. The sitting room was in half-darkness, and the day-light outside was showing, very clearly, that a greater part of the curtains hung off their hooks than on. There were plates and newspapers on the floor, and glasses on the television and half Justine's clothes lay on the sofa, strewn about in a way which, in the morning, only managed to look pathetic. Titus sighed. He stubbed his toe on a stray shoe, and swore.

From the bedroom, he could hear Justine giggling. She'd laughed a lot the night before, through the red wine and the curry attempt, even through a lot of the sex. At the time, Titus had found the laughing rather a challenge, as if he had to rise to immense heights of inventiveness and sensation to extinguish it, but now it was only annoying. Justine's giggles were as annoying as was her inevitable girl's ex-pectation that, as they'd had sex together, he must not only feel something for her, but also say so. He trudged into the bedroom. Justine was half-sitting up against the pillow, with the duvet pulled up just far enough to cover her nipples. Even in the gloom, he could see her eyes were shining. He dumped the tea down on the chest of drawers, out of her reach.

"We're going to be late," he said.

Marnie had thought about telephoning. She had thought, changing the children's bedding and replacing Petey's up-stairs toys in their hamper, that she would put in a calm, reasonable call to Nathalie and ask, in the steady voice she was now managing—most of the time—to use to and about David, if she might come and see her. But it occurred to Marnie, fitting together various component plastic parts of Bob the Builder, that Nathalie might ask what the call was about, and whether they might not, whatever it was, sort it on the telephone. And, contrary to what she felt was her normal conduct, her usual, steady, reasonable conduct, Marnie did not want to have this particular conversation on the telephone. It was a conversation that needed to happen face to face if Marnie was going to derive any satisfaction from it, and satisfaction, Marnie thought, was right now not just something she craved, but something that she was somehow entitled to.

She put Bob the Builder into the hamper and closed the lid. The older children were at school and would not be home until the afternoon. Petey, at present in front of the television with his sleepy rag, in defiance of all Marnie's long-held principles about stimulating amusement for even the youngest of children while awake, could be put into the car and taken to Nathalie's flat where he might play on the floor of her kitchen with all the amenableness he seemed unable to display at home. She could take his juice and some rice cakes, or she could rely on Nathalie having something for him, the kind of thing, Marnie thought with sudden savagery, that he would reject with screams at home but would probably eat with enthusiasm at Nathalie's. Marnie held on to the hamper and took a breath. This was ridiculous. This was in fact worse than ridiculous; this was really dangerous, building up more and more illusory reasons for resenting Nathalie when the real reason—the fundamental reason—for resenting her lay, as it always had, with David.

She went downstairs. Petey sat, glazed and absorbed, in front of a video of Walt Disney's *Sleeping Beauty*. At eighteen months, he had worked out how to use the video, and was now given to murderous yells if prevented. He loved buttons and plugs, switches and keys, anything that clicked and whirred and sent lights flashing and noise roaring. All Daniel had wanted, Marnie remembered, had been bats and balls and running, anything faintly connected with sport, even as a baby, and Daniel had been impervious to any other temptation.

Marnie went back to the hall and dialed Nathalie's number.

"Hello?"

"Nathalie, it's Marnie—"

There was a tiny pause, as if Nathalie was rearranging a response.

"Oh, hello—"

"Will you be there in the next quarter of an hour or so?"

"Well, yes—"

"May I bring Petey over? Just for twenty minutes?"

Nathalie cleared her throat.

"Of course. I haven't seen Petey for ages—"

Marnie put the telephone down and went back into the family room.

"Time to turn that off—"

Petey yanked his fingers out of his mouth.

"No!"

"Yes."

"No! No! No!"

"Petey," Marnie said, stooping to heave him off the floor, "we are going in the *car.*"

"You OK?" Nathalie said.

Marnie looked down at the floor. Petey was eating a breadstick Nathalie had given him and arranging Polly's Noah's Ark animals in a long unsteady line.

"It's just," Marnie said, "that he screamed all the way."

"He'll stop," Nathalie said. "They all stop. How many twelve-year-olds scream for hours? Would you like some coffee?"

Marnie nodded. Nathalie indicated a chair.

"You sit."

Marnie sat. She could feel her shoulders slumping. The balance of power in Nathalie's kitchen was not what she had visualized, not what she had intended. She made an effort and squared her shoulders.

"This isn't about Petey."

"No," Nathalie said.

"I imagine," Marnie said, "that you have some idea of why I'm here?"

Nathalie paused in spooning coffee into a jug.

"David—"

Marnie looked at the tabletop. There was a ring on the surface, a ring left by a glass or a mug, a glass or a mug used by, perhaps, someone who had been sitting here last, talking to Nathalie.

She said, abruptly, "How could you?"

The coffee spoon in Nathalie's hand clanged against the glass of the jug.

"Sorry?"

"How could you?" Marnie said again. "How could you let him tell you before he told me? How could you let him come here first?"

Nathalie turned slowly and leaned against the kitchen counter.

"It wasn't a question of let."

"What?"

"I didn't let him," Nathalie said. "I didn't, as you imply, allow him or encourage him. He just came. He just arrived."

"As he always has!" Marnie cried. "As he always has because you *have* encouraged him! You've always made him feel that no one understands him like you do, that no one can share his inner life like you can!"

Nathalie moved away from the counter, and leaned on the table.

"They can't."

"How *dare* you—"

"I'm not daring anything," Nathalie said. "I'm not taking anything that's yours. But there's something David and I know, an—an unhappy kind of knowledge that, I promise you, you wouldn't want, that we can't help sharing. You know that. You've always known that."

"You're missing the point," Marnie said. She held her hands flat to stop them clenching. "You've always deliberately missed the point. You make me sick."

Petey's face appeared above the tabletop, visible only from the eyes upwards. He reached up and put an elephant and a porcupine on the table. The elephant fell over.

"No," Nathalie said. She stretched out a hand, and set the elephant upright. "No. You're just so possessive you can't stand him loving anyone else, you can't stand anyone else understanding him better than you do."

Marnie said nothing. She glanced down the table. Petey's eyes, as blue and round as marbles, were fixed on her with inscrutable intensity.

"If he came here," Nathalie said, "to tell me about meeting his mother, don't you think that says as much about you as it does about him or me?"

"Like?"

"Like why are you jealous of his mother? Like why are you jealous of me?"

Petey's eyes vanished.

Marnie said, her own gaze not leaving the spot where Petey's had been, "Wouldn't it unsettle you?"

"No," Nathalie said.

"If Steve came and told me things before he told you, wouldn't that drive you crazy?"

"You know your parents," Nathalie said. "So does Steve. You both know exactly where you come from."

Marnie gave a stifled small shriek.

"Oh my *God*. It always, *always* comes back to this, doesn't it? It always comes back to this adoption bond, to this deprivation, to this—this *thing* that makes you so special, so deserving of privilege, so entitled to anything you want, even if it legitimately belongs to someone else, because nothing will ever, ever make up to you for this terrible injury, this wound that's been inflicted—" She stopped, gasping slightly.

Nathalie said, in a low voice, "It is a wound."

"So it's OK to punish everyone else?"

"I'm not punishing."

"You are. You may not mean to, but you *are*."

"And you?"

"What about me?"

"Don't you," Nathalie said, "punish David for not being able to love back like you want him to?"

"How dare you—"

"Don't keep saying that," Nathalie said.

The top of Petey's head emerged again above the edge of the table. His gaze traveled slowly round to Nathalie and then stopped.

"More bic," Petey said.

Nathalie looked down.

"Of course, darling." She glanced at Marnie. "Is that OK?"

Marnie made a dismissive little gesture. Nathalie turned to the cupboard behind her and took down the box of breadsticks.

Marnie said bitterly, "He would never eat those at home."

"Of course not."

Petey took a breadstick in each hand. He looked up at Nathalie and gave her a wide, gorgeous smile.

"Marnie," Nathalie said, "I'm not his wife or the mother of his children. But I've known him since he was this size, smaller. I know about the kind of shadow we both have inside, the shadow that stops us quite releasing ourselves—"

"Please stop."

Nathalie straightened up.

"OK."

"You made him go on this journey. You made him find Carole. But now stop. *Stop*. This isn't to do with you any more."

Nathalie put the breadsticks box down.

"I can't stop him coming—"

"You can stop him coming here *first*. You can stop him telling you how he feels."

"Stop him?"

"Yes."

"You *want* that? You want David to do something just because he's been *told* to do it?"

Marnie bent her face over the table. She felt suddenly insecure, suddenly tearful. She shook her head.

"No—"

Nathalie said, "Do you want to meet Carole?"

Marnie nodded.

She said, "Can I have a tissue?"

Nathalie reached for a roll of paper towels and pushed it across the table.

"Why d'you want to meet Carole?"

Marnie blew her nose.

"She's David's mother—"

"Or do you want to fight *her* for David, too? Are you going to tell her where to get off? Are you going to tell her that no one has rights like a wife does?"

Marnie's head came up.

"You haven't been tested! You don't know what it's like!"

Nathalie said nothing. She put a hand on Petey's head.

"You wait," Marnie said. "You just *wait*."

If her room was completely dark, Polly understood, the glowstars on the ceiling would shine better. However, if she insisted that her teddy bear nightlight was still on, and her bedroom door was left open enough to be wedged by her slipper, this not only represented a triumph over Nathalie's wishes, but also the opportunity to hear whatever else was going on in the flat. Mostly whatever was going on was quite boring, but sometimes, and quite a lot lately, there was an edge to the atmosphere. It wasn't anything Polly could actually have described, like Daddy shouting or Mummy crying, but more a feeling of tension or energy in the air that made her feel that she had better stay awake in case she missed out on something. The feeling also made her restless, and a bit uncertain, so that it was extremely necessary to put Nathalie to the test, over and over, by doing things which, while not exactly naughty, were not precisely good either. Polly was not particularly happy teetering on this borderline, but while things were as they were it seemed the only possible place to be.

She lay, and looked up at her glowstars. They seemed dim and furry, and she could hardly see the points of the moon, the points that made it look like a *c*, which was the letter for cat and candle and car crash. Polly said "car crash" to herself, several times, savoring it. She turned her head to one side and stretched her eyes wide to see better. If she really stretched them, she could make out her doll's house and all her Barbies piled in a plastic laundry basket and her Noah's Ark in its box. When she got home from school that day, her Noah's Ark animals had been all over the floor because Petey had been playing with them.

"You shouldn't have let him," she'd said to Nathalie.

"Oh? And why not?"

"He might have broked something."

"I was there, Polly. I was watching."

"Not all the time," Polly said. "You weren't watching *all the time*."

She had gathered up the animals with elaborate care, and laid them reverently in their box.

"Very commendable," said Nathalie, in a voice that made Polly suspicious.

She looked at her supper. It was one of her favorites except that the carrots were in rounds, not sticks.

"Not hungry!"

"Fine," Nathalie said.

"Don't like penny carrots."

"No," Nathalie said, "nor you do. I've got something to tell you."

"What?"

"I can't tell you till you're sitting in your chair."

Polly sighed. Slowly she hitched herself into her chair and absently picked up a cube of ham.

"I'm going away for a couple of days."

Polly let the ham fall out of her hand.

"Just two days," Nathalie said.

"Why?"

"Eat your ham."

Polly bent down to her plate and seized the ham in her teeth.

"Polly!"

Polly smirked.

"How disgusting."

"Dogs do it," Polly said.

"And are you a dog?"

"Yes."

"Well, be a good Fido and eat another mouthful and I'll tell you."

Polly picked up her fork and speared a piece of carrot. Nathalie said, "I'm going away to see a friend."

"Why?"

"Because I haven't seen her for years and years."

"Since I was born?"

"Long before that."

Polly chewed her carrot.

"Are you going on an airplane?"

"No," Nathalie said, "on a train."

"Am I coming?"

"No. You're staying here with Daddy. Daddy and the grannies will look after you."

Polly threw her fork across the table.

"No!"

"It's only two days. Two days and one night."

Polly thrust her lower lip out.

"Like," Nathalie said, "you having a sleepover with Hattie."

"Why are you going on a train?"

"Because it's a long way."

Polly screwed up her eyes.

"As long as—Australia?"

Nathalie retrieved Polly's fork and handed it back to her. "Not quite."

Polly flicked her fork about.

"What's her name?"

"Who?"

"What's your friend's name?"

Nathalie looked away. Polly watched her. The mood had suddenly gone from one thing to quite another thing. Polly gave her plate a shove and morsels of food scattered across the table.

"Cora," Nathalie said.

Going back to the flat had become, Carole decided, something almost to be dreaded. It wasn't the place itself, the place that had once been such a pleasure to decide about, to choose things for, but more a question of what she might find there. Once she had known it would only be Connor. Connor whom she knew, and knew how to manage, Connor back from a game of something or an auction room, or a meeting with somebody's respectful son seeking advice on the basic principles of setting up a small business. Now it was certainly still Connor, but a more unpredictable and vigilant Connor, a Connor on the lookout for any tiny telltale sign in her that she had been anywhere or contacted anyone that he should know about.

And if Connor was out, then there was always Martin. Work kept Martin occupied until the early evening, but he never now seemed to do anything after that but come home. He said he had no money, and he didn't want to see his friends because he couldn't face them. Carole had tried to say that one of the essential elements in friendship was that it was there when you really needed it, in bad times, but Martin had looked at her as if she didn't know what she was talking about. On the whole, she preferred that look to his other one, the slightly suspicious version of Connor's new alertness, which suggested strongly to Carole that she was being tested, in every detail, for any change she might display in demeanor or attitude since producing David and introducing him to the family.

It was exhausting, having their eyes upon her in this way. Even if she felt, to some degree, that Connor's behavior was justified, Martin's only maddened and sometimes alarmed her. She felt that he had already judged her, and come to his own conclusion, and was merely watching her to obtain evidence of the verdict he had pronounced already. He had, it seemed, decided that David, on account of his looks and his provenance, and the fact that he had been her private secret for all these years, had risen effortlessly to the head of the list in her affections. He was her eldest son, her first-born. He was successful enough to run his own business. He had produced two sons of his own. He must be what every mother hopes and longs for, and Martin was going to keep his eye on his mother for as long as it took to prove himself right.

"Have it out with him," Euan said. "Get it out in the open. *Tell* him."

Carole twisted her wedding ring.

"He takes everything I say the wrong way—"

"Oh," Euan said, "that's just Mart. Perfectly balanced, chip on each shoulder. Tell him David's just an add-on."

Carole looked at him.

"Would you come too? Would you help me?"

Euan hesitated. He wanted to help, he wanted his mother and brother to find some solution to their age-old difficulties, but the fact was, he was a bit tied up just now. He'd spent so much time with his family recently, what with the David business, that Chloe, who was as demanding as gorgeous girls so often turned out to be, was beginning to kick up a bit of a fuss, check up on him, want treats and compensation. David's arrival had been pretty shaking, for God's sake, but the thought of Chloe being dissatisfied enough to get restless was very much more so. He scratched his head.

"Sorry, Ma. Bit difficult at the moment, I've had so much time off—"

"Of course."

"Anyway," Euan said, "you ought to do it alone. Mart wouldn't like me holding your hand. Who invented sibling rivalry?"

Carole laughed.

"You're right. Of course you are. It's just—"

"I know, Ma. It always is."

Now standing in the hall outside Martin's bedroom door and surveying with exasperation the growing heap of bags and boxes he had begun to pile up outside it, she felt an enormous weariness. There always seemed to be a mountain to climb, just now, and the scaling of one peak only led to another, and another. That was why, she supposed, people kept secrets. The moment they stopped, and confessed, was the moment their own control over whatever it was vanished and everyone else joined in, clamoring and criticizing and claiming their slice of the action. She took a step forward and raised her hand to knock on Martin's door.

The door opened. Martin stood there, wearing tracksuit bottoms, a Manchester United T-shirt and bare feet.

Carole said, almost diffidently, "I was just coming to see you."

"Oh."

"Were you on your way out?"

"Only to the kitchen. To get some juice."

Carole said, "Then perhaps I could talk to you. While you drink it."

Martin moved past her and headed across the hall.

"What about?"

Carole followed him.

"David."

Martin was by the fridge, his back to her.

"Thought so."

"Darling," Carole said, "nothing has changed, nothing in the way I feel about you or Euan or Dad."

Martin opened the fridge and took a carton of juice out of the door.

"Good-looking bloke."

"What's that got to do with it?"

"Isn't it gratifying," Martin said, tipping the carton up so that he could drink from it, "to have such a handsome son?"

"I have two already."

Martin snorted.

"Don't give me that."

Carole came closer.

"I didn't think about him. Not for months on end—"

"But you thought about his father."

Carole hesitated.

"Sometimes."

"And he looks like his father."

Carole looked straight at Martin.

"Darling, all that is over. *You* are my family, Dad is my husband, this is now and the future; that was the long, long ago past."

Martin slammed the carton back in the fridge.

"But it happened."

"Yes," Carole said, "I can't undo that. I can't. I've said sorry till I can't say it anymore. What am I supposed to do now, what more *can* I do?"

Martin swung the fridge door shut. He stood facing it a while and then he turned round.

"Get rid of him," he said.

"Get rid—"

"No," Martin said. "No, on second thought, I'll get rid of him. I'll tell him he's not wanted." He eyed his mother. "Is he?"

CHAPTER SIXTEEN

A man a bit further down the railway carriage had been looking at Nathalie all the way from Birmingham New Street Station. He wasn't staring exactly, and he didn't look sinister or threatening, but he was obviously, frankly, interested. He had a heavy-looking, thick book, but he spent more time gazing at Nathalie than he did at its pages. It was as if, Nathalie thought, he was trying to work something out about her. It was as if he had first noticed her because she attracted him, and then he'd noticed something else, something more elusive and beguiling than mere looks, and was held in thrall to it. She'd tried, once and unwisely, giving him a brief glance and smile, but he hadn't responded or changed his steady, open gaze. He was plainly concerned with something much less commonplace than flirting.

Nathalie looked steadfastly out of the window. She too, had a book, but she couldn't even contemplate concentrating long enough to get through a single sentence. She wasn't, if she was honest, particularly surprised that the man should be looking at her: in fact, she was more surprised that everyone in the carriage wasn't looking, that there could possibly be a person sitting within yards of her who couldn't see the difference, the difference between all of them in the accepted certainty of their lives and her, on the brink of this extraordinary change in hers, this change that was going to bring solution and resolution and—and *discovery*. And yet it wasn't a change, in reality. The change had been all the years leading up to this moment, all the years when she didn't know who her mother was, didn't know that her mother cared so much. She kept replaying that first telephone conversation in her mind, with Cora crying, Cora asking so—so anxiously, if Nathalie was angry, if Nathalie could ever forgive her. When she went back through those minutes on the telephone together, Nathalie felt a surge of something so pure and strong and pleasing that she supposed it must be joy.

Elaine Price had offered to come to Northsea with her. She'd said she often did that, often came to the first meeting just to get it started, just to help those first few moments when it was so dauntingly difficult to start on the business of repair and reconciliation. She said it was her practice to pull out as soon as she could, but that as these meetings were often an anticlimax, neither side daring to reveal their true feelings, it was usually a help to have someone there to help that daring along.

"If you hold back on emotion," Elaine said, "you'll hold back on progress."

Nathalie had been very sure that holding back on emotion would not be a problem. The problem, she thought, would be that there would be too much emotion, too little holding back. She wasn't sure she wanted Elaine there while she cried, and Cora cried, as she was certain they would; not because she didn't like and trust Elaine, but because this moment was going to be so supremely private that it should have no witnesses. There shouldn't, Nathalie told herself, be anyone present at a kind of rebirth; it wasn't right or natural. Two adults who were going, in their separate ways, to remedy the great loss in each of their lives should be able to perform this precious and extraordinary ritual in an appropriate seclusion.

"Thank you," she said to Elaine, "thank you, really. But I have to go alone. I want to go alone."

She hoped Elaine had understood. She hoped that Elaine meant what she said when she had explained that she was no more than a midwife to a form of rebirth, that when it had happened she would step quietly back and attend to other clients, those clients who were always, always coming along. Nathalie hoped—though not to much effect, if she was candid—that in her exhilaration at what lay ahead of her she hadn't forgotten, somehow, to include Elaine in all she was thinking and feeling.

She glanced away from the window. The man with the book was, slightly disappointingly, now reading it. He seemed to be reading it—so male this—with exactly the attention he had given to her face only minutes, probably, earlier. She pulled back her cuff to look at her watch and felt a sharp clutch of panic in her stomach. In thirty-seven minutes the train would pull into Northsea Station, where Cora would be waiting on the platform wearing, she said, something red, or orange, and carrying flowers.

"Cornflowers, if I can find them," she said. "I love cornflowers. I've never seen them growing in corn, but I'd love to. Cornflowers and poppies in a field of corn."

Nathalie closed her eyes. For the last few weeks, there'd been an image of herself that kept coming into her mind, as clear and precise as an old snapshot. She was six perhaps, or seven, wearing the kind of dress Lynne liked her to wear, a puff-sleeved, full-skirted dress with a smocked bodice and a sash tie. It was pink, or blue, something pale, and her hair was tied up on top of her head with a ribbon with long ends falling down to her shoulders. She had white socks on, and bar shoes, and she was standing in the back garden at Ashmore Road by a lilac bush, with her hands demurely clasped in front of her, as they had to be at the beginning of her dancing classes. She couldn't remember where this tidy

241

and formal child had been going, but she knew where she was going to go now. It was a scene she had played over and over in her mind of the child with the hair ribbon and bar shoes stepping down off the train and holding her arms up to a woman in a red dress holding a bunch of cornflowers. In some moods, she could bring a lump to her throat, just picturing it.

She opened her eyes. Better not to think about that now, better not to hope and plan too much, better to look out of the window and see that, astonishingly, the gray-blue North Sea was only a hundred yards from the railway line, glimmering under a cloud-blurred sky. They must be close, very close. In fact, people were beginning to stir in the seats around her, struggling into jackets, stuffing newspapers into bags, adopting the wary, shuttered expressions necessary for abandoning the brief and blessed release of a journey for the pressures of daily life again.

"Northsea," the conductor's voice said over the speaker. "Northsea next stop."

Nathalie stood up unsteadily. Oh, the terror of great moments, the terror of facing them coupled with the accompanying terror of having them somehow taken away. She reached up to the rack for her bag, the bag containing her night things and a picture Polly had drawn—insistently, deliberately—of a large dog beside a small house and three tiny people with "For Cora" written at the top with the r's backwards.

The train was sliding past houses now, gray-walled houses with gray slate roofs, and then a warehouse and a garage and a football stadium with craning lights rearing up above the stands. Then more houses, and a park, and railway lines running together and apart in a seemingly liquid sequence that made you dizzy to look at. And then the train slowing, nothing to stop it, gliding under the dirty glass canopy of Northsea Station, gliding along beside the platforms, beside the piles of mailbags, the luggage trolleys, the scattered passengers, the dog on a lead, the newsstand, the signs saying "Taxis" and "Toilets." And then, stop.

Nathalie grasped her bag. She stepped forward. In the aisle between the seats, the man with the book was standing looking at her.

"Good luck," he said.

She nodded. He made way for her to precede him and she went clumsily past, holding her bag up in front of her, down the carriage, out of the door down the steps, and onto the platform.

There was someone there, someone waiting, someone in an orangey-red garment, a loose, coatlike thing. She was holding flowers, but they weren't cornflowers, they were something ordinary, something like carnations, whitish-green. And this person wasn't mother-sized, this person was small. Tiny. You couldn't, Nathalie thought wildly, hug up to this person. You'd have to hug down.

"Hello, dear," Cora said.

It had taken determined courage to telephone Carole. Marnie had performed all kinds of steadying rituals before-hand—folding the laundry, re-plaiting her hair, checking that Petey hadn't kicked his rug off during his nap—and had then made herself walk into the hall with resolute steps and dial the number David had given her. He hadn't wanted to give it to her, of course, protesting that, as it didn't look as if there was much future in any of this anyhow, there was no point in Marnie joining in the dance. But Marnie had insisted, holding out her hand as if he was a chastised child who had to surrender something he had stolen.

"If it concerns you, it concerns me. We agreed that, from now on. Remember?"

Carole had not sounded welcoming. David had told her that Marnie would be calling her, but she still managed to sound as if she had been caught out unfairly, and didn't like it. Marnie tried to remember all David had said about Carole's inability to deal with confrontation, which in turn would require great patience on the part of the confronter.

"I don't want anything from you," Marnie said. "I'm not after anything at all. But I'm his wife, so I'm involved." She stopped abruptly. She'd been about to say, "I can't be left out of this," but that was exactly the kind of thing she was schooling herself *not* to say. So she said instead, "This touches all of us."

There was a pause, and then Carole said reluctantly, "I suppose so."

She'd wanted Marnie to go to London. She'd suggested they meet for lunch somewhere, maybe in the restaurant of a gallery, a place, she implied, that was both acceptable and anonymous for women in such a highly charged situation to meet. But Marnie was ready for her. Marnie was having no truck with emotional airbrushing, not after having seen Nathalie, with the gloves off.

"You should see his home," Marnie said. "You should see his life, where his family is."

"OK," Carole said surprisingly. She sounded, irritatingly, slightly amused and not in any way taken aback. "OK. I'll come to Westerham."

And now, here she was, in Marnie's sitting room, in one of Marnie's blue upholstered chairs, accepting a cup of Marnie's coffee and refusing one of Marnie's specially baked pecan squares. She was looking round her in a way Marnie couldn't fathom, neither avidly curious, nor indifferent, taking in the clean walls and polished floor and the books and pictures and the model child on the hearthrug with his fingers in his mouth and an ecologically sound wooden train set strewn around him. Marnie watched her, watched her gaze travel over the flowers in the stone vase, the photographs, the sofa with its unmistakable signs of having been jumped on more than sat on, and wondered what, if anything, she had forgotten.

Carole took a sip of coffee.

"Lovely."

"I come from a long line of coffee makers—"

"I meant the room. The coffee too, of course."

Marnie waited for Carole to say something to Petey. Petey was, after all, being perfect, upright on his bottom with his blue stare fixed upon the visitor, his little boot-clad feet so charmingly thrust out among the decorative clutter of his train. But, apart from a brief greeting, Carole had appeared oblivious to Petey. So oblivious, in fact, that Marnie was beginning to wonder if she was avoiding looking at him because she couldn't bear to, because the sight of a small blond boy was too painful, brought too sharp a recollection.

Petey took his fingers out of his mouth and picked up the wooden train. He held it out, towards Carole.

"Thomas," Petey said.

Carole gave him a quick glance.

"He means Thomas the Tank Engine—"

"Lovely," Carole said again. "Lovely train."

Petey dropped the train, leaving his arm stiffly still in the air.

"*Not* Thomas," he said.

"No."

"Thomas *blue*," Petey said scornfully. He put his fingers back in.

"He's two," Marnie said.

Carole looked at her coffee.

"I'm rather out of practice at guessing ages." She took another sip. "I haven't had a two-year-old for over twenty-five years."

Marnie put her cup down on the floor by her chair. She disliked drinking coffee out of cups. Cups were for tea, English-style. Coffee should come in mugs, in pints and half-pints. But somehow, seeing Carole's hair and suede shoes, her conviction about the Canadian way of coffee had faltered and given up. Just as her resolve had given up about not changing out of her jeans, about not washing the kitchen floor. She had determined to do neither and then the recollection of what David had said about Carole's clothes, Carole's flat, had weakened her.

"I expect David told you," Marnie said, "that Petey is the youngest of our children. Ellen is twelve and Daniel is ten." She indicated a photograph on a bookshelf four feet away from Carole. "That's them, in Canada last summer."

Carole turned her head towards the photograph. She made no movement to lean to pick it up.

"Lovely."

"We spend each summer in Canada," Marnie said, "staying with my folks. It's a wonderful life for children."

"I'm sure," Carole said. She turned her head back again. "I've never been."

Petey got slowly and carefully to his feet. Then he trotted across to Carole and stood by her knee, looking intently at her.

"Hello," Carole said.

Petey said nothing. Marnie looked at his solid small back in its striped T-shirt, at his smooth pale head, at his endearingly stoutly shod feet, and marveled that anyone could refrain from touching him.

"When my Martin was two," Carole said to Petey, "he liked tractors. Do you like tractors?"

Petey took a step back.

"Thomas," he said loudly.

"Of course—"

"Thomas!" Petey shouted.

"Don't shout, sweetheart," Marnie said.

Petey turned and went back to the hearthrug. He bent and picked up his train and then trotted purposefully out of the room with it.

"He can't go far," Marnie said, as if Carole cared. "There's a stair gate."

Carole reached out to set her cup down. Then she leaned back and put her hands on the arms of the blue chair.

"Why did you want me to come?"

Marnie was startled.

"But that's obvious—"

"Is it?"

"Of course. You are David's mother and I am his wife and the mother of his children—"

"Oh," Carole said, lifting one hand, "I see all that. I see all the settled-ness, this house, this family establishment. But I could see that anyway, I could see that from meeting David. David doesn't look like a man with no one to care for him."

"I should hope not—"

Carole looked at her.

"And you do care for him. Don't you?"

Marnie looked away. The plate of pecan squares, now softening in the sunlight falling through the window on to them, seemed suddenly forlorn, pathetic, a truly amateur gesture.

"It's not about that."

"No?"

"No."

"Then what? What is it about? Why did you want me to come down here?"

"I needed you to know something. I needed you to be very certain of something."

Carole clasped her hands together under her chin, her elbows on the arms of the chair.

"Like what?"

Marnie took a breath.

"I want you to know," she said, "that as David's mother, you are very welcome to join in our family. But please don't think that there was a gap here, waiting for you to fill it. Because there wasn't."

Petey appeared in the doorway. He was holding Daniel's outgrown baby cricket bat, clasped in his arms, like a teddy bear. Carole didn't glance his way. She was looking at Marnie.

"What makes you think," she said, "that such a thought ever crossed my mind?"

Marnie leaned forward.

"I just want you to know," she said. "I just want there to be no doubt about it. You're very welcome, but on our terms."

"Bat," Petey said loudly.

"You poor girl," Carole said to Marnie. "You poor girl. You really love him, don't you?"

It was so strange, Lynne thought, to consider the things that gave you comfort down the years, and how something that could once be utterly relied upon for consolation later turned out to be of no use at all. There'd been a time—a long time, it seemed then, a reliably long time—when contemplation of a cake baked for the weekend, or David's rugger kit successfully washed, could bring with it a sense of extraordinary fulfilment, and peace. But of course, that time had passed. It had passed not just of its own accord, but also, Lynne was sure, egged on by Nathalie who had wanted an end to dependency, an end to this child life of routine and small, sweet comforts. Lynne had sometimes had visions of Nathalie deliberately unpicking this careful structure Lynne had made, partly to test its strength and partly to test her own capacity to do without it. Lynne couldn't, in her heart of hearts, blame Nathalie for wanting to grow up and away, but she had always blamed her— unreasonably, she knew—for not leaving anything behind to take her place.

That was where, Lynne knew with a degree of shame, that television came in. She was sure that there were thousands and thousands of other people like her, people for whom television had become a boon companion, a source of friendship and fantasy. It wasn't that Lynne spent whole afternoons watching old Hollywood movies with a bottle of what her mother had witheringly called grocer's sherry, but more a creeping addiction to home and garden-improvement programs. She didn't want love and improbable romance: she wanted an escape from the present, a magic carpet back to the place where she was the power in the land, the wife and mother, the heart of the household. Sitting watching these shoddy and theatrical transformations of rooms and spaces of earth, and seeing the touching hope for an echoing transformation of their lives on the faces of the participants, took Lynne back to a time when she knew she'd been happier than at any other time, a time when two clean, well-fed, sleeping children upstairs had, for a while, made her believe that she not only had a purpose, but that it was a purpose she was wonderfully fitted to fulfill. There'd been moments—or more than moments, maybe—when she had almost been reconciled to infertility, to not going through a pregnancy, and now, bizarrely, watching stage-set bookcases stapled up against a hastily painted wall on screen, she could recapture a lingering taste of that peace of mind, see a fantasy brought down like a balloon on a string until you could hold it in your hand. It was pathetic, she knew, but why should pathos diminish the real capacity of cheap nonsense, in whatever form, to help?

She preferred watching her programs when Ralph was out of the house—right out, not just tinkering on in his workshop. He'd joined a chess club again—not the superior one where David played, but a more random group, including several asylum seekers from the old Soviet republics, who met in a pub near Westerham Station and were tolerated as long as they bought a drink each an hour. Ralph didn't say why he'd started wanting to play again, and Lynne didn't ask him. It was, on the contrary, something of a relief to see him go off, two nights a week, with an air of purpose that, in its turn, set her free for—the television. Settling down in front of it gave her the feeling, every time, of putting down a burden, of giving herself a respite from something arduous and demanding.

"You can't," David's voice said from the doorway, "be watching *that*."

Lynne gave a little scream.

"David!"

He indicated the screen. Two cheerfully blethering men and a big girl in a boiler suit were positioning boulders and cacti across a blond carpet of gravel.

"Mum, it's rubbish!"

"I know—"

"That garden'll last ten minutes, and where did they get those plants? Those are *desert* plants. They ought to be in Arizona."

"You gave me such a fright," Lynne said. She aimed the remote control at the television, and the screen sank into blackness.

"If I'd rung first," David said, "you'd have killed the fatted calf and cleaned the bathroom."

"I *like*—"

"But I didn't want you to," David said. He bent over her chair and kissed her. "I wanted to see you and I didn't want a whole lot of cooking and stuff to get in the way."

Lynne looked away.

"Oh."

David sat down on the sofa close to her chair.

"Dad's chess night. You watching telly. Perfect."

"Do you know," Lynne said uncertainly, "I don't think I'm up to any more revelations."

"Nor me."

Lynne looked up.

"Let me get you some coffee."

"No."

"David—"

"No," David said, "I don't want anything. I didn't come for anything like that."

"I like to do it."

"I know." He looked at the blank television. "Mum, I know."

Lynne said in a small voice, "I've been so frightened."

"I know that too."

"I thought—"

"Yes."

"I don't know what happened. When—when you went to see her I thought perhaps you, or Nathalie—"

"That's why I'm here," David said.

Lynne nodded.

"You don't need to worry," David said.

She shut her eyes tightly and held her hands together hard, in her lap.

He said, "I kind of liked her. She's impressive in a way, sort of polished, *accomplished* is perhaps the word. She gave me a lot of answers about my father and stuff. But—" He stopped.

Lynne didn't open her eyes.

"There's no connection," David said. "Or at least, not the one I might have been looking for. There's something there, but it's feeble, sickly. Mum," David said, leaning forward so that he could touch her clasped hands, "it's at least twenty years too late."

Lynne began to cry. David watched as the tears seeped slowly out from under her lids and slid down her cheeks.

"I was terrified—"

David leaned forward.

"But not now. Nothing to be afraid of now."

Lynne said unsteadily, "Find me a tissue, dear. On the side."

David stood up. A box of tissues stood on the cabinet which housed—had always housed—Ralph's set of *Encyclopaedia Britannica*. He put the box in Lynne's lap.

He said, "Seeing her laid some ghosts."

Lynne blew her nose. She looked up at David, damp-eyed.

"Like what?"

"Like who my father was. What my name is."

"Your name is Dexter."

"That's Ralph's name," David said, "Dad's name. It's not yours or mine or Nathalie's."

"Why does a name matter?"

David sat down again.

"It matters."

"So," Lynne said, attempting a weak smile, "your mother doesn't matter but your name does?"

"Don't be daft. You're my mother. I came to tell you that. That's why I'm here."

Lynne pulled out another tissue.

"Don't start me off again."

"I don't mind—"

"You're a good son," Lynne said fiercely. "A *good* son."

David spread his hands.

"I'd hope so—"

"And your father?"

"Dad?"

"No, not Dad. Your birth father—"

"I know his name," David said. "I don't know anything else."

"Do you want to?"

"I don't know."

Lynne said softly, "I wonder how Dad would feel."

"Yes."

"This chess club—"

"Yes."

Lynne put the tissue box on the little table by her chair.

"There's no dress rehearsal for anything, is there? There's no chance to practice anything."

David leaned across to give her a little nudge.

"Very philosophical, Mum."

She smiled at him.

"Thank you for coming."

He moved his hand so that he was holding her wrist.

"There may be changes ahead, Mum, more changes. But there's one thing that won't change. Are you sure of that? Are you sure of that now?"

Lynne looked up at him.

"Nathalie—"

"Forget Nathalie," David said. "It's me we're talking about. Yes or no?"

"I'll try," Lynne said.

"Not good enough."

She looked down at his hand on her wrist.

"Yes," she said.

Betty paused outside Cora's door. There was a line of light under it, but no sound. Betty had been up to bed at her usual time, and had lain there counting the exasperating rhythm of Don's snores for over an hour, as wakeful as anything, and could then stand it no longer. So she had got out of bed and put on her dressing gown and formidable slippers—running a bed and breakfast taught you never to emerge onto the landing in only a nightgown—and padded downstairs to Cora's door.

She put her ear to the wood. No sound. Nothing. She raised her knuckles above her head and knocked gently. There was a faint rustling inside, and then silence.

"Cora," Betty whispered.

More silence.

"Cora," Betty said, slightly louder. "Are you all right?"

There was more rustling and the door opened. Cora stood inside, still in her orange dress, and barefoot.

"Oh Cora," Betty said. "It's after midnight."

"Is it?"

"Why don't I get you some hot milk—"

"No thank you," Cora said, "I'm not ill. I'm just not sleepy."

Betty moved past her sister into the room. It was tidy, as if Cora hadn't been there, as if she'd just been standing on the carpet, not moving.

"Did she upset you?"

"No," Cora said.

Betty peered.

"You sure? You look all in."

"I'm fine," Cora said.

"Don't give me that," Betty said. "Don't tell me she didn't upset you."

Cora gave a little sigh.

"She didn't. I upset myself."

"What?"

"I wasn't what she was expecting. I'm her mother but she wasn't expecting me. And I wasn't expecting her."

"Oh come on," Betty said. She sat down heavily in Cora's small, uncomfortable chair. "You'd seen her *picture*."

"It wasn't the one I had in my mind," Cora said. "She was lovely, don't get me wrong, lovely to look at, lovely manners, sweet. But she's different now."

"Different?"

"She's not my Samantha—"

"I told you," Betty said triumphantly. "I *told* you, didn't I? I told you you'd only get hurt, seeing her."

"I'm not hurt," Cora said.

"What, standing there fully dressed at midnight, staring into space—"

"I'm working things out. But I'm not hurt. I'm upset, but I'm not hurt."

"And I suppose madam has flounced off back down south—"

"No, she hasn't," Cora said. "She's in the guest house, where I booked her. I left her there just after ten. She was exhausted."

"And she's exhausted you."

"Of course she has," Cora said. "What d'you expect?

Important emotions are exhausting." She looked at her sister. "I think you'd better get back off to bed."

"I need to see you're all right."

"I am."

"But you're upset. You said so yourself."

"I'm adjusting," Cora said. "I'm adjusting to—Nathalie. I'm adjusting to everything I've felt for so long being—well, being *over*."

Betty heaved herself to her feet.

"Sometimes," she said, "you are very hard to follow."

"Perhaps."

"I do my best," Betty said. "I try my hardest to prevent you from getting any more knocks and you go all perverse on me and go chasing after knocks anyway."

Cora picked at something on the front of her orange dress.

"This isn't a knock, exactly. It's more like another version of a story I've lived with nearly all my life."

"No more riddles," Betty said, moving towards the door, "it's too late. Was she kind to you?"

Cora looked startled.

"Oh yes—"

"Not just polite. *Kind*."

"Yes," Cora said. "She was very kind to me."

Betty put a hand on Cora's shoulder.

"I knew it," she said, "I knew it. *Kind*. What sort of a daughter is that?"

255

CHAPTER SEVENTEEN

The studio lay bathed in early evening light. Steve hadn't realized this when he bought the building, but the crooked rooflines outside the west-facing window were so arranged that long shafts of late sunlight could come sliding in, during spring and summer, straight, it seemed, from the horizon of the world. It gave him the same sensations that contemplating the roof beams did, the same eerie, wonderful sense of being, quite by chance, part of something timeless, and endless, and, ultimately and superbly, careless of little human things.

He sat now just outside one of the great dust-furred beams of light, with his stool turned back to the wall. His computer was still on, the lit screen trivialized by the natural brilliance pouring softly past it, because he had promised himself he would finish his invoices for the month, so that Meera could insert them into her scrupulously detailed accounts.

"It's not like you to be late," she'd said, standing by his desk with her perfect posture, which enabled her hair to hang straight down her back in a blue-black sheet. "Not like you at all."

"Sorry," he said, not looking at her.

"Is something the matter?"

He gave a rueful smile at his keyboard.

"You don't miss much—"

"No," she said, "specially things I don't like."

He'd sighed. It was a moment to say something, a moment to spread out the tangle of all that was going on under an objective and practical eye, and ask for advice in sorting it out. But he let it pass. He sighed again and looked up at her. She was wearing an expression of surprising sympathy.

"I'll get those invoices to you tomorrow. Promise."

He had done more than half of them. It was only a question of checking, a task he knew his mind was not only suited to, but rather liked, but all the same it refused to stay focused and slid about like a raw egg on a plate, into the subject of Nathalie, and then Sasha, and Nathalie's visit to Northsea, and then Sasha, and Polly, and Polly's impending time in hospital, and then Sasha. Invoices might, in fact, have brought respite and relief, but he couldn't fix upon them, he couldn't stop the sliding, and the great sloppy burdens of anxiety and love and remorse that so heavily accompanied it.

Sasha had wanted to see him that afternoon. She had wanted to quite insistently, quite demandingly, in a way he might, a few weeks earlier, have found flattering, especially coming from someone who made such a point of leaving people free, herself in particular. But she had rung four times on his mobile—her name had come up, almost menacingly, on its tiny screen—and then tried on his office line until he had to say no with a kind of finality he'd never had to use before.

"What do you mean, no?"

"I mean I have to work. I mean I have some work to finish by six o'clock tonight."

"Then I'll see you at six o'clock."

"I'm going home at six o'clock."

"To put," Sasha said, with a distinct edge, "your child to bed."

"Yes."

"Then have a coffee with me now. Coffee for half an hour. That'll leave you three hours still to do whatever stuff you have to do."

"No."

"It's this Nathalie thing again, isn't it?"

Steve shut his eyes, holding the phone.

He said, "It was something very big for her—"

"Another behavioral interlude."

"Enough—"

"Another look-at-me-I'm-adopted moment."

"I said enough—"

"You're a fool," Sasha said.

"Maybe."

"The chances you throw away—"

"Maybe that too—"

"I need to see you!"

Steve kept his eyes closed.

"Not today."

There'd been a pause, a highly charged small pause, and then Sasha had said, quite casually, "Bye," and put the phone down.

And since then, he'd sat here, fiddling about on the screen, conscious of Titus and Justine answering their phones, going out on various errands, of Meera pursuing her steely purpose at the far end, of a desire to telephone Nathalie for no precise reason he could think of. Nothing just now, he thought, skimming the cursor about mindlessly, was quite on track, nobody seemed to be cheerful or simple or light of heart. Even Titus, usually so reliably and robustly spirited, appeared to be deriving nothing from his new affair with Justine, an affair that had given Steve—no use at all pretending otherwise—just the illusory permission and excuse he needed to see Sasha. Titus looked sullen, Justine looked miserable, Meera looked disapproving, Nathalie looked, was—oh *hell*, Steve thought, spinninng his stool back, how on earth had everything become so unraveled? And how had he so departed from all the codes of conduct he had followed all his life that he now found himself in the middle of a most despicable maze with not the first idea of how to make his way back to the beginning?

He looked at his watch. It was ten past six. Meera had left at five-thirty, Justine had followed her ten minutes later, and Titus had disappeared two hours ago without explanation, and would presumably not now reappear until the morning. He should have told Steve where he was going, and Steve should have given permission, and ascertained how long he'd be, and made a few reliably Steve-like comments about the state of his desk. But neither of them had done either. Titus had merely put the telephone down on some call, called out, "Got to see to something," and gone, followed by Meera's steady and eloquent dark gaze. Justine hadn't looked up. She'd merely kept on working, head bent, shoulders hunched, every atom of her unhappy body visibly conscious of his departure.

He glanced at the screen. He'd done three weeks out of four. Perhaps he'd go home now, and see Polly, and let Nathalie say whatever it was she wanted to say at the moment, and then come back to the office early in the morning, to finish, so that the disc would be ready and waiting on Meera's desk before she even arrived. As he would like to be, all braced for a return to the brisk ordinariness of things, to the jokes and the busyness and the tickings-off.

The door to the stairs opened. Titus appeared round it, and stood, holding the edge, almost as if he needed support. He looked down the length of the room at Steve, and lifted his chin.

"You bastard," he said loudly.

For some reason, Steve stood up. He put his hands in his pockets.

"Where have you been?"

"Where do you fucking think?"

"This is work time, Titus. I pay you for the day's working hours. What you do outside that is your affair, but between nine and five-thirty—"

"Shut up," Titus said.

He let go of the door and advanced down the studio towards Steve.

"You're a rat," Titus said. "A sanctimonious, two-timing shit of a *rat*."

Steve licked his lips.

"You've seen Sasha."

"She called me."

"Ah. Of course."

"Don't use that fucking tone!" Titus shouted.

"I wasn't aware—"

"You betray your wife, you nick my girlfriend—"

"I didn't—"

"I knew," Titus said, coming up close and thrusting his face at Steve's, "I knew you were meeting. I knew there was all this kissy crap in wine bars masquerading as heart-to-hearts about Nathalie. I knew all that. I could just about take all that. But I didn't know, until two hours ago, that you'd fucked her."

Steve felt his hands clench into fists in his pockets.

"Once."

"Oh!" Titus cried. "Once, is it? One little mistaken, innocent, ooh-what-a-naughty-lapse time? A fuck is a bloody fuck, Steve, and you bloody well know it."

Steve glanced away. A red tide of something terrible, shameful, was burning up his throat.

"Yes."

"I'd like to put you through that fucking window. I'd like to chop up that pretentious sign out there and ram the pieces up all your fucking orifices."

"Titus—"

"Don't start explaining. Don't start justifying. Don't give

me any of your control-freak *crap*. You *knew* what Sasha meant to me. You *knew* it."

Steve nodded.

"And now," Titus said, "I've gone and buggered up poor old Justine."

"Yes."

"Yes," Titus said in sarcastic imitation. "Yes, yes, sorry, didn't mean to, sorry, Titus, sorry, Sasha, sorry, Justine, sorry, Nathalie—" He stopped and then he said, "What about Nathalie?"

Steve said in a low voice, "She doesn't know."

"That you've been seeing Sasha? That you've fucked her?"

"No—"

"Will you tell her?"

Steve looked up at the ceiling.

"I don't know."

"You will," Titus said.

"Titus—"

Titus rose up on his toes until his face was almost level with Steve's.

He said, "You'll tell her, you fucking wimp, or I will."

When Ellen woke, she knew it wasn't morning. It wasn't just that the birds were still quiet and that the brief spring night sky was still dark, but also because there was this feeling, the atmosphere the house always had when life in it got switched off for a few hours. She rolled over and looked at her clock radio. The squared green numbers said 12:40. She'd been asleep for an hour and a half. What on earth could make her wake up after only an hour and a half? What was it that had made her wake up and feel as if it was the morning already?

She sat up in bed and looked at her closed door. There was no line of light under it, so that meant that everyone was in bed, that the landing light was off, that the only lights in the house would be the little red standby lights on the television, and the computer monitor. Even Petey slept in the complete dark. When she and Daniel were little, they'd had a lamp like a dim green mushroom, with plastic rabbits molded round the base, which she'd fallen in love with during a stopover in Montreal Airport, but Petey had shunned the mushroom and slept like a grown-up—about the only thing about him, Ellen sometimes thought, that was grown-up—in the dark.

She twisted round and slid out of bed. It occurred to her to do something she'd never done before, something that people in books did when they had a problem or were in the middle of an adventure, and go down to the kitchen. She might have some cereal, or make herself some hot chocolate, and then she might go into the family room and turn the computer on and do a bit of research for her current obsession which was summer tennis camps in Canada. She had already told Zadie and Fizz, untruthfully, about being enrolled for one of these camps—she'd found a particularly beguiling-sounding one, in British Columbia—and was now playing with the idea, shortly to become a requirement, of putting the proposition to her parents while they were still in a weakened state because of this Carole woman.

Ellen tiptoed across the room, and put her hand on the doorknob. She hadn't actually met Carole, but she knew she'd been to the house, leaving a coffee cup with lipstick on it and a disturbed atmosphere. Marnie hadn't volunteered much about Carole's visit, and Ellen, now that she knew more than she'd ever wanted to know, hadn't asked. There seemed, in fact, to be a kind of pact among them all, a silent complicity about not budging, about not making way, in the family, for any new person, for any change in dynamics. That was fine by Ellen, absolutely fine. She had watched Marnie turning over the cushion in the seat of the chair where Carole had been sitting, and felt a surge of relief at the gesture.

Out on the landing, she checked in the gloom to see that

all the bedroom doors were shut. Daniel's was, her parents' was, only Petey's was wedged open with a small beanbag hippo, its pink-felt tongue lolling. She took a step or two along the carpet, and noticed that a light was shining from downstairs, a lamp someone had left on, probably the lamp just inside the kitchen door. She peered over the banisters. The door to David's office was open, and through it Ellen could see her father's computer was on, and that her father was sitting in front of it, sideways on, and that on the desk between himself and the computer's monitor stood his chess set, his old one, the one Grandpa Ralph had given him when he was about eight, and that, because of the way everything was arranged, the light from the computer screen was throwing the shadows of the chess pieces onto the wall beside the desk, and making them look much bigger, taller and stranger, and inhuman somehow, like those statues on Easter Island with monster eyes and mouths. Ellen swallowed. She watched her father's huge shadow hand swoop up a crowned piece and hold it there, like a prisoner, lit by the hard green glow from the computer. It was rather horrible, watching him, rather unsettling, as if he was exercising a power which wasn't quite natural, which made him seem to be someone other than her father. She leaned forward a bit further, gripping the banister, and opened her mouth to call out to him, to bring him back to her, when she saw him lift his left arm in a sudden sweeping gesture and crash all the chess pieces across the board and off the desk and onto the floor. And then, while her mouth was still open and her voice stuck dry in her throat, he pushed a button on the monitor and the light on the screen went out, leaving them all in the sudden dark.

"Where's Daddy?" Polly said.

She had been to tea with her friend Zoe, and was, in consequence, not in the least interested in her supper. It lay

263

in front of her, on the plate she preferred, bright and appetizing and untouched.

"At work," Nathalie said.

Polly picked her fork up and inserted it down the neck of her T-shirt.

"Why?"

"Because there's a lot to do, I expect."

Polly patted her lumpy front.

"Look."

"I'd rather look at you eating."

Polly sighed.

"We had tea at Zoe's house."

"One day," Nathalie said, "you'll learn what it feels like to carefully make supper for someone who couldn't, in return, care less."

"My fork's stuck—"

Nathalie put a hand briefly to her face.

"Get down and shake it out then."

"And *stay* down?"

"Polly," Nathalie said, "if you don't eat now, there will be no more food until the morning. Did you hear that? No more food."

Polly's expression declared that the threat was a matter of absolute indifference to her. She bent sideways and pulled the fork out of one leg of her shorts.

"Will you play with me?"

"No," Nathalie said.

"Why?"

"Because I want to do some thinking."

"Why?"

"Because my mind is full of things that need sorting out."

Polly eyed her.

"You're quite dull."

"I expect so."

Polly flipped the fork in the air so that it clattered across the table.

"I'll be in my bedroom," she said grandly. "Waiting for Daddy."

Nathalie went round the table and picked up Polly's supper plate. She remembered the long-ago days, the before-Polly days, when the only children she knew were Ellen and Daniel, and how she had thought of them as representative children, because they were all she knew, just as she had thought of love and motherhood and parenthood within the parameters of familiarity. Watching Ellen and Daniel eat their wholesome suppers had been as emblematic of an aspect of family life as watching Lynne and Ralph get into their car together had been emblematic of a certain kind of married habit. It amazed her, looking back, how much she had accepted, how much she had never thought to examine, or question, or try to see through. It horrified her to think how cowardly she had been.

Well, there was no opportunity for cowardice now. She had traveled to Northsea, she had spent six or seven hours in her mother's company, she had slept the night—no, not slept, *passed*—the night in a strange guest house, and had brought back with her a new and fragile cargo of reactions and emotions that were taking more courage to unpack than she could ever have imagined.

"I don't know what to think," she'd said to David on the telephone. "I mean, I felt lost before, but this is different. I don't know where my mind is going."

"Yes," he said. "Yes." He'd sounded distant, she thought, almost as if he wasn't listening.

"I don't want to be let down," Nathalie said. "I don't want to find that that phone call was the high moment."

"What phone call?"

"That first one," Nathalie said, "that first one, when she was crying."

"No," he said, "of course not."

Nathalie scraped Polly's supper into the bin. She hadn't

265

rung David since then. She hadn't had the inclination. It was amazing, disconcerting, but she hadn't really felt that she could, that, if she did, he'd be listening. And even if he was listening, as he always had, she wasn't quite sure that she could describe what she now felt to him, could make him see the confusion and awkwardness and affection and guilt and shame and disappointment that had been jostling about together in her mind and heart since she had stepped down off that train and said to herself, with a cry of silent dismay, "This is my *mother*."

She put Polly's plate down, and bent over her balled fists on the kitchen counter. Cora had been sweet, very sweet. Nathalie was absolutely certain that Cora's sweetness of nature was something she would defend to her dying day. Cora was sweet and affectionate and humble and appealing. But—and why did this have to be the but Nathalie had never considered?—she wasn't what you would think of, for a mother. She was too uncertain for motherhood, too childlike, too submissive and stubborn all at once, too simple, too—too *odd*. When she told Nathalie about the party, about the sailor, about the Salvation Army home for unmarried mothers, about the Child Welfare Officer who took the baby away, Nathalie could see all that. She could see the schoolgirl, see the terror and the oppression, see the bullying mother, see the despair of knowing one had neither voice nor weight in the matter. But what she couldn't see was Cora as a mother. All she could see was herself, standing on that platform, sitting at that coffee-shop table, lying in that inhospitable bed, thinking, It's not her. It can't be.

And, what was worse, what was haunting her, was seeing that Cora could see too, could see what she was thinking.

"Sorry," Nathalie whispered now to her fists. "*Sorry*."

She raised one up and pushed it into her eye socket. Then the other. If she pushed hard enough, she could obliterate images with blocks of violent color. There came to her, as there had been beginning to come to her, ever since she had returned, a desire to tell Steve how she felt, a need to lay all this complicated, contradictory, not entirely proud-making stuff out in front of the boy from the Royal Oak, the boy who didn't feel he belonged where he'd begun either, and have him tell her that he understood, that to become something is not necessarily a betrayal of what came before, that love means acceptance but not, by obligation, emulation. She took her fists away from her eyes. She wanted Steve to give her permission, the permission he'd had to award himself so painfully, in such a solitary way, unhelped by her, to be the person she felt she truly was, mother or no mother.

"What time is it?" Polly said from the doorway.

"You tell me."

Polly leaned in the doorframe and stared at the clock.

"Half-past eight."

"Seven. Bathtime."

Polly transferred her stare to her mother.

"Where's Daddy?"

There were thirty young oaks to be planted, thirty tall, slender, expensive young oaks imported from Holland, with their huge root balls carefully wrapped in specialist bubbled plastic. David had explained to the owner of this field, which was being gradually landscaped into a park, that the oaks should ideally be planted while still dormant, but the owner, who was disinclined to heed advice that conflicted with his wishes, in this case to have an avenue planted before midsummer, had instructed the planting to go ahead. So David, plus two men and a digger, was making a long double line of huge holes and wondering, not for the first time, if this kind of work was bringing him the pleasure it once had, or even that he had supposed it would. You could stay interested in trees, of course, but maybe that was the trouble, maybe you swung, over time, so much on to the trees' side that you could only see the people who wanted them planted in avenues leading to specially dug lakes as the enemy.

He got down off the digger and went over to where he had slung his jacket on the grass to find a bottle of water. From the direction of the house across the rough grass, someone was approaching, no doubt the owner who was, David reflected sourly, the kind of man who would wait until you had dug thirty holes big enough to drop a small car into before saying that he wanted them another foot apart. David found his water bottle and, affecting not to have noticed the approaching figure, turned his back towards it to drink, as if thoughtfully contemplating the prospect down towards the lake.

"David," someone said.

He turned, holding the plastic bottle. Martin Latimer stood there, in jeans and a T-shirt and absolutely black dark glasses.

"What are you doing here?"

"They said I'd find you here—"

"Who did?"

"At your office. I went to your office. I said I was a new customer."

David capped the water bottle and threw it down on the ground.

"This isn't a good moment, Martin."

"It won't take long."

"Why didn't you telephone?"

Martin put his hands in his jeans pockets. He was wearing a sort of zipped pouch round his waist like a skiing bumbag.

"This isn't—something ordinary, something you arrange—"

David looked across at the digger. Andy and Mick were standing by it, waiting.

"Keep going," David shouted. "I'll be ten minutes."

"Five," Martin said.

"Five," David said heavily, "five. Sure it was worth your coming?"

Martin took his hands out of his pockets and pushed his sunglasses up on top of his head.

"Yes."

David began to walk away across the field.

"Did she send you?"

"Who?"

"Carole."

"Oh," Martin said, and then with emphasis, "*Mum*. No, she didn't."

"She's been to meet my wife."

"I know. And it's the last time."

David stopped walking.

"What?"

Martin pushed his glasses back down.

"We don't want you."

David said nothing.

"We don't want anything more to do with you," Martin said. "We don't want any more contact. Not my mother or father or brother or me."

David glanced at him.

"Who sent you?"

"No one."

"Who knows you've come?"

"None of your business."

"Why," David said, "do you feel so threatened?"

"I don't. I just don't want you around. We don't need you. We don't want you." He took a small step nearer David. "What do you want, anyway? You've seen her, you've got your pathetic story. What more do you want?"

"If I stay away," David said, "you won't feel any better."

Martin's chin went out.

"I will. I feel better already."

"Already?"

"Yes," Martin said.

"Well, good—"

"My mother had three children," Martin said. "Three sons."

"Yes."

"Two she chose to keep. *Chose* to keep. You weren't one of those two."

David took a quick breath. The impulse—which he was sure his Canadian brothers-in-law would competently have obeyed—to flatten Martin was almost overwhelming.

"You pathetic little *jerk*—"

"She didn't want you," Martin said. "She didn't want you then and she doesn't want you now."

David began to run clumsily away from him across the grass. When he got to the digger, Andy and Mick were leaning against it, Mick thoughtfully rolling a cigarette.

"Move," David shouted.

They looked up at him, slow, astonished and normal.

"Move!" David yelled again. "Move! Get back to fucking *work*!"

CHAPTER EIGHTEEN

"Look," Meera said, "it's not worth crying over."
Justine put her chin up and sniffed.
"I'm not crying."
"No man's worth humiliating yourself over."
"But I've done it," Justine said, "I've already done it. Haven't I? I *am* humiliated."
Meera began to order things on her desk, picking up paper clips, parking her computer mouse tidily on its mat.
"You don't have to *show* it," Meera said.
"You mean you wouldn't—"
"We're not all made the same," Meera said. She flicked her hair behind her shoulders. "Maybe I'll never feel as much as you do. Maybe I'm just not made for it."
Justine leaned across Meera's desk to twitch a tissue out of her box.
"I didn't want to. I didn't like myself. I didn't like *him*, even—"
"No."
"You think I'm pathetic—"
"Only if you let it get to you. Only if you let it affect your decisions, what's right for you."
Justine blew her nose.
"What should I do now?"
"You don't take my advice," Meera said. "You never have. Why should I waste any more on you?"

"Sorry—"

"I think everyone in this office has gone mental recently. Mental. In fact I'm wondering whether to stay."

Justine's eyes opened wide.

"Not stay!"

The door to the staircase opened, revealing Titus.

Meera glanced at him and said, a little more loudly, "I'm thinking about it."

"About what?" Titus said, advancing.

"Never you mind," Meera said, "I was talking to Justine." She picked up her handbag.

Titus looked at Justine.

He said, "I don't suppose she'll talk to me."

Justine said nothing.

"You look awful," Meera said. "You both do."

"No change there then," Titus said, still looking at Justine.

Meera put out a hand and lightly touched Justine's arm.

"Will you be OK?"

Justine nodded.

"Sure?"

"I'm too beaten up," Titus said, "to be a trouble to anybody."

"Do you want to come with me?" Meera said to Justine.

Justine looked up. She glanced at Titus.

Then she said, "In a minute."

"OK then," Meera said. "If you're sure. Bye, then."

They watched her go, and the staircase door shut decisively behind her.

"I keep," Titus said, "feeling that there's no further shit to feel like, and then I feel like more."

"Yes."

Titus turned and sat down heavily in Meera's desk chair. He said, "She's gone."

"Who has?"

"Sasha," Titus said. "She's just gone."

"What do you mean, gone—"

"I went round to Della's," Titus said, "and Della said she went on Tuesday. Tuesday night. After I'd seen her."

Justine leaned on Meera's desk.

"Rubbish. People don't do that, except in soap operas, they don't just *go*, they can't, they have to arrange stuff—"

"She's gone," Titus said. "Her room is empty except for that Japanese girl picture. She's paid Della, and she's gone."

"Well, find her—"

Titus tipped his head back and closed his eyes.

"She doesn't want me."

"She might, when she's calmed down a bit—"

"No."

Justine straightened up.

She said, too quickly, "Now you know how it feels."

There was a pause. Titus raised his head and slowly opened his eyes.

"Sorry."

She shrugged. He sat a bit further upright.

He said, "I suppose—" and stopped.

"Well, don't," Justine said.

"Maybe, in time, if there isn't Sasha—"

"No."

"Babe—"

"I'm leaving too," Justine said.

"What?"

"I've decided," Justine said. She put her hand up to the wisps of hair on her neck, and twisted some. "I'm going."

"Does Steve know?"

"Not yet."

Titus stood up.

"Where'll you go?"

"I don't know yet—"

"Babe, don't go till you've got another job, don't go just because of me—"

She looked away.

"It's got nothing to do with you."

"That," Titus said, "*really* depresses me."

"Don't make me laugh," Justine said desperately. "Don't make me like you."

He reached forward and put a hand on her arm.

"Stay—"

She jerked her arm away.

"Don't."

"Sorry. It's just that I'm so bloody miserable."

She looked at him hard. Her eyes were full of tears.

"Yes," she said furiously. "*Yes.*"

When Marnie was small, and her parents weren't getting on too well, her father used to clear out the basement. It never looked much different when he'd finished, except all the lumber would be piled in a different corner, and the boys' pool table would be cleared of boxes, and the little thick glass window, through which you could see the pilot light for the furnace, would have been polished. After he'd been crashing about down there for a few hours, her father would come upstairs to take a shower, and then he'd put a gun in the back of his pickup and roar off to the cottage and Marnie's mother would glance up from whatever work she was doing—she was always doing work then—and ask someone to bring her some coffee. It was only years later, long after Marnie's parents had divorced, and her mother had married Lal, who was a philosophy professor and more than her intellectual makeweight, and Marnie had had a row with her mother about her choice of career and her decision to go to England, that she found herself, almost without meaning to be, down in the basement hurling broken lampshades and splitting boxes of out-of-date academic magazines into a pile to be put out for the trash.

It had occurred to her then to call her father. He'd gone to live near Halifax, to lead the kind of practical outdoor life that suited him, with a woman called Sandie who believed in self-sufficiency. Once he'd gone to Halifax, it didn't seem to cross his mind to come west again, even to see his children, but if he was called, he sounded both delighted and interested, and Marnie would picture him in a checked shirt and overalls, standing in his rural kitchen, smiling with real affection into the telephone. She pictured him saying, "You do what you have to do, hon," so vividly that she did indeed call him, and he answered on an early mobile telephone—he'd always been interested in technology—from his pickup, and said, "Now, hon, if it's what's in your heart to do, and England is the place to do it, you go do it in England."

Now, nearly twenty years later, sitting on the kitchen floor with, as a basement-clearing substitute, the contents of the tin and pan cupboard strewn around her, her father came into her mind again. He'd had a hip operation but was back at home now, being nursed by Sandie, and so it would be perfectly possible to call to ask how he was, and then just gradually let the call slide into telling him that she seemed to have lost her way, and that all the clarity of purpose and intention that had guided her for almost forty years had become blurred in the last few months, and that she had never felt so foreign in this land which had been her home now for almost half her life.

She couldn't quite imagine what her father would say. Anything too philosophical, or metaphysical, unsettled him and made him tense and anxious, as life with her mother had done. But she knew he not only had her real welfare at heart, but was also not temperamentally inclined to judge. Were she to ring her mother—so mellowed now, so relaxed by living with Lal who saw no merit in a life that was exclusively a life of the mind—her mother might be sympathetic, might be ready with advice, but there would always be, at the back of everything she said, the unspoken admonishment that as Marnie had chosen, deliberately, this bed of an English life, and marriage to an Englishman, she now had to lie on it.

Marnie sighed. She picked up a muffin tin and shook the dried corpses of two daddy-long-legs out of it. From the family room came the strains of the theme tune from *Thomas the Tank Engine*, which meant that Petey had eluded his nap—and she had been so certain he would sleep, after his swim group—and his room, and had come downstairs to watch a video. It was incredible to Marnie that he had no fear of being caught, and reprimanded. His purpose was always so focused, and so steely, that it plainly overrode, obliterated, all that he knew—he *knew*—about the consequences of forbidden actions. You could talk all the child psychology you liked, comfort yourself with the knowledge that this two-year-old behavior was unlikely to translate into similar twenty-year-old behavior, but nothing helped the exhausting and sometimes frightening business of dealing with Petey, day in, day out, *now*.

Wearily, Marnie put the muffin tin down and got to her feet. At the same moment, the front door opened, and then slammed, followed by the sound of Petey's feet running into the hall.

"Hi there," David said to him. "How're you doing?"

He appeared in the kitchen doorway holding Petey in his arms. He looked at the floor.

"Going to make a cake?"

Marnie looked at the clutter round her feet.

"I was thinking of calling my father."

David set Petey on the floor.

"I don't get the connection—"

"No," Marnie said, "you wouldn't. It isn't a connection to anyone but me." She glanced up. "You're home early."

"Yes."

"Something wrong?"

David ruffled Petey's hair.

"I just had enough."

"Yes," Marnie said. "It's a hard feeling."

Petey leaned against his father's leg.

"Bic?"

"No, he may not," Marnie said. "He didn't stay in bed."

"I climbed," Petey said truthfully.

"And now," Marnie said, making a move towards the door, "I am going to unplug that television."

David leaned to try and catch her arm.

"Could he watch it?"

"No."

"Ten minutes?" David said. "I want to say something."

"Oh please—"

"No," David said, "not another thunderbolt."

Marnie swallowed. She looked down at Petey. He looked back, calm and unconcerned.

"Till the end of this video."

They watched him trot out of the room, back to the television.

"The others were never this—this willfully disobedient. They wanted to please me. They wanted to get it right."

"Maybe," David said, "you were different."

"Let's not make something else my fault, huh?"

"I didn't mean—"

Marnie kicked a cake tin.

"What do we do with the possible theory, then, that I was a more able mother when I worked than I am when I don't?"

David picked his way towards her among the pans and put his arms round her. She stiffened.

He said, "I came home to talk to you."

She closed her eyes. It was almost unbearable that he should think he could claim her full attention, from whatever else was preoccupying her, simply by putting his arms round her. It was even more unbearable because it was true.

He held her a little tighter.

"I want to say some things," he said against the side of her head, "that I can't say to anyone else."

She held her breath. If she didn't, she knew she would say, "Nathalie?" in a tone of voice whose neutrality she couldn't guarantee.

"Not even Nathalie," David said. "Not now."

Marnie let her breath go.

She said, "Do you want me to make some coffee? Do you want to sit somewhere more comfortable?"

"No."

She relaxed a little. She felt him adjust his hold on her, moving his arms until they were behind her shoulders.

He said, "Marnie, I am so tired of all this going back."

She didn't move. She opened her eyes and looked into the buff brushed cotton of his rolled-up workshirt sleeve. Then she looked down his arm a little to that fine tracery of scars, like the veins on a leaf, scars she'd always known about and never, for some reason, mentioned. She brought her hand up and laid a finger on his skin.

"Not back to this," she said.

He took a tiny breath.

"Never to that."

She took her finger away.

He said, "You knew."

"Yes."

She felt him sigh.

She added, "It doesn't matter, my knowing."

He said, "It's a relief. Like—like not having to keep going back to the past is a relief. It's—it's being freed from something because—well, I haven't just been doing it the last few months, you see. It might look like that to you, but I now know I've done it always, I've always been conscious of the gaps and the questions, I've always had this where-do-I-come-from stuff at the back of my mind. Now that I know some answers, I realize how much I needed to know them. I mayn't like some of them much, but I know them."

"OK," Marnie whispered.

He took his cheek away from her hair.

He said, "I never realized, you see, that just going on living wasn't going to take me away from my past. I thought it would, I thought it had to, that time would just sort of cover it over, after a while. But it didn't. It didn't just take me somewhere else, it just kept taking me back to my childhood, back to all those things I didn't know. And that place, that childhood place, was the one place I didn't want to be."

He bent his head a little lower.

He said softly, "Do you get me?"

She nodded. He moved a hand behind her to hold her pigtail.

He said, "I have no regrets about finding Carole. I feel kind of sorry for her. I don't even seem to mind that she couldn't really love me because I wasn't the one she wanted. Maybe I ought to mind, but I don't."

Marnie raised her head a little.

She said clearly, "Lynne loved you."

"Yes," David said, and then, after a pause, without any anxiety or questioning in his voice, "And you do."

She nodded again, pulling her plait free of his grasp.

He said, "Maybe, if your mother can't love you, you're never very certain of your own lovableness. Maybe you don't quite know how to *do* love, even if you'd like to."

Marnie took a small step back, freeing her arms. She raised them and rested them on David's shoulders.

"I think your mother would have liked to love you now," she said. "But it's too late. She's trapped."

"And so is Martin."

"Martin?"

"He came. He came and found me at work. He came to tell me that none of them wanted another thing to do with me."

"Oh David—"

"He told me that she'd had a choice of three sons, and had only chosen two—"

"How dare he—"

"Because he's unhappy. He's not sure of her. He wanted me to think he'd come as a family deputation, but I think he just came because he couldn't stand not to."

279

"Poor, sad guy."

"Yes."

Marnie looked up at him. She moved one hand so that she could touch his neck with her forefinger.

"David—"

"Yes?"

"Nathalie—"

"She's had a hard time," David said. "I get the feeling she got even harder answers than I did, less straightforward."

"That's not what I meant."

"No."

"I meant—" She stopped and took her hands off David's shoulders. Then she put them flat on his chest and regarded them sternly, as if something important was written on the backs of them. She said, "Why have you said all this stuff to me and not to her?"

"Because you are the right person."

"Even if I almost never have been before?"

"That was part of the problem," David said, "the being stuck in the past problem. She was stuck there with me."

Marnie said hesitantly, "Is—is something rather amazing happening?"

"I don't know. I don't know about the amazing, I mean. I hope so. But I do know about the happening."

The door to the garden swung open. Daniel, fresh from school, stood there carrying his bookbag and wearing his cycling helmet. He looked at his parents.

"What's going on?"

They said nothing. He dropped his bag on the step, and came further into the kitchen. He looked at all the cake tins on the floor.

He said, "Is it someone's birthday?"

Fifty yards ahead of them, Polly was pedaling furiously on her Barbie bicycle. She had refused to let Steve detach the stabilizers, just as she had refused, during her swimming lessons, to remove her armbands. Steve could see her clearly, curls flying, riding with purpose straight down the center of the main asphalt path in Westerham Park. Boys on boards and blades and mini-scooters were swooping respectfully round her in a way, Steve thought, that could only, when she was older and more vulnerable, end in tears or triumph.

It was easier, he was finding, to focus on Polly than on Nathalie. Nathalie, who had never been very demonstrative, was holding his arm, actually closely linked to him, leaning on him, her head occasionally turning towards him, so that her hair brushed his shoulder. She had taken his arm as soon as they entered the park, and she was talking to him as she had been talking the last few days, earnestly and confidingly, as if he, instead of being the man she happened to live with who also happened to lack the required degree of emotional intelligence, had been transformed into a soulmate, into the kind of person who would, uniquely, understand the complexity and conflict of emotion that she was currently going through.

It was, Steve thought, feeling the pressure of her arm through the cotton of his shirtsleeve, agony. He felt terrible, awful, base. He could hear her talking on about Cora, about motherhood, about the long painful journey to reconciliation with self, however disappointing, and could sense, in the way she was talking, that not only did she want him to understand her and comfort her, but also that she knew he would, because he could, because he had suffered a similar disillusionment, a similar feeling of not being perfectly matched to his actual beginnings. She was talking in a way, in fact, that he would have sold his soul for, up to a week or so ago, a way that he had longed for her to talk to him, a way he had jealously feared, all the years they had been together, that she had reserved exclusively for David. And now here it was, pouring out of her, sweet and confiding, and he had put himself in a place where he was, quite simply, too grubby to receive it. He looked ahead at Polly on her pink bicycle and longed, with a childish anguish, to change places with her.

"Do you know something," Nathalie said. "Do you know something really unexpected? It's—it's how humbling this has all been, how it's made me feel I made myself a tragedy queen I'd no right to be. I mean, I sort of saw myself—awful to admit it—as the center of the world, I saw a kind of *glamour* in my situation, a kind of pathos. And now I know Cora's story, I feel terrible about that, I feel that what she's been through in terms of loneliness and being just, well, *forgotten* is ten times worse than anything that's happened to me. And then I feel worse because I can't see her as my mother. I can see her as a sweet person who got caught up in something she didn't intend in a million years, and has been paying for it ever since, and I feel desperately sorry for her. But I can't feel that sort of blood link I expected to feel, that I feel for Polly—"

"Look at Polly," Steve said, interrupting.

Nathalie looked. Then she looked at Steve.

"Aren't you listening?"

"Yes—"

"Aren't you interested? I thought, I really thought you were interested—"

"I am. I *am*."

"I expect I'm repeating myself. I mean, you do that, don't you, while you work stuff out—"

"Nathalie—"

"What?"

Steve stopped walking. He looked at the sky.

He said, "It isn't that."

"Well, what?"

"I'm deeply interested in what you're saying. I'm really concerned, I love having you talk to me like this, I've longed for you to talk to me like this—" He stopped.

Nathalie slid her arm out of his and took his hand. "What's the matter?"

Steve could feel tears coming.

He said with difficulty, "I can't let you. I can't let you talk like this. I can't let you be so—so—*trusting*—"

"Why not? What's the matter?"

Steve pulled his hand out of hers and turned his back on her. His head was bent.

He said, as inaudibly as possible, "I've had an affair."

"What?"

He raised his head a little.

He said again, not turning, "I've had an affair."

There was a silence, an apparently interminable and complicated silence. And then Nathalie walked round him until she could see his face.

"An affair?"

"Yes."

He couldn't look at her. He could see her face, so close to his, and he stared just past it, just past her ear and a dark cloud of her hair.

"Why?" Nathalie said in a kind of whispered shriek.

He shook his head.

"I was lonely."

"Lonely?"

"I didn't think I was of any account to you. I didn't think I was enough for you—"

"An affair," Nathalie said, with horror.

"I'm so sorry, so *sorry*—"

"Who was she?"

"You know."

"No, I don't. Who—oh my God," Nathalie said. "Not her, not Titus's girlfriend, not that pseudo—"

"Yes," Steve said.

Nathalie took a step back and put her hands to her face. "Why *now*—"

"It was because of now. And it's over."

Nathalie said nothing.

"It's over," Steve said. "I slept with her once, and it's over. I ended it and she's gone."

Nathalie took her hands away. She looked straight at him.

"It's over?"

"Yes. I promise. And it was never to do with love, never, ever to do with love—"

"Over—"

"Yes."

"For you," Nathalie said. Her eyes were huge. "For you, maybe. But can't you see, for me, it's only just beginning?" And then she turned away from him and began to run down the path towards Polly and her bicycle.

CHAPTER NINETEEN

"Do you need a Scotch or something?" David said. Steve shook his head.

"It doesn't seem to make any difference. But thank you."

"A pint, then."

"Yes—"

"I'll get it," David said. "You stay there. I'll get it."

Steve watched him walk away across the pub and then, as big men so often seem so peacefully able to do, through the crowd at the bar to a place directly opposite the bartender. He thought, shamefacedly, that even if he'd had the collectedness of wit to offer to get the drinks first he might not have made it to the bar, might, quite simply, not have been able to walk across that floor with David watching him, David knowing what he had done, David knowing and then doing something he had almost never done in all the years they had known each other—telephoning and suggesting a drink.

"A drink—" Steve had said, as if David had suggested a trip to the moon. "With—with you?"

"Why not?"

Steve had shifted his mobile against his ear. Nathalie had been round to see David and Marnie the night before, had been gone hours and had then returned and made it plain that, for the third night, she preferred Steve to sleep on the sofa in the sitting room.

"Because—"

"What?"

"Nathalie saw you last night—"

"This isn't about Nathalie. Or, only peripherally about Nathalie. It is, in fact, something I would rather tell you than tell Nathalie. I would rather *you* told Nathalie."

"OK," Steve said uncertainly.

"Good," David had said. "Good. The Seven Tuns at lunchtime."

And now here he was, on a padded bench covered in exactly the kind of harsh velour fabric favored by his father for the Royal Oak, being bought a pint by David.

"There," David said, setting it down.

"Thanks—"

David sat down on a chair opposite Steve, and hitched it closer.

"Look," David said, "let's get this over with. Last night, when Nathalie came. We're very sorry, but we're not getting involved. It's for you guys to sort out."

"I thought," Steve said, "that you'd want to call me all the names I've been calling myself."

"Nope."

"Didn't she—"

"She didn't call you names, either. She's shocked, but she isn't calling you names."

Steve gave his glass a nudge.

He said, "*I'm* shocked—"

"I bet."

"And ashamed."

David said nothing. He leaned forward and put his elbows on his knees.

"And now," Steve said, "as of this morning, it looks as if my entire workforce is walking out."

David glanced up sharply.

"What's the matter with them? Titus you'd understand—"

"Justine because of Titus, and Meera because she says I

286

am not concentrating on the business and I mind most about her because she's right."

"She looks to me the kind of girl who is usually right."

"She's brilliant. She'll be impossible to replace. But do I want to replace her? Do I want to replace any of them? Do I—"

"Look," David said, "I don't want to seem unsympathetic, but that's exactly what I wanted to talk to you about."

"My business?"

"Mine," David said.

Steve picked up his beer and put it down again.

"You're not in trouble, surely—"

"It's doing fine," David said. "It's not growing like it was, but it's OK. I like it, but I don't love it, not anymore. I'm going to sell it."

Steve looked startled.

"Sell it!"

"Yes," David said, "because we're going to Canada."

"You always go to Canada—"

"I mean go to Canada for good."

Steve leaned back and let out a breath.

"Wow."

"All this family stuff," David said, "the way it's turned out, this finding my mother, and then a brother who wants to murder me, and realizing my name isn't my name, and putting Marnie through it all, well, it's sort of made me feel I've got to start again somewhere. I've got the answers now, I've got the knowledge, I can start with those, I can live somewhere where people only know me with those."

Steve said, "Will you change your name?"

"I might."

"To your father's name?"

David shrugged. "Maybe. Or it may be too late—"

"Will you try and find your father?"

"Maybe that, too."

"I think—I see what you're doing."

"No conjecture anymore," David said, "no wondering. No walking down a street having fantasies that this mythical mother might have walked down it before. She didn't. She's Carole Latimer, and she never came to Westerham."

"But why Canada?"

"Think about it," David said. "Think about living in Winnipeg and just being accepted, quite easily, as the person I *actually* am, without having to lug all the adoption baggage round with me. My parents have names. I have a name. I have wonderful adoptive parents but they live in England so that dynamic can actually, thankfully, stay in England. It gets simple, at last, it gets straightforward at last, it gets *honest*."

"Yes."

"And Marnie gets to go home."

"Yes."

"And perhaps I will find, in a way, that I've gone home too."

Steve looked at him.

"And if it doesn't work?"

"What do you mean, not work?"

"What if you don't like it," Steve said. "What if you aren't happy?"

David looked back.

He said, "Have you been listening?"

"I think so—"

"What have I just said about the way my life has been? How can Canada be *any*thing other than better than that?"

Steve glanced down.

"I bet the kids are thrilled."

"They don't know yet."

"And—and you want me to tell Nathalie."

"Yes."

"Why don't you tell her yourself?"

"Why do you think?"

"Because you don't want to be the one to upset her further—"

"No," David said. He picked up his beer glass again. "Because I can't be there for her anymore. And you can."

Steve said nothing. Then he glanced away across the room, towards the comfortable crowd by the bar.

"Suppose I can't," he said. "Suppose I've blown it."

David drank his beer, then held the glass and looked down into it.

"Then you'll have to think again. Just like I have."

In ten minutes or so, Betty would knock on Cora's door, and say tea was ready. Often, in the past, when she hadn't got classes to teach, Cora would go into the kitchen and try to help with slicing onions and peeling carrots, even though she never did it quite the way Betty would have liked. She'd be given an apron and a board and a knife just as if, she thought, she was a good child, and then be set a task at the table with Betty watching, alert to the inevitable disappointment of Cora's performance. But lately, since Nathalie's visit, Cora hadn't felt like too much time in the kitchen, too much time alone with Betty who was as congenitally incapable as their mother had been of keeping the smallest thing that was on her mind to herself. And as none of the opinions that Betty currently—and strongly—held coincided with Cora's, it was better, really, to stay out of the way unless Don was in the room to neutralize things, to say, "You leave her now, Betty, you just let her alone."

Well, she was alone. But, contrary to Betty's insistence that she was desperate in her loneliness, she was not, in her own view, any more alone than she'd ever been. She suspected that some people were just like that, alone all their lives, with this odd sense of not quite belonging, not quite fitting in. It wasn't particularly painful, once you got used to it; it was just a state of being that people who needed close communication with other people would never understand. In fact, Cora sometimes wondered if, had the opportunity for close communication with someone ever come up, had she ever surrendered to any of the offers made by Betty's paying guests, she would have liked it at all. At least with herself, she knew who she was, she was in a place of familiarity and control. How must it feel, then, to embark on unknown human terrain, to take chances and make bargains and compromises? How must it feel to give up—be required to give up—the ultimate freedom of self?

Anyway, if she was truthful, she hadn't expected any change in the alone department when she met Nathalie. She might have made her little shrine, and pored fascinatedly over those photographs, but she had never deluded herself that she'd be embarking on some fabled episode of happy families. Meeting Nathalie had been about something quite different, about the unspeakable relief and comfort to be derived from realizing that she was forgiven, that Nathalie wasn't angry or resentful of the past, that Nathalie had managed to salvage something out of a life which had started so wretchedly. It was so difficult to make her see that she'd never had any idea of playing mother and daughter, of trying to retrieve what was lost and gone forever.

The trouble was—and Betty, ever lynx-eyed, had pounced upon this—that the meeting hadn't been easy. It hadn't been exactly difficult, but it had been undeniably awkward. It was inevitable, when she thought about it, that there'd be a tension between their blood bond and their differing ways of life, but it wasn't until she saw Nathalie, and heard her voice, and watched the way she sat and drank her coffee, that she realized that courtesies were going to have to substitute for candors. Nathalie hadn't put a foot wrong, but she hadn't relaxed either. When the door of the guest house where Cora had booked her a room closed behind her that evening, Cora knew that Nathalie was relieved to be alone, and so was she. She might be hurt, in the way you can't help being if you feel you've made a bit of a fool of yourself, but she was also free to go back to her room where she lived not just with the inside of her own head, but also with baby Samantha. And that, she knew, was where the pain lay, the pain that had to be faced and dealt with. It didn't really lie with Nathalie and her southern ways, or only obliquely; it lay with the realization that baby Samantha, idealized, lost and precious, was, in hard, cold reality, no more. She supposed that this was how you felt if you lost your faith. If, indeed, you'd ever had one.

Betty's fist crashed on the bedroom door.

"Tea's ready!"

Cora stayed where she was, sitting on her bed.

Betty turned the door handle and looked in.

"I don't like to see you brooding."

"I'm not brooding," Cora said. "I'm thinking."

Betty came further into the room.

"Same thing—"

"I'm not *resentful*," Cora said. "I'm not wishing what happened *hadn't* happened. I'm just thinking about it."

Betty stood in front of her.

"What'll you do now?"

Cora gave a little shrug.

"Nothing."

"Has she rung you?"

"Once," Cora said, "to tell me that she's safely back and Polly's having her ear done on the twenty-seventh."

Betty gave a little snort.

"That all?"

Cora glared at her.

"What d'you expect her to talk to me about? The weather? The television?"

"You know exactly what I mean."

"I'm not expecting anything," Cora said. "I got what I wanted and I'm not looking for anything more."

"Good."

"Why good—"

"Because," Betty said, holding out a hand as a signal for Cora to get up, "you can now start accepting that it's over."

Cora looked with distaste at Betty's hand.

"Over—"

"Yes," Betty said. Her voice had a ring of finality to it. "Yes. Chapter closed. At *last*."

Lynne stood by her kitchen sink, waiting for the tap to run really cold. Looking through the window above the sink, she could see Nathalie just where she had left her when she'd said she'd come in and get them both a drink, sitting on the bench by the lilac bush, staring in front of her.

"I don't need a drink," Nathalie had said.

Lynne put a hand on her arm.

"You do, dear. You've been crying."

Nathalie had turned a wan smile on her.

"You always say that. You always did, when we'd been crying. D'you suppose a drink will fill up our tear ducts?"

Lynne had put elderflower cordial and ice cubes in two tumblers. It was a silly gesture, she knew, making a drink, but her instincts always drove her to the consolingly practical and, in any case, she'd needed a moment in the kitchen to collect herself, to steady her mind in the face of Nathalie's wild, tearful claim, made only minutes before, that the two most important men in her life had betrayed her, Steve by sleeping with this Sasha girl, and David by going to Canada for good.

"How could he?" Nathalie had wailed. "How could he do it? And how could David leave me?"

It had occurred to Lynne to point out that she was as much affected by David's departure as Nathalie was, but with an enormous effort of will, she had restrained herself.

"I can't believe it," Nathalie said. "I can't believe they

could *both* do this to me. And in this *conspiracy*. David telling Steve to tell me—"

Lynne picked up the tumblers one by one, and held them under the tap. There was so much, it seemed, to feel at the moment, so many conflicting things that it was hard to know what was uppermost. Her own shock and dismay at David's news and Steve's infidelity had, after all, come hard on the heels of an exquisite relief at the outcome of David and Nathalie meeting their mothers. It was—as it so often was, she reflected—yet more evidence of life only allowing you to have something you longed for if it took away something equally important simultaneously, as compensation. She put the tumblers on a tray and looked at a packet of salted almonds. If she put those on the tray too, Nathalie would tell her that eating was no cure for emotional torment. Her hand hovered a moment, and then left the nuts where they were.

She carried the tray out into the garden and set it down on the table that Ralph had made years ago, when eating outside had graduated from what you did on the beach to something you might stylishly do any fine day of the year.

"He hardly knew her," Nathalie said, turning her head away to look down the length of the garden. "I mean, what does that say? What kind of man goes to bed with someone he hardly knows?"

Lynne took a breath. She pushed a tumbler towards Nathalie.

She said, in a voice whose firmness quite surprised her, "In Steve's case, a bewildered and unhappy man."

Nathalie's head whipped round.

"What do you mean?"

"He couldn't get through to you. None of us could. You were going on this mission, and whatever effect it had on anyone round you, you weren't going to stop."

Nathalie stared at her mother.

"Are you saying that Steve screwing around was *my* fault?"

293

Lynne picked up her drink.

"There's no need to use that disgusting language to me."

"Oh, for God's sake—"

"But if you want my view, dear, you didn't exactly drive him to it, of course you didn't, but you gave him a very strong impression that you didn't want him, that you didn't need him. You'd got David and you'd got this mission, and you didn't need anyone else."

"So in your opinion, that excuses screwing around?"

Lynne put her glass down. She turned and looked full at Nathalie.

"As he appears to have slept with the girl once, and feels terrible about it, I would say yes."

"And what would you know about such things?"

"Enough," Lynne said crossly, "to try and get you off your silly high horse."

Nathalie took a breath. "Stop it—"

"I'm not afraid of you, dear," Lynne said. "I have been, in the past, but I'm not now. You've had terrible things happen to you but you've had wonderful things happen too. I haven't helped in the past, either, I know, because I was so insecure about a lot of things, but *all* this, the last few months, has made me feel a bit better about life in general. I know I can't lose you now, however angry you are with me, and if I can't lose you even if you won't speak to me, I can get on with loving you without worrying."

Nathalie stared at her.

"Of course," Lynne said, "I'd like to punish Steve for what he's done. Just like I'd like David not to have married a Canadian, so he hasn't got this option. But even more, I'd like to see you really take stock of what you've got, and make something of it."

Nathalie was still staring.

Hardly moving her lips, she said, "Like what?"

294

Lynne shifted. She smoothed the front of her overshirt, aligning the buttons.

"Well," she said, "you could start by seeing that what Steve did was wrong but part of what you did was wrong too. You don't betray people just by sleeping with someone else, you can betray them by taking someone else, not them, into really important confidence."

Nathalie dropped her glance.

"I think," she said, "I've had enough of this."

"I expect you have."

Nathalie shifted on the bench.

"I think I'll go now—"

"All right, dear."

"I think I'll go before you tell me that if I'd married Steve in the first place, none of this would have happened."

Lynne glanced at her.

"It hadn't crossed my mind."

"No," Nathalie said, "too many other little homilies crossing it already." She stood up. "Nothing's as simple as you make it look."

"No?"

"No!"

"It only has to be a drama," Lynne said, "if you want it to be."

Nathalie flung her head back. "*Look* who's talking!"

"Maybe," Lynne said, "but we can all learn."

"Platitudes," Nathalie said, "clichés. All you ever do—"

"Then why did you come round? If I'm so unsatisfactory to talk to in every way, why did you come to see me?"

There was a pause. Nathalie clenched her fists, then unclenched them, and said, in a low fierce whisper, "Because you're my *mother*."

Lynne stood up slowly, too. She put her hands together, and held them, to prevent herself from putting her arms round Nathalie.

"What about your real mother, then? What about Cora?"

Nathalie looked away.

"I don't know—"

"Are you going to just drop her now? Are you going to let all that effort and pain and discovery go to waste? Are you going to tell her that now you've got what you wanted, you've no more use for her?"

"Mum—"

"Well," Lynne said, "I can't do any more about you and Steve. I've said all I'm going to say, and it's up to you two. But I'm not going to let that poor woman languish up there in Northsea, thinking nobody cares."

"Mum—"

"Think what she's been through. All these years. *Think*."

"I do think," Nathalie said, "I do. But I don't know what to do."

"Well, I'll do it," Lynne said. She unclasped her hands, and folded her arms instead. "I'm going to telephone her."

On the coffee table close to the wing chair in the sitting room, Connor had left a brochure for Elegant Resorts. He had left it there especially, pointing it out several times, and telling Carole that she was entirely free to choose, that whether this special holiday he was planning—he hadn't actually uttered the words "second honeymoon" but he intended them as plainly as if they had been stenciled on his forehead—took place in Mauritius or Thailand or the Maldives was a matter of absolute indifference to him. The point was, he said, holding Carole's gaze with his deliberately significant one, that she should be taken somewhere entirely to her liking, somewhere that could, in a blur of white sand and blue sea, gently, completely and finally erase the deeply disturbing few months and land them back on the serene shore of all their familiar former securities.

Carole had opened the brochure a few times. She had looked at pictures of vast white beaches and vast white beds and supine people being restoratively massaged in bowers of frangipani. She had remembered previous holidays of this nature with Connor, holidays of extraordinary, immediate routine in a cocoon of improbable comfort, almost stifling in their regularity and impeccable, unbearable service. She remembered coming out of the sea once, the warm, clear, aquamarine tropical sea, to find yet another respectful immaculate boy waiting, crisp in the hotel's livery, holding both a towel for her and a glass of iced water on a tray, complete with an orchid, thinking to herself, This is completely, utterly *idiotic.*

So in her view was the purpose of the brochure. It was idiotic to suppose that anything could be changed, or retrieved, by going somewhere else, by living in a bubble of la-la land for two weeks. It was idiotic to suppose that she was the same person, that their marriage was the same institution, that Connor could, just by shelling out thousands of pounds, reinstate himself in the place he presumed he had been all these years, the place he had chosen to see as both acceptable and unassailable to her. And it was the most idiotic of all for her just to go along with it all, just to get carried off on a plane and be dumped like a helpless parcel for a whole lot of indifferent people, directed by Connor, to unpack.

She picked up the brochure and looked at it. Then, still carrying it, she went across the hall of the flat to Martin's closed bedroom door. She knew he was behind it. Because it was Saturday afternoon, he had refused to play tennis with his father, and had announced loudly, in the injured tone he adopted habitually now, that as he couldn't afford to go out day *and* night on weekends he preferred to economize during the day and just stay at home.

Carole knocked.

There was a pause and then Martin said, "Come in."

He was lying on his unmade bed, trainers on the duvet, reading a copy of GQ. Carole held out the brochure.

"Did you see this?"

Martin snorted. His eyes didn't leave his own magazine. "All right for some."

Carole sat down on the edge of the second bed, pushing aside a heap of Martin's clothes to make room.

"I don't want to go."

Martin's body tensed.

He said with elaborate indifference, "Oh?"

"No."

"You always used to like it—"

"No, I didn't. I went along but I didn't like it."

"Lucky old Dad then."

"He liked it. He wanted to go. He booked those holidays. He wants to book this one."

Martin looked sideways at her.

"Why're you telling me?"

Carole dropped the brochure on a pile of sweaters.

"I want you to help me tell Dad."

"*What?*"

"I want you to help me tell Dad that I don't want to go on this holiday. I want you to help me tell him that this won't make any difference, that we can't pretend what happened didn't happen, and just go back to where we were. Or where we *thought* we were."

Martin put the magazine down and eased himself into a sitting position.

He said sourly, "I don't need you sucking up to me."

"If that's how you choose to see it—"

"I do. You'd have gone on seeing David if I hadn't made sure you didn't. I *know* you would and don't try and tell me otherwise. And don't try and get round me now."

Carole looked down at the floor.

"I know I can't see him."

"What?"

"I know I can't see David. I don't know if I wanted to see him for him or because he's so like his father to look at. If it's any consolation, he didn't feel like my son, he didn't feel

298

like my child. He just felt like someone I'd been missing, someone I can't have, so it's better not to pretend I can. I'm grateful to you for putting a stop to it, I'm grateful."

There was a small silence, and then Martin said grudgingly, "You're a mess, Mum."

"Probably."

He made a gesture towards the floor.

"This holiday—"

"I can't."

"What'll you tell Dad?"

"That it will be a terrible waste of money, that it won't change anything, that it can't put the clock back."

Martin said unexpectedly, "He won't get you."

Carole looked up.

"No. And there's something else."

Martin's knees came up, almost involuntarily, and he held them hard against his chest.

"You're not bloody leaving—"

"No."

"But you've thought about it—"

"Not really."

"Why not?"

She looked away.

"Because of you."

"Don't give me that!"

"True," she said. "I may be a lousy mother but I am capable of attempts at redemption."

Martin let his knees go.

"Don't expect *me* to be bloody grateful—"

"I don't. I'm doing it as much for me as for you."

"So it's a line to give Dad—"

Carole stood up and walked to the window.

"I shan't even mention this aspect to Dad."

"Well then," Martin said, "why would he buy all your reasons for not wanting the holiday then?"

Carole swung the blind cord.

"Because I want the money."

"You have such a *nerve*."

"I want the money he would spend on this holiday," Carole said, "to add to some of my own to set up another business."

Martin snorted.

"He'll never agree. Set up a business without him? In your dreams."

Carole took the wooden acorn at the end of the blind cord in her hand, and inspected it.

"It would be without him, certainly. But I think he'd agree if I told him it was with you."

"Enough," Martin said.

Carole turned.

"I mean it."

"You think I'm useless," Martin said. "You think I couldn't organize a piss-up in a brewery."

"But I could."

Martin shouted, "Don't patronize me!"

"Your IT skills are better than mine. You can do accounts even if you couldn't do a business plan. I can do business plans."

Martin rolled over.

"Go away."

Carole let the acorn go.

"I can't make it up to you in all the ways you want me to make it up to you if you won't even let me try."

Martin said nothing.

"We'll fight," Carole said, "we'll get on each other's nerves. We may lose every penny."

"We fight anyway—"

"Only," Carole said, "because you insist we do."

"You *lied* to me!"

"I lied to everyone."

Martin rolled back.

"So what'll convince me you won't do it again?"

Carole shrugged.

"There's nothing personal to lie about anymore. You know everything. And if it isn't personal, it can't hurt you. Also, I think I can say I've never told a business lie in my life."

"Crap."

"Well, a *personal* business lie then."

Martin got slowly off the bed and stood up. He bent and picked up the holiday brochure from the floor.

He rifled through it then said, with his back half turned to her, "When's Dad back?"

CHAPTER TWENTY

Polly, Steve thought, had rather liked being in hospital. The ingenious operation had left no outward evidence and amazingly little discomfort.

"Ow," Polly said loudly when anyone came within inches of her head. "Ow, ow, *ow*."

"Point to the place where it hurts you," the surgeon said, sitting on Polly's bed.

"Here," Polly said, pointing. "And here and here and here."

The surgeon laid his hand on her knee.

"And here?"

She glared at him.

"Sometimes."

He smiled.

"You'll probably have to wear earmuffs because every-thing will sound so loud."

"It won't," Polly said, "it will be exactly the same."

He gave her knee a pat, and stood up.

"You do it your way, Polly." He glanced across at Steve and Nathalie. "It's healing nicely."

"Ow," Polly said.

Evie had come in with new pajamas, and Lynne had sent flowers and Marnie had made chocolate brownies the size of dice. Everyone had come to see Polly, trooping into the hospital in that half-fearful, half-respectful mood that hospitals induce, bearing grapes and jelly beans and plastic puzzles. In the bed next to Polly a sad, slablike boy who never removed his baseball cap lay and watched her visitors and tributes with open resentment.

"What's his name?" Nathalie asked Polly.

Polly glanced at him. She was wearing sunglasses that Ellen had brought her with frames like pink glitter daisies.

"He's just a boy."

"He must have a *name*—"

"No," Polly said, "some of them don't."

Nathalie went over to the boy's bed.

"Would you like a brownie?"

He stared at her for a moment, and then he raised one hand and slowly tipped the peak of his cap down until it obscured his face.

"Another time," Nathalie said.

She came back to Polly's bedside and the blue plastic hospital chair. She didn't look across at Steve but then she hadn't looked at him much. In fact, she hadn't, he thought, looked at anyone, not her parents or his parents, or David and Marnie and the children when they came. He'd wanted her to look at David and Marnie particularly so that he could see if she thought that they were changed somehow, that a sheen of confidence had gone off them, that, standing there by Polly's bed with Marnie's arm through David's, they had looked, for the first time Steve could remember, vulnerable, almost doubtful.

Marnie had done something to her hair, too. There seemed to be less of it somehow, and instead of being in a plait, it was loose behind her shoulders, in a strange rippled curtain, making her face look younger but also less certain, as if some sort of control had slipped from her, and she hadn't yet found a replacement for it. And the way she held David's arm was uncharacteristic too, more dependent than anything Steve had seen in her before, and David had her arm pressed against his side, and when they looked down at Polly, they were looking with great intensity, as if they were trying to memorize every detail about her.

"We're going to Canada," Daniel said to Polly, sprawling on the foot of her bed. She didn't look up.

She said, "You always go."

"No, to live, stupid. Go to school and everything. And skiing."

Polly said nothing. Ellen had held out the sunglasses in their pink plastic envelope.

"I expect you'll come. To stay with us."

"Yes," Nathalie said.

Polly took the sunglasses.

"I'll come," she said, "when I'm not too busy."

"Polly!"

"In the holidays," Ellen said. "In the summer."

"It nearly is the summer—"

"Well," Ellen said, "when you're free."

Polly put the sunglasses on.

Nathalie said, too quickly, "Polly's got someone to meet here, first, someone important. She's coming a long way to meet Polly."

Steve put his hand on Nathalie's arm. She shook it off.

"She's called Cora," Nathalie said.

Daniel glanced up.

"Who's she?"

"She's—another granny. Another granny for Polly."

Polly sighed. She removed her sunglasses.

She said loudly, "I've got enough of them already."

David began to laugh. He took his arm away from Marnie's and put his hands over his face, laughing and laughing.

"Oh Polly—"

She regarded him. Steve bent and kissed the top of Polly's head.

"Thanks, Poll."

"Ow," Polly said.

He glanced at Nathalie. Her face was expressionless.

"Come on, Nat—"

David took his hands away from his face.

He said, in the tone he used to reprove his children, "Lighten up, Nathalie."

Marnie gave a tiny gasp.

"It's OK," Nathalie said tightly. "It's OK." She shot David a lightning look. "It's just that there's a lot to get used to all at once, don't you think?"

Marnie nodded.

"You just wonder what'll work out and what won't—"

Ellen's head came up sharply.

"What do you mean?"

"I mean," Marnie said, swallowing, "that Canada's a big adventure, but it's very different. It'll be very different for me, too."

"Sh," David said.

"I'll miss you," Marnie said, dropping suddenly to her knees beside Polly's bed. "I'll *miss* you, Polly."

Polly looked embarrassed. Marnie looked up at Steve and Nathalie.

She said, "I'll miss you, too. I'll miss all of you, I will, I really will, I didn't realize—" She bent her face into the blue cotton of Polly's bedcover and said thickly into it, "I thought I wanted to do this, I thought I wanted—"

David bent and put his hands under her arms to lift her.

"Come on, Marnie, come on—"

Marnie was crying now.

"I mean it, I mean it, I didn't mean to drive you all apart, I didn't—"

Nathalie leaned across Polly's bed and put a hand on Marnie's arm.

"It's all over. Promise. All that, over—"

"But it's *changed* things!"

"It was bound to," David said. "Change had to happen." He got Marnie clumsily to her feet.

"We were all part of it," Nathalie said. "We *all* were."

"What?" Ellen said.

There was a silence.

Ellen said sharply, "This adoption business?"

"Well," Daniel said, reaching for another of Polly's grapes, "*I'm* going to Canada."

David held Marnie upright.

"We're coming with you, mate."

Marnie put a hand out towards Polly.

"Promise you'll come soon. Promise."

Polly said loftily, "When my ear is completely better."

"Of course."

"Which may be *ages*."

Marnie bent and kissed Polly's head lightly.

"Bring them all—"

Polly nodded. Steve glanced at Nathalie. Nathalie was looking at David and David had his gaze fixed above all their heads, at the hospital's cream-painted wall.

"Bring some stuff for the blackfly," Ellen said to Polly. "They are *vicious*."

Now, a week later, Polly was back at home and behaving badly and Nathalie had permitted Steve back into their bedroom but was wearing pajamas. He felt himself to be on remand, electronically tagged as to his whereabouts, required to show remorse and the capacity to reform but, at the same time, to be capable of demonstrating a desirable, powerful maleness which Nathalie, in her present state, could not do without. It was because of this latter quality, this need to be strong and sheltering, that Steve had not told Nathalie about the business. He had told her that Titus was quitting—in fact, she had asked in one of her first outbursts after the revelation of his affair with Sasha how Titus could stand to work with him for another minute—but he had not revealed that Justine and Meera were going too, that Justine had, in fact, already gone, leaving her desk in a state that would have looked like a childish revenge if Steve had felt less unhappily responsible for her state of mind. He had not said a word about Meera because it was, in a way, the departure he felt most keenly about, the one that most pointedly showed up his own weakness, his own inability to put the professional before the personal, his own folly and destructive risk-taking. To fail in Meera's eyes was something he could not, in his own mind, even tiptoe towards without wincing. And when she offered to stay, while he found a replacement, as long as that period didn't exceed a month, and he accepted with pitiful alacrity, he knew he'd sunk in her estimation about as low as he could go.

"One month, then," she said. "From this Friday. No overtime."

He glanced up at the clock on the wall above her desk. It said ten to six. She had left precisely at five-thirty, leaving no sign behind her that the evening's departure was any different from any other evening's. Her desk was immaculate, her bin empty, and a faint breath of Issey hung in the air like the ghost of a reproof. Steve sat down in her chair and looked up at the ceiling beams. They did not appear to him a source of comfort tonight, but merely old, interesting pieces of ex-tree which had seen every kind of human stupidity and were perfectly indifferent to his. He thought, staring upwards, that someone else might have to work under them soon, that he might have to sell everything he had worked for because he had let so much slide, because he had made a mess of things, because he had done exactly what his angry, disappointed father had said he would do if he turned down the Royal Oak in favor of art college.

Somebody knocked on the door to the staircase. Steve sat up, alert.

"Come—"

The door opened slowly.

"I saw the light was on," Titus said. "I wondered if you were working—"

"Have you ever knocked on a door in your life?"

"Not since school—"

"No."

"I wasn't sure," Titus said, "what you'd be doing. If you see what I mean."

Steve put his hands behind his head.

"I am contemplating the future."

"Oh."

"I don't like the look of it."

Titus came further into the room and stood a foot away from Meera's desk.

"None of it?"

Steve eyed him.

"Why do you ask?"

Titus looked away. He cleared his throat.

He said awkwardly, "I—I'm sorry about Nathalie."

"What?"

"I'm sorry," Titus said, "that I insisted you tell Nathalie."

"You were angry—"

"I was. Steaming. I wanted to bloody kill you. But I didn't want to kill Nathalie, I didn't want to hurt her at all."

"Titus," Steve said, "why are you here?"

Titus gestured. He was wearing a denim jacket and half the collar had got tucked in.

"I—um—wanted to see if she was OK. With Polly in hospital and all that."

"Nathalie?"

"Yes."

"Do you mean, has she forgiven me?"

"Yes."

"I don't know," Steve said.

Titus put his hands in his pockets.

"Are you talking—"

"Sort of."

"And her brother's going to Canada, isn't he?"

"Yes."

"So she feels a bit, well, abandoned—"

"Yes," Steve said. He unlocked his hands and leaned forward. He said, "It wasn't you. I had to tell her anyway."

"I don't know," Titus said. "I don't know about all this soul-bearing. I wasn't brought up to it. I shouldn't think my parents have ever talked about love in their lives."

"And have they been faithful to each other?"

Titus shrugged.

"Haven't the faintest. Don't want to think about it."

"Well, Nathalie is the kind of person who does. And so am I."

Titus gave him a quick glance.

"So there's a long way to go."

"Yes."

Titus took his hands out of his pockets and gestured towards the rest of the room.

"What about this?"

Steve stood up slowly.

He said, "Maybe it will have to go." He took a breath, thinking of Meera, and then he said, "I've neglected it."

Titus took a few steps away and then said, his back to Steve, "I could stay."

"You what?"

"I could stay. If you like."

"Well—"

"You're a nightmare to work for," Titus said, "but I like what you do."

"Thanks."

"And to be honest, I'm not in a mood to start looking, I'm not in a mood to go to London and chance my arm."

"Titus," Steve said, "it mightn't work. It might have gone too far to rescue."

"We could start again. We could be bloody associates."

"I don't know. I can't promise you anything. I can't even plan anything until I get down to a cold-towel session—"

Titus turned round.

"Are you turning me down?"

"I think so."

"What kind of stupid death wish is this?"

"Maybe," Steve said slowly, "I have to do something with Nathalie now. Maybe, if she'll agree, we'll have to re-think everything, including how the money's earned."

"Don't you think," Titus said angrily, "that you *owe* me something?"

"An apology, yes. But not a job."

"*Jesus*," Titus said.

Steve moved forward. He put a hand on Titus's arm.

He said, "I couldn't handle you now. I'd like to, but I couldn't."

Titus glanced at him.

"At least that's honest."

Steve said nothing. Titus moved his arm and stepped away towards the door.

"So it's the open road for me."

"Yes."

"Will you write me a reference with bells on?"

"Of course."

Titus paused in the doorway. He gave a quick look at the photographs hanging on the wall beside Steve's desk.

He said, "You're a lucky sod. You always were," and then he went out onto the staircase and slammed the door behind him.

Steve walked down the length of the studio, and looked down into the street. He saw Titus pause on the pavement below him and collect himself for a moment, squaring his shoulders, lifting his chin. And then he saw him walk purposefully out across the road, deliberately not looking, deliberately making a car swerve to avoid him. And then he crossed the far pavement and vanished into an alley that led to the center of town.

Steve turned, and went back to his desk. It was covered with papers, papers he had not attended to, requests, complaints, estimates, invoices, papers that just at this moment represented an aspect of life which had no savor to it at all. He would, he decided, leave them. He would leave them just as Titus would leave them, and instead, just as Titus would do, he would pick up the telephone and make contact again with the essence of things.

He looked at the phone in his hand. Then he dialed the flat.

"Hello," Polly's voice said at once, and imperiously.

"Hello, darling—"

"Oh," Polly said, "it's you."

"Yes."

"It's Daddy," Polly said over her shoulder, and then in her former tone, and quickly before Nathalie could take the phone from her hand, "Have you finished your work?"

Steve looked round him, down the length of the room, up into those mysterious and remote old beams above his head.

"Yes," he said, "yes, I rather think I have."

There was a pause, and then Polly said briskly, "Well, you'd better come home then," and put the receiver down.

A NOTE ON THE AUTHOR

Author of eagerly awaited and sparklingly readable novels often centered around the domestic nuances and dilemmas of life in contemporary England, Joanna Trollope is also the author of a number of historical novels and of *Britannia's Daughters*, a study of women in the British Empire. In 1988 she wrote her first novel, *The Choir*, and this was followed by *A Village Affair, A Passionate Man, The Rector's Wife, The Men and the Girls, A Spanish Lover, The Best of Friends, Next of Kin, Other People's Children, Marrying the Mistress* and, most recently, *Girl From the South*. She lives in London and Gloucestershire.

A NOTE ON THE TYPE

The text of this book is set in Linotype Sabon, named
after the type founder, Jacques Sabon. It was designed by
Jan Tschichold and jointly developed by Linotype, Monotype
and Stempel, in response to a need for a typeface to be
available in identical form for mechanical hot metal
composition and hand composition using foundry type.

Tschichold based his design for Sabon roman on a font
engraved by Garamond, and Sabon italic on a font by
Granjon. It was first used in 1966 and has proved an
enduring modern classic.